ATTRACTION & REPULSION

ATTRACTION
&
REPULSION

Maloree E Anderson

Printed in the United States of America.

Cover design by Beautiful Book Covers by Ivy

Edited by Addison Horner avocadotreepress.square.site

Proofread by Heather Hudec simplyspellboundedits.com

Paperback ISBN: 979-8-9926904-0-8

Paperback KDP ISBN: 9798336018264

eBook ISBN: 979-8-9926904-1-5

*Topics portrayed in this novel may be upsetting to some. Reader discretion is advised.

ATTRACTION & REPULSION

To my sister, who has loved me even through my worst.

SUICIDE & CRISIS LIFELINE
Call or text 988

CHAPTER ONE

I t only took two swipes to satisfy the craving.

The damage was done.

Carson's vision faded in and out as a hazy memory flickered in her mind: lifting her shirt and pressing a sharp object, the first sharp object she could get her hands on, to her rib cage. The pocketknife had been cold as it made a clean cut, followed by goosebumps texturing her entire body.

Now she was slumped over the oak kitchen table, her long, black hair swept across her face, blindly staring at the gleaming blade in her hand as it mocked her. Closing her eyes, she took a deep breath and winced as it stretched the fresh cut. The pain felt like ice water being thrown in her face, waking her from the trance and back into reality.

She ran to the toilet to vomit.

After flushing, she sat back against the wall as hot tears burned a path down her cheeks. Once again she had succumbed to a catatonic state where she numbly sabotaged her body. She hated the self-harm, she feared it, yet she still mutilated her body and, worse, *liked* it? Even desired it at times. The way the blade sliced through her fragile skin, leaving mark after mark after mark, was pleasure. It was agony.

The self-disgust continued to rage within Carson as she picked herself up off the floor and rummaged around for the first-aid kit in the cabinet under the sink, where she had tossed it the last time. Mechanically, she cleaned the drying blood that had trickled down her stomach, applied ointment, and secured a bandage—a ritual carried out by muscle memory.

Shoving the kit back under the sink, she grabbed her phone sitting on the bathroom counter. Three new messages sat patiently on her screen, all from Raegan.

> How are you doing today? Been thinking about you all morning.

> What are you wearing to the softball tournament? It's supposed to rain. UGH.

> Hunter left already. I might be late. If you're there before me, find us a place to sit.

Carson typed a thumbs up, then leaned on the counter to stare at herself in the mirror. Under her emerald eyes were dark shadows, a contrast against her pale skin. What would Raegan, her best friend, say if she found out her secret? Her stomach turned once more at the pathetic humiliation of being a woman in her thirties who cuts her skin on purpose. She had lost all control of her mind, of the body that betrayed her five years ago.

What had become of her?

This monologue would play in her head on repeat, over and over, always ending with a seemingly simple answer: just stop cutting.

Ignoring the familiar stinging on her side, Carson wrapped her arms around her chest. She could just stop. If only she wanted to.

Chapter Two

B eing stuck outside in bleachers with dozens of sweaty people on a blistering August evening was the last place Carson wanted to be, especially today.

The crowd cheered as the batter hit the ball into the outfield, then sprinted past first base and second before sliding into third. Carson choked down a grumble when the trio of young women beside her whooped and giggled at the City of Prescott's firefighters and police officers on the field. Trying to dispel the ringing from their shrill laughs, Carson shoved her pinky finger in her ear and wiggled it around.

It didn't matter, though, because Raegan was hollering just as loud as the badge chasers on her other side.

"That's my man right there!" Raegan belted, cupping her hands around her mouth like a megaphone. On the field, Hunter flashed a smile up at them while dusting the dirt off his black-and-red uniform. She blew him a kiss, then planted herself back in her seat, her wavy golden bob bouncing. "Damn, he looks so fine in that uniform. I'm going to make him keep it on later tonight."

Carson rolled her eyes, then shifted in her seat trying to bring blood flow back into her legs. Her backside needed a break, and her skin needed . . . more pain. "I'm going to run to the bathroom."

Raegan peeled her eyes away from the tournament. "Do you need me to go with you?"

"No. I'll be right back."

Shuffling past a sea of legs and feet with apologies, even receiving a few irritated grunts in return, Carson managed to make her way down the stands and onto the concrete path toward the mediocre facilities. A roar erupted from the bleachers as the announcer called a home run for—as Hunter had proudly helped name his softball team—the Super Soakers. Carson could imagine the groans coming from their competitors, the Boys in Blue.

Rushing into the bathroom she shut the door behind her, muting the game. After checking that the stalls were empty, she leaned her head back and closed her eyes. The cacophony of the stands still echoed in her ears.

"One more hour and it's over. You're doing this for Raegan. Luke would want you to be out having fun today," she whispered.

Wanting to inspect the bandages on her ribs, she lifted her shirt. Only a little blood had seeped through. There was a reason she always wore black.

Then her eyes darted around the bathroom, yearning for something sharp. Just to get her through the rest of the night—to get her through another year. Nothing behind stall door one. Two. Three. She let her fingers slide across the corner of the sink, the hand dryer, the trash can. Dull. Round. Useless.

Carson harrumphed. The pain would have to wait until she got home. After allowing herself another minute of silence, she stepped back outside, ready to brave the crowd again.

The setting sun waved its final goodbye as it disappeared below the Arizona horizon, leaving traces of cotton candy-colored clouds. The field lights flickered and buzzed, and a small breeze teased the promise of an evening thunderstorm. In anticipation, Carson pulled her sleeves over her hands and crossed her arms, holding them tight to her body.

As she walked along the building's brick wall, one of the doors came flying open. The heavy metal smashed into her skull with a sickening thud. Her head snapped back, causing her to lose her balance and fall to the ground.

Black—

A buzzing reverberated in Carson's ears, making the pain in her head intensify. She was twisting her neck to find the source when the vibration stopped, followed by another sound she couldn't distinguish. Bending metal?

Then a blinding light hit her eyelids. Cringing, she blinked a few times. The light, she realized, was coming from the sun.

Squinting, Carson looked through a shattered windshield at a semi-truck stalled in the middle of the intersection, its front crumpled. Bystanders stood huddled on the side of the road. Lights—reds, yellows, blues—spun atop a fleet of emergency vehicles.

A blanket-covered mound lay in the rain-soaked road. She knew who was under that blanket.

Carson screamed—

She was back on the concrete, stars pulsating in her vision. Groaning, she reached up to touch her throbbing head and found a hot, sticky substance. A voice as deep as the sea cursed somewhere near her. Then a pair of ocean-blue eyes appeared just above her, inducing a fleeting moment of déjà vu. So familiar . . .

"Are you okay?" the voice asked.

"Ow," she mumbled, trying to sit up, but large hands held her shoulders down.

"Don't get up. You're bleeding."

She rolled her head to look at the person talking to her. Like Hunter, he wore a black-and-red softball uniform. He knelt beside her body, one hand on her shoulder to pin her down while the other rifled through a duffle bag. While he was turned away, Carson noticed a silhouette of flying ducks displayed on his hat, turned backward on his head. Black hair stuck out from under it. His hand reappeared with a white rag and pressed it to her forehead, his dark eyebrows furrowed with concentration. Under thick stubble, a frown touched his lips. His eyes were serious. Too serious.

Damn. How much blood was there?

Those serious and still-familiar eyes glanced down, full of concern, and locked with hers.

"I am *so* sorry," the man said.

"Don't be," Carson said, a little annoyed at herself. "I wasn't paying attention." It was she who shouldn't have been walking so close to the door's swinging radius.

Peeling back the cloth, he grimaced. "Yeah, I got you pretty good. You may need stitches."

"Well, that sucks," she muttered. "Can I sit up now?"

"Let me help you." The man grabbed her hand and placed it on the towel, letting her take over. "Keep pressure on that," he instructed before sliding his arm under her back and hoisting her to a sitting position.

Carson sat for only a second before getting to her feet.

"What are you doing?" he asked, seeming surprised.

"I need to go find my friend and let her know I'm going ho—" That was when the earth tilted to the side, causing Carson's legs to buckle.

"Oh-kay." The man caught her around her waist.

Confirming her legs were stable, Carson tried to push him away. It was like struggling against a brick wall.

"Thank you, but I'm fine," she said. "I just need to go home and lay down." She needed to get away from the noise and the crowd. Away from the smack of the leather ball against the aluminum softball bat. Away from those infuriating girls who swooned over the first responders on the field at every annual tournament. Away from her dead husband laying in the middle of the road—

"Um, no, you need to go to the hospital." The stranger kept his hold on Carson's half-limp body.

"I told you, I'm fine," she snapped. After the accident, she had vowed never to step foot in a hospital again.

"If you say so," he said, letting go of her waist. Carson didn't realize how much weight he had been holding, because as soon as he released her she started to drop back to the ground. Before she could crumble, he was supporting her again.

"That's what I thought," the man said.

Carson shot him a glare from beneath the towel. Partly because of his smart-ass remark, partly because she realized she needed his assistance. She envisioned herself crawling up the bleachers, searching for Raegan. How insane she would look to everyone.

A chuckle rumbled in his chest at her expression. "Come on. I'll take you." Before she could protest, he bent down, scooped her up, and began walking with her cradled in his arms. The sharp movement pulled at her scabbed ribs, making her gasp.

"How's the pain?"

"Bearable," she said through gritted teeth. The rocking was making her regret the concession stand nachos she had earlier, now churning in her stomach. *I swear if I throw up one more time today* . . . "Just feel like I'm going to puke."

"Damn. I might have given you a concussion."

"That would be my luck," she grumbled. It didn't help that the game continued to boom around her, making her brain pulse against her skull. Though she was surprised how the pain didn't bring the attraction she was looking for earlier.

"Who's your friend?" he asked.

"Huh?" She tilted her head back to look up at him.

"You said you needed to tell your friend you're leaving. Who's your friend?" he repeated while keeping pace, his voice never faltering from the exertion of carrying her and his duffle bag.

"Oh, uh, her name is Raegan. She's in the bleachers."

"Raegan Olson? Hunter's wife?"

"Yeah . . . how did you—" Then it clicked. His uniform matched the Super Soakers, which could only make him one of the firefighters. He must work with Hunter.

The firefighter stopped walking, and to Carson's surprise, they were in the parking lot standing next to a large, red truck. Keeping her eyes closed for most of the trip, she had figured he was taking her back to the stands. Without any effort, he opened the door, barely shifting her weight.

"What are you doing?" she demanded.

"Like I said, taking you to urgent care," he retorted, lifting her into the passenger seat with ease.

"*Like I said*, I'm fine. I need to find Raegan. She's probably wondering where the heck I am." Carson grabbed the handle and tried to slide off the seat, but he blocked her.

"Relax. I'll call Hunter, and he'll let her know," he said.

"Can't you or one of your buddies just glue it here instead?"

"Maybe if we were in the middle of the jungle with no access to a medical facility."

Carson bit the inside of her cheek, her tongue sliding over the years' worth of bite marks. Urgent care technically wasn't a hospital, so she didn't have to worry about breaking her vow. Annoyingly, her head continued to throb like a heartbeat where the door had smashed into her forehead. She was officially over an already shitty day. And whether she liked it or not, if a firefighter thought she needed to see a doctor, there was a very good chance she needed to see a doctor.

The firefighter, who was still standing in her way, watched her carefully as she mulled over her situation. Concern was still evident in his face. Every few seconds his eyes flitted to the rag pressed to her forehead. First responder mode, she thought, itching to address her injury.

Her hesitation gave him enough assurance to push her legs back to face the dashboard. This time, she didn't resist.

Letting her head rest against the seat, she closed her eyes. The seatbelt zipped as he pulled it from the slot and clicked it into the lock. The pressure of the strap against her lap and chest felt nice, but a frown pulled her lips down when the door slammed. Why did everything have to be so loud?

The truck's cab smelled old and dusty, like driving down a dirt road toward a grandparent's house. Or at least that's how Carson imagined it, having never met hers. The saddle-blanket seats' coarse fibers poked at her exposed thighs as she adjusted to get comfortable.

When the driver's door opened, her eyelids lifted. The stranger was sliding into the truck, a phone with a STLHD Gear sticker on its case held to his ear.

"Hey, Hunter, it's Jax. I know I was up next, but I left my duffle bag in the locker room and ran to grab it. Something happened, and now I'm taking your friend"—he leaned over to her—"what's your name?"

"Carson."

"I'm taking Carson to urgent care." Jax waited for Hunter's response. "I slammed a door into her head. She's got a nice laceration and may even have a concussion, but I haven't checked." Another pause. "She says she's fine, but I'm still taking her. Anyway, let Raegan know that's where she went. Text me if she wants to meet us at the urgent care."

CHAPTER THREE

T he pounding in Carson's skull never stopped, making the short fifteen-minute drive to the walk-in clinic feel like two hours. Jax parked the truck and came around to her side. She already had the seatbelt undone when he opened the door.

"Think you can walk?" he asked, offering his hand to help her down onto the sidestep.

"Yes. I'm not as dizzy anymore."

"Just keep the towel on it."

Once inside, he guided her to one of the empty chairs and went to speak to the receptionist. Hushed murmurs drifted about the waiting room from the other patrons. An older couple sat reading magazines in the corner. A mother and father distracted their coughing child with a colorful, wooden toy. A group of teenage boys snickered, as their mother slumped in her chair.

"Are you able to fill this out?" Jax was back, holding a clipboard.

Sitting up, Carson took the paperwork from him. As soon as he lowered himself into the seat on her left, his pocket buzzed. He snatched his phone to read the incoming texts.

"It's Raegan. Want her to come by?"

Carson finished scribbling her insurance information, which gave her a moment to think. If Raegan showed up, Carson would have to talk . . . a lot. More talking than she could handle at the moment. She was too exhausted to entertain anyone or replay the whole door-to-head incident. But she had no other way home; they had driven together to the tournament.

"Or I can just drive you home," Jax offered. "If that doesn't weird you out."

She squinted at him. "You're not some sort of perv, are you?"

He laughed. "I'm a lot of things, but that I am not."

"Then sure, I just want to go home—wait." Leaning forward, she patted her back pocket for her forgotten phone and was thankful to find it still there. Her sigh of relief was short-lived when she saw the stack of alerts—five missed calls and fifteen messages—waiting on the screen.

"I can text Raegan and let her know," she told Jax. "I live in Chino Valley, though."

Propping one arm on her chair, Jax lay back, calm for being in a place full of pain and sickness. Carson surmised it was because he was used to it. Besides, isn't that what firefighters are? Comfortable in chaos.

"No problem," Jax said. "It's the least I can do after knocking you out."

They waited in silence. Jax was fixated on a hockey game on the flatscreen mounted in the corner while Carson slouched in her seat, dreaming about her plush bed.

"Carson West?"

Both Jax and Carson turned to see the triage nurse holding a door open, her eyes scanning the waiting room. Jax stood and reached a hand toward Carson. When she got up, the room didn't spin like a carnival ride, which was an improvement.

"Need me to go back with you?" he asked.

Too exhausted to care, Carson nodded, and they followed the

nurse—Cindy, according to her name tag—through the door, down a hall, and into a tiny patient room. Bland blues and creams covered the walls, and a wooden "Keep Moving Forward" sign too tiny for its canvas hung on one wall. Beneath it was an arrow pointing to nowhere. Carson believed it was a sad attempt to liven up the drab space.

"Have a seat on the bed so I can get some vitals," the nurse instructed. Short and sweet, she reminded Carson of Raegan's mother.

The tissue paper crunched beneath Carson as she took her place. Jax sat casually in one of the chairs in the back corner. An ankle rested on one knee while his arms, hands, and fingers loosely lay on the arms of the chair.

Cindy unhooked the blood pressure cuff from the rolling tray. "I'll need your right arm, honey."

Carson's stomach lodged in her throat. She sure as hell wasn't going to roll her sleeve up right now. Not for the nurse, not for the doctor, and *not* in front of Jax.

"Can I keep my sleeve down? I'm . . . cold," she lied.

Cindy gave her a sympathetic smile. Carson's own mother would have rolled her eyes.

"Sure, dear," Cindy said. "It makes no difference."

The dread released from the pit of Carson's stomach. With her left hand still holding the rag to her head, she offered her right arm. Cindy wrapped the cuff around it and pressed a button to automate the machine. The tight pressure on her bicep was oddly comforting.

"So, you hit your head?" Cindy asked, holding a thermometer to the side of her forehead the towel wasn't covering.

"I wasn't watching where I was going and ran into a door," Carson said.

Jax broke his silence. "That is not how it happened."

The nurse's large, round eyes darted between her and Jax. "Oh?"

13

"I swung the door open, and she was on the other side," he said.

"Yeah, but if I was watching where I was going this wouldn't have happened. It's my fault we're here," Carson confessed.

Cindy's face softened. "It sounds like it was nobody's fault. Freak accidents are very common." She reached over to the counter and grabbed a pair of gloves. "Now, let's see what all the fuss is about." When Carson peeled back the rag, Cindy's lips pursed. "I think it's safe to say you'll be needing stitches."

Taking the cloth from Carson's hand, Cindy tossed it in the waste disposal, but not before Carson caught sight of the large maroon spot staining the pristine color. How many bloodied rags had Carson thrown away herself? Too many to count. While the nurse taped a sterile gauze over the open wound, Carson shook her arms out, attempting to release the tingles from holding them up for so long.

Cindy went on to ask the typical intake questions. Carson had always loved the clacking sound that keyboards made. Cindy's acrylic nails made the experience even more satisfying as she took down Carson's answers. No concussion, no double vision, minimal nausea at the beginning that was gone now, no confusion.

As Cindy stepped out to fetch the doctor, Carson reached up to rub the knots that had formed in her shoulders, eyeing the jars of clinical disposables that sat on the counter next to the sink. How ironic that she was back in a medical facility on the anniversary of the car accident. *Just my luck.*

"Feeling any better?" Jax asked, sneaking a peek into one of the drawers.

Dropping her hands into her lap, Carson rubbed them down her thighs to her knees before answering his question. "Just ready to get home."

"I don't blame you." Jax closed the drawer then tilted his head. "You know, you look kind of familiar. I swear I've met you before."

Carson shrugged, having thought the same thing. "Maybe. It's a small town."

"Hmm." Jax continued to study her face, causing Carson to nervously look down at her shoes.

Then the door squeaked open, and Carson was transported back five years.

A young man wearing a white coat—far too young to have gone through medical school and residency—entered the room. Heavy doses of sedatives and narcotics coursed through Carson's veins, making her feel like stone. The doctor's face had been emotionless when he stood at the end of her bed reciting the words: dead, dead, dead. That was the only part she had understood. She clung to that word. They were dead. Dead because of her . . .

"Carson?"

It was Jax who brought her back to the present. Carson wasn't in the hospital, hadn't just woken from a coma. The doctor hadn't just told her that her family was dead.

Blinking, she squeezed the cushion beneath her, trying to ground herself. She cleared her throat. "I'm sorry. Yes?"

The urgent care physician in front of Carson looked nothing like the doctor from her memory. In fact, he appeared very experienced with his white hair and well-worn lab coat.

"The nurse tells me you hit your head but doesn't think you have a concussion." The physician pulled a flashlight from his front pocket as he stepped up to Carson, just as Cindy returned with a cart full of supplies. "Just look at the button on my shirt." Carson obliged as he shone the light in her eyes.

"Looks good. Not feeling sluggish or sick?"

She shook her head.

"Very good. Go ahead and lay back. We'll get you stitched up and out of here in no time."

As Carson reclined, Cindy pulled out a slate so her feet wouldn't hang helplessly off the bed.

"Oh, you are cold. You're shaking," Cindy said.

Yes, cold. That's why Carson's bones and joints were twitching, and her jaw hurt. Why her heart was pumping so hard she was sure she would wake up with bruised ribs. Cold. That's all it was.

A weight covered her legs, and she glanced down to see Cindy had placed a knitted blanket over her. She wanted to cry at the gesture.

The doctor and the nurse began the procedure, their movements routine as if they had done it hundreds of times. It happened so quickly: gauze was removed, plastic ripped open, sterile drapes placed on and near her. A spotlight clicked on, blinding her.

She dropped her gaze and found Jax's face. Worry lines creased his forehead, and his mouth was slightly open. Perhaps it was because Carson's breaths were short and quick, or because her eyes appeared wild and panicked. Jax was leaning toward her as if he wanted to scoop her up and rescue her from this place. If he did, she wouldn't resist.

Carson fought to keep from squirming under the physician's touch. Her fingers dug into the plastic on the edge of the medical bed hard enough to leave marks. She was good at leaving marks.

Then Jax did something she would have never imagined a stranger to do. He brushed the tops of her fingers. From his touch, the tension released, and Carson grasped his offered hand. Closing her eyes, she squeezed tighter as the thread tugged on her skin. Instead of listening to the physician, she focused on the warm hand that held hers.

Touch. Skin. Solace. How long had it been since she had held a hand? She couldn't remember.

Carson released a raspy exhale. The physician was going to chastise her if she didn't get her breathing under control. She tried to breathe in through her nose and release it through her mouth. The snip of the scissors announced that the physician had finished sewing her skin back together. It was almost over. She could suffer through a little more, especially now that someone was holding her hand.

"All done," the old physician announced, standing up to dispose of his gloves.

Cindy quickly gathered the soiled gauze and drapes and helped her sit back up. Carson noticed she was still squeezing Jax's hand. When she released him, the tips of his fingers were slightly purple. How hard had her grip been?

"You did great," the physician said before bidding farewell and slipping out the door.

How observant, Carson thought.

Cindy shoved the remaining medical waste into a hole carved out of the counter. "I'll get you some ice, then you'll be free to go."

As Cindy stepped out Carson turned to Jax, catching him mid-yawn while he ran a hand through his shaggy hair and readjusted his baseball cap. A twinge of guilt hit her stomach as she wondered how late it was.

"Thank you again for bringing me and for . . . holding my hand." Carson's face pinched, a little embarrassed that she needed her hand held like a child in the first place. She wondered what he thought of it, of her.

Jax grinned. "I didn't mind."

Carson pressed her lips together but didn't say anything further because whether he minded or not, she did.

Then his face shifted, looking upset. "I still can't believe I smacked you with a door," he said. "I feel really bad. You're going to have to let me make it up to you somehow."

"How 'bout you promise to never hit me on the head again?" Carson offered, hoping to show him it wasn't that big of a deal.

He barked out a laugh, making Carson happy that he was no longer frowning. That was when Cindy came back with an icepack and post-procedure instructions, giving Carson the okay to go home.

It was late into the night, which left old Highway 89, connecting Prescott and Chino Valley, dark and barren. Carson directed Jax with simple instructions to her home as she kept the icepack in place. By now the adrenaline of the night had worn off, and she was ready to crawl into bed.

When they turned off the dirt road and drove through her front gate, Carson instructed Jax to take the gravel driveway that looped around her home where she could access a side entrance. After parking the truck, their footsteps crunched against the rocks as they walked, using the headlights and porchlight to illuminate their path.

"Do you have everything?" Jax asked when they reached the door.

Carson patted all her pockets with one hand. "Phone, key"—she lowered the icepack from her head and wiggled it—"ice. It's all here."

Jax glanced at her forehead and frowned. Then he reached up as if to touch the bandage but stopped half-way and let his arm fall back to his side.

"I'm fine, really," she said, pretending like she didn't want him to touch her.

Jax opened his mouth as if to argue but must have decided against it because, instead, he gave her a soft smile.

"Get some rest. You need it," he said before turning.

She watched as Jax retreated to his truck and drove away. And while she was excited for the day to be over, Carson knew she would be lying in bed awake reliving her evening with the blue-eyed firefighter.

Chapter Four

It took Carson a moment to realize the vibration that had awoken her wasn't coming from the throbbing pain in her forehead but from her phone.

Rubbing the sleep from her eyes, she reached across her bed to answer the incoming call.

"Are you alive?" Raegan screeched.

Carson pulled the phone away from her ear to deflect Raegan's shriek on the other end, which only intensified her headache.

"Yes, I'm fine. I'm alive," Carson promised.

"You didn't answer my calls or texts last night. You didn't call me to let me know you were home safe." There was a small break in Raegan's voice. "I've been worried sick about you. Hunter finally had to call Jax just so I wouldn't drive to your house to make sure you didn't die in your sleep!"

Carson let her friend scold her. She deserved it. After Jax had dropped her off at home, Carson had immediately plonked into bed without changing her clothes, or messaging Raegan that she was home, or even plugging her phone in to charge. She peeked at the battery symbol. It was dangerously low. Quickly, she jammed the charger into the port and leaned back into her pile of down pillows, wiggling until she was comfortable again. But the pain in her skull made the pillows virtually useless.

"I'm sorry. There was so much going on, I completely spaced texting you," she tried to explain.

Raegan sighed. "I'm just happy you're okay. How's your head? Jax said you had to get stitches?"

"Five."

"I can't believe it was Jax who hit you with the door."

"I was going to ask about him. Does he work with Hunter or something?"

"Not anymore," Raegan explained. "They were at Station 74 for a while before Jax transferred to Station 71. I'm surprised you haven't met him already. He and Hunter are really good friends."

"Maybe I have and just don't remember him," Carson said, thinking about her brief conversation with Jax while waiting for the urgent care physician. Raegan and Hunter regularly hosted parties at their house with hordes of people. Surely Jax was amongst them. But with so many people, it was impossible to remember everyone.

"Jax is, like, the nicest person you'll ever meet," Raegan said.

Images of Jax cradling Carson in his arms flooded her mind—the concern on his face, the way he'd stroked her clammy fingers and held her hand to keep her from dropping over the edge of panic. "Yeah, he seems very kind."

"He *is* kind." Then Raegan changed the subject. "Oh! Have you talked to your boss about junior partner?"

Carson sat up and pushed her covers off, swinging her legs over the edge of the bed. "I did. He said he'll talk to me sometime today."

"Let me know what he says. I can't think of why he wouldn't promote you. You're an amazing lawyer, and he has to be smart enough to see your potential."

Pride filled Carson's chest. She had dedicated a lot of her time to her career, but she didn't want to be an associate attorney forever. Eventually she dreamed of opening her own firm, but she didn't have experience running one. Becoming a junior partner would provide her opportunity to learn the ropes and, hopefully, open her own business one day.

"I'll let you know what he says. Speaking of work, if I don't start getting ready now, I'll be late."

"Okay. Bye!"

Hanging up, Carson slipped out of bed, went into the bathroom, and flicked on the light to inspect her injury in the mirror. She was met by a gruesome sight. The skin around the stitching had swelled up, and dried blood clung to her matted hair. Was this what she had looked like last night? How embarrassing. Would it leave a scar?

Just another in the collection.

Twisting the knob three-quarters of the way to the left, she started the shower so it could rise to her preferred heat level. It wasn't as scalding hot as Luke had liked it, though. Whenever he went to bathe, she would joke, "Have fun in the inferno flames of hell."

The pain continued to pound in her skull, so Carson rifled through her medicine cabinet, looking for the bottle of anti-inflammatories. But as she eyed the little red tablets in her palm, a memory fought to expose itself. Before the image could fully develop, she quashed it back into the recesses of her mind and dumped the entire bottle in the toilet.

As she stepped into the shower, she caught a glimpse of herself in the full-length mirror on the bathroom door. It was almost ritualistic of her to examine her butchered body before she showered. So many lines. But, for the first time, she took concern at her gaunt form, identifying her bones prominently sticking out, especially her rib cage and hips. Had she always been this skinny?

Her mother had always thought she was pudgy. She would call Carson her "little chunky monkey."

Carson continued to stare, her body reminding her of a sunken skeleton. She looked ghastly. She looked dead.

She huffed. If only that were true. With a shrug of resignation, Carson stepped into the steaming water.

As Carson waited for her office computer to wake, she flipped through the stack of papers in her wire-tray inbox. How had it grown in size over the weekend? Lips pressed into a thin line, she tossed the sheets back into the tray and diverted her attention to her monitor. The login screen had a different image every time the computer powered on. Today it displayed a disheveled tabby cat clawing at a thick rope, its back paws swinging in the air. At the bottom it read, "Hang in there!"

"Ha," Carson scoffed.

"What's so funny?" Garrett Hoover, the senior attorney and her boss, was standing in the doorway. A grin was already glowing on his face, his white teeth a stark difference against his deep-brown skin.

"Oh, nothing." Carson quickly typed in her password and hit Enter.

Stepping into her office, Garrett relaxed in one of the cushioned seats in front of her desk. His tall, lean frame made it look like a children's chair.

"I have a favor to ask of you," he said. "Can you take over a consultation for me? I need to meet with the hospital district this morning."

"Of course," she said, eager to show him that she was a team player at every chance she got. "What time?"

He glanced down at his watch. "At nine. It's for modification of spousal support."

Carson had never dealt with a spousal support case before, or any family law matter, but she wasn't going to let that stop her. She was a team player *and* versatile.

"I can do that," Carson confirmed, scribbling the time on her notepad.

"Thanks. I also wanted to talk to you about the promotion we discussed last week."

Carson immediately held her breath. All her hard work was going to finally pay off.

"I'd like to see you succeed in this career. I really would, but"—Carson's heart hit the floor with a thud—"you're not quite there. You're passionate, and a damn good lawyer." Garrett eyed the stacks of case files on her desk before he continued. "I think becoming a partner may be too much for your plate right now. And that's why I'm not going to grant the promotion today."

For a second, Carson had the urge to argue. Working her ass off over the past six years at this firm had to count for something, right? Then she took a second to ponder Garrett's words. Was it too much for her plate right now? Her scar-covered body flashed into her mind.

Despite the tension lingering in her neck, Carson nodded. "Yes, sir. I understand."

Garrett tilted his head to one side, maybe noticing the slight twitch in her eye. "I'm not saying no. Becoming a partner is loads more responsibility. As your boss, and your friend, I'm advising you to focus on getting control of the cases you already have. In a couple of months, if I see improvement, we can talk."

Even as Garrett left for his office, his words continued to echo in her mind. *Focus on getting control of the cases you already have.* How was she supposed to be junior partner, let alone run a successful private practice, if her own boss thought she didn't have control of her workload?

Before Carson could wallow any more deeply, she was interrupted.

"Good morning, Car—what happened to your head?" Dan, another of the firm's attorneys, was standing in her doorway. His buggy, sunken eyes were zeroed in on her forehead. When Carson had first met Dan, his appearance reminded her of Gollum from *The Lord of the Rings* trilogy Luke had made her watch years ago.

"I just hit my head. That's all," she said. Apparently, the nude-colored Band-Aid she applied that morning wasn't as subtle as she hoped.

"What happened to Carson's head?" a voice beyond Dan asked. Rookie paralegal Noah slunk into the doorway, pushing his thick-rimmed glasses over the bridge of his nose. He was slouched over to keep from clipping his yellow highlights on the doorframe as he slipped into the room.

"Carson hit her head," Dan said.

Noah glanced at Dan, then back at Carson. "How'd you hit your head? Did it split open?"

Carson sighed. "I got hit with a door. It's only a small cut." It was the only one of her cuts that didn't feel good.

"Ouch," Dan said, at the time Noah said, "Nice."

"I'm taking over Garrett's consultation at nine," Carson told Noah, deviating from the subject. Despite Noah's cheeky humor, she could always rely on him to get stuff done. He was the best paralegal she had ever worked with.

"Got it." Noah shot finger guns her way and walked back toward the front reception desk with Dan following behind.

After skimming through only half of the dozens of emails waiting in her Outlook, Carson decided to light the lavender-and-vanilla candle Raegan had gotten her for Mother's Day. Maybe its calming properties would make her headache go away.

Just as she was sniffing the melting wax, Noah rapped on the door. "Consult is ready for you."

As Carson approached the conference room, she summoned what little she learned about family law in law school. Just as she pushed open the partially shut door, she halted with one foot inside the room. Jax was sitting at the large, granite-topped table. The morning sun bathed his silhouette from the window behind him. Instead of a baseball cap and the Super Soakers uniform, he looked more professional in a navy-blue shirt with a Maltese cross on the left side of his chest. His inky-black hair spilled across his forehead. A crisp manila folder was laid out in front of him next to the complementary water bottle.

"Jax?"

"Carson?" His tone echoed her surprise as he stood up. When the shock on his face turned into delight, Carson was a bit perplexed as to why her heart stuttered.

"I see you survived the night," he continued. "How's the brain?"

"Not dead," Carson quipped, gaining her composure and shutting the door behind her before choosing the chair opposite him. He waited until she was seated before he sat back down.

"You're Mr. Hoover?"

She snorted. "Mr. Hoover had a last-minute emergency. He asked that I take over this consultation. I didn't know it was you when I agreed."

"Are you still able to do it?"

"Yes. Although there may be a conflict of interest meeting with the person who assaulted me."

Folding his arms across his chest, Jax leaned back in his chair. "Does that mean you're going to press charges?"

She spun her pen on the stone tabletop. "Maybe . . . depends on how much you're willing to bribe me."

Jax smirked.

"If you would like to reschedule with Mr. Hoover you are welcome to. I would not be offended if you're uncomfortable with talking about personal matters with me," Carson said.

"I don't mind. Are you uncomfortable?"

"Nope." A lie, perhaps, based on her heart rate. "It's my job."

"Good." He surveyed her, his eyes trailing her up and down. "So, you're a lawyer, huh?"

"Yep." Carson popped the *p* at the end.

"Do you like it?"

"I do. There's enough drama that I don't have to pay for Netflix anymore."

"Then you'll appreciate my ex-wife's drama," Jax grumbled.

Carson's eyes flitted to his left hand. There was no ring or indentation. Not even a tan-line. Maybe not a recent divorce, or maybe he'd never worn a wedding ring.

She crossed her legs. "Is that what brings you in? Mr. Hoover mentioned spousal support."

"I've been paying for a year, since the divorce. But I recently found out that she moved in with a guy and got a job. My previous attorney told me if either of those two things happen, I could stop paying."

Carson pinched her pen between her fingers and tapped it on her palm, recalling her law school education. "In simple terms, yes. There must be a substantial change in circumstances in order to amend your support payments. Do you mind me asking why you're not using the attorney who represented you in your divorce?"

"He retired a few months ago."

"Alright. Do you have anything that shows she's got a new job and is living with someone?"

Jax opened the folder that was in front of him, pulled out a piece of paper, and slid it across to her. It was a screenshot of a webpage for a local hair salon, Modern Locks, and it displayed images and short bios of their hairstylists.

"Kristen at the top is my ex-wife." He pointed her out.

The name Kristen Miller was written in creamy calligraphic letters. Underneath she was described as Modern Locks' newest stylist. A picture next to the name showed a poised woman with long, white-blond hair and an oblong facial structure, showing off two rows of perfectly white teeth.

"Don't let her looks fool you."

Carson glanced up at Jax, whose demeanor had changed. A scowl had taken over his face, and his chin was raised a bit higher than she had remembered it.

"Let's just say she was"—his fist clenched then relaxed—"unfaithful for our entire relationship."

Carson detected Jax's anger in the stiffness of his shoulders, the twitching of his jaw. "I'm so sorry."

"It's not your fault. It took me a long time to figure out that it wasn't my fault either. I'm just the naive dumbass that didn't recognize what was happening."

She grimaced, not liking the idea of him feeling guilty about Kristen's transgressions. "Cheating isn't typically obvious."

A corner of Jax's lips turned up. "So I've been told. At first I didn't . . . handle it very well, but I eventually got my life back to normal."

Normal again. If only Carson could have that luxury.

"Is this Kristen's first job since your divorce?" she continued. Even though she was curious to know more, she had a job to do. "Has she been unemployed this entire time?"

"Yes. She uses the guys she is with, and me, to pay for everything."

"I see. And she moved in with someone?"

"I know she's been seeing this guy for a while now." Jax rifled through the stack of papers before him until he found what he was looking for. "Her boyfriend posted on Instagram about a housewarming party last week."

He held out the paper to Carson. It was a picture of Kristen with her arms around a stocky man in a cowboy hat and Pit Vipers. Surrounded by balloons, they stood in front of a ranch house.

"We'll want to have this," Carson said. "Is this your only copy?"

"No. You can keep both of the pictures."

"Perfect." Carson jotted a few notes down on her notepad for Garrett. "Did you bring in your divorce paperwork? Specifically, the current decree and order that the judge signed?"

Jax handed her a few stapled papers, which she scanned for anything that could complicate the process of amending his spousal maintenance, taking note of Judge Callaghan assigned to his case.

"Good news is initially it looks like we can reduce your payments, if not end them altogether," Carson said. "No guarantees, though. If you would like to hire us, our office can definitely represent you. Noah at the front desk can prepare the hiring agreement."

"Will you be my attorney?" Jax asked.

He seemed troubled that she would be. Was he uncomfortable having a friend-of-a-friend represent him?

"No, I don't handle divorce cases in the office," Carson said, "Mr. Hoover will represent you." Maybe she should look into taking on some family law matters. It would give her a wider berth of legal knowledge for when she opens her own firm.

"Good. So no conflict of interest."

Her eyebrows scrunched, but instead of investigating his statement further, she let it go. "No, there is no conflict of interest. Do you have any other questions?"

"No, Mr. Hoover," he deadpanned, "I believe you've answered them all."

Carson began gathering her things while Jax mimicked her, creasing his folder and palming the bottle of water. She guided him from the conference room to the reception area, where Noah's fingers were flying across a computer keyboard.

"Mr. Miller will need a fee agreement," Carson told him before she turned to Jax. "It was good seeing you again."

"Good seeing you too. I'm happy my stupidity didn't kill you yesterday," Jax said, his blue eyes flashing up to her forehead.

"Wait," Noah said, looking from Carson to Jax with a confused expression. "Ms. West said she hit her head on a door."

Carson stifled a groan. "I did."

"Did she tell you that I was the one who hit her with the door?" Jax asked.

Noah's eyebrows shot up. "No, she did not."

"It was an accident," Carson said.

"I slammed a door open, and she was on the other side," Jax explained. "Nearly killed her."

"Did not," Carson argued, galled.

"Your head was bashed open, and you were on the ground bleeding all over," he countered.

"I was not bleeding all over."

"Wanna bet?"

She opened her mouth to dispute but gave up. Noah's eyes were bouncing between her and Jax.

"Anyway . . ." Carson grabbed a business card off the elevated counter space in front of Noah's desk and gave it to Jax. "Here is Mr. Hoover's card. At the bottom is our main office line and his email."

Jax took the card from her, scrutinizing the front and back of the small rectangle, before giving Noah side-eye. "Do you have one? You know, just in case I have any other questions."

"Mr. Hoover and Noah are able to ans—"

Noah shot up and reached for another card on the counter, thrusting it into Jax's hand, looking pointedly at her. "Yes, Ms. West does have a card. It's right here *with* her cell phone number."

"Thank you." Jax tucked her card into his back pocket. "I hope to see you again . . . soon."

Carson's mouth was still open from being cut off mid-sentence. "I'm sure we'll see each other in passing."

There was a slight fall in his shoulders. "Right. Thank you again." He turned to walk out the glass front door. Carson eyed his robust frame while Noah whistled behind her.

"Are you going to jump on that?" he asked when the door had shut.

Face flushing, Carson whirled. "Noah!"

"What?" he said innocently. "He was totally digging you, and you are totally digging him."

Her nostrils flared. "He does not *dig* me. I do not *dig* him. There is no *digging*."

"So, you're telling me that you haven't checked out that hot piece of ass?"

"No," she lied.

One of his eyebrows raised. "Mm-hmm, and I don't wear glasses."

She gave him a trenchant glare, but he continued anyway. "The guy totally has the hots for you. He literally asked for your phone number."

"That's because he's a client."

"No, that's because he wants to talk *casually*."

Just then the office phone rang, interrupting their conversation.

"He likes you and you know it." Noah spilled out the words and answered the phone before she could contend. "Hoover & Associates, this is Noah."

Once again in her office, which now smelled like a lavender farm, Carson skimmed through her emails, forgetting she had already read most of them. Her conversation with Noah continued to resound in her ears only causing her to become more flustered with him. She didn't—*shouldn't*—like Jax. At least, not in that way. But the guilt was like a rock settling in her stomach. What would her dead husband think about her liking another man?

She shook her head, trying to clear it out, and pulled the lit candle closer. She had too many unresolved cases to be thinking about some hunky fireman.

CHAPTER FIVE

Tap. Tap. Tap.

Carson's arms were crossed, finger hammering against her forearm. Twenty minutes and still waiting. Raegan could at least have the courtesy of arriving on time, especially since she had begged Carson to be her plus-one at the charity auction.

Standing at the main entrance of Ponderosa Pines Conference Center, Carson observed event attendees dressed in fancy cocktail dresses and tuxedos bustling through the revolving glass door. She'd extracted her own little number from the back of her closet: a floor-length, ebony gown with long sleeves. It was one of Luke's favorite dresses on her, particularly because the back exposed a great deal of skin from her neck to her hip line. The dress fit a little looser than Carson remembered it, though.

A light breeze rustled the leaves and brushed against her spine. The sun was on the verge of setting for the night, turning the sky sherbet orange. The venue sat on top of one of the highest hills in the area. Its grand architecture towered over the residents of Prescott, demanding attention from all those within sight. Except, Raegan was nowhere in sight, so Carson was left standing on the sidewalk like a lost puppy.

For the fifth time that night, Carson fished her phone out of her clutch.

Scrolling through her work calendar, she wrinkled her nose. It was not looking any better than the past three weeks. Ever since she'd been denied the promotion, she'd chosen to take Garrett's advice seriously and pour herself into her work. Carson was going to show him she had what it took to become junior partner. From early mornings to late nights, she'd had little time to think about anything else but her cases. Because her hands were busy with drafting court documents, she hadn't harmed herself since the morning of the softball tournament . . . until last night.

Carson slid her palm down her side, feeling the hint of bandages just beneath the polyester. From her rib cage down to her hip were strewn new lines, the consequence of withholding for so long. Her body and mind were so numb, she hadn't realized the damage until it was too late. The cuts were nearly all scabbed over, but the pain remained to remind her of how weak she was.

"This is ridiculous," Carson said aloud, shoving her phone back into her little purse and snapping the clasp shut. Just as she was about to turn and walk back to her truck, she heard her name called. She spun around to find Raegan gliding up the side path, her turquoise gown shimmered in what was left of the sun's light.

"I am so sorry. I had an emergency cavity filling at work. I got here as fast as I could," Raegan apologized.

Carson plastered a smile on her face. "It's fine. Where's Hunter?"

Raegan adjusted her plunging neckline—a little too revealing, in Carson's opinion—pulled out a tube of pink lipstick from her purse, and started applying it while she spoke. "He drove separately since I was running late. He should already be inside and checked in." Then her eyes focused on something behind Carson. "Speaking of handsome firemen up for auction . . ."

Carson turned to find Jax strolling up the main pathway between a few couples.

"Jax!" Raegan yelled.

Having only seen him in casual clothes Carson's breath caught when she saw him in black tie. His short beard was tidier than the last time she had seen him at the consultation three weeks ago. Carson didn't understand how his dark hair could appear harmoniously unruly and professionally styled at the same time. Her heart stammered in her chest. Maybe this event wouldn't be as awful as she had thought.

Jax looked around, trying to find who called for his attention when he spotted the two friends. Recognition flashed across his face.

"Mr. Hoover, long time no see," he said as he approached them. From the corner of her eye, Carson caught Raegan curiously tilting her head.

"Are you part of the auction too?" Carson asked.

He rubbed the back of his neck. "Unfortunately."

Now that he was closer, Carson noted how stiff the fabrics of his suit were. No signs of wear and tear. No dust smudges. Not even a speck. Luke always had some sort of stain on his clothes. It annoyed Carson beyond reason. Either Jax was an absolute clean freak, or he had just purchased this ensemble.

"You are the sexiest bachelor in all of Arizona," Raegan said. "The ladies will be fighting over you. Now get inside. You're going to be late for check-in."

After surrendering their tickets, Carson and Raegan were ushered into the grand ballroom. Wide swooping canvases hung from the ceiling, giving the illusion of a large outdoor tent. Dozens of tables covered in black-and-white tablecloths filled a majority of the great room. The effect reminded Carson of a checkerboard. Centerpieces, stained glass and metal intricately forged to take on the shape of a flame, rested in the center of each table. A flickering light illuminated from within making the colors of the glass sway and dance. A band of strings and winds produced classical melodies that drifted about, filling any empty space. It felt extravagant and cozy.

Raegan pointed to one of the last empty tables. "Over here."

They were only seated for a few seconds before a server stuck a silver platter filled with skinny glasses and exotic hors d'oeuvres underneath their noses.

"Something to eat or drink?" he offered in a nasal voice.

"Yes, please," Raegan enthusiastically answered, swiping one of the tall glasses. The server picked up a pair of miniature, silver tongs and pinched a few of the morsels—morsels which Carson couldn't identify, let alone recognize as edible—onto the plate already placed in front of Raegan.

He turned to Carson. "And for you, ma'am?"

The waft of alcohol accosted her nose, her stomach spasming. Never again. "No, thank you."

As the young man pivoted, Raegan snatched another glass off the tray. "She still wants this."

Sometimes Carson believed Raegan enjoyed having a sober friend. If only she knew the reason why Carson had chosen sobriety . . .

"Who are these smoking hot ladies?" Hunter slipped his big frame into the chair on the other side of Raegan. Like Jax, he wore a suit, only instead of a black bow tie, he had a thin turquoise tie that complemented Raegan's dress, which had no doubt been her doing.

"I hear you're a bachelor tonight," Carson said.

Hunter rubbed a hand through his auburn hair, ruffled it a bit, then smoothed it over before leaning an arm on the table. "I'm a happily married man who has no idea why his wife wants to pimp him out."

Raegan waved her hand dismissively. "I'm thinking of the children and all the money you're going to raise for them."

"Uh-huh." Hunter placed a hand on his wife's shoulder. "Before it starts, I want to introduce you to someone."

As Hunter and Raegan disappeared into the crowd, Carson continued to observe the variety of people around her, impressed at how well attended the event was. She wondered if it was like this every year, or if it was because this year's live auction consisted of hot firemen. Additional stewards drifted around the room, serving those who were waiting for the main event to begin.

"Is this seat taken?"

Jax had come up from behind, gesturing to the chair next to Carson.

Butterflies. Little, tiny, cliché butterflies whirled in Carson's gut before immediately turning into culpable moths.

Still, she shifted to make room. "It's all yours."

He slid into the seat, his cobalt eyes dazzling her. "I haven't seen you in a while." Then his gaze flicked to her forehead. "You got your stitches out." With no hesitation he reached up to brush her curled hair out of the way, inspecting the scar. She was startled at his nonchalant touch, but even more startled by how it made her heart skip with trepidation.

"I got them out about two weeks ago, on my birthday," she said, remembering how she had thought it was a treat getting her stitches out on her special day. Like a little birthday gift to herself. The surgical thread was starting to get annoying, and it was a relief to finally have them removed.

He lowered his arm. "When was your birthday?"

"August twenty-first."

"Happy belated birthday." He gave her forehead one more peek. "The doctor did a very nice job stitching you up. You probably won't see it in a couple of years."

Disappearing scars would make my life a whole lot easier, Carson thought.

"You look beautiful, by the way," Jax added.

Carson flushed and raked her hands through her dark hair, hoping to tame any flyaways. Ever since the consultation, Noah had relentlessly tried to meddle, constantly asking if Jax had called her yet. Which Jax hadn't. Carson forbade herself from deciphering what his lack of communication could mean and ignored why it made her feel disappointed.

"Thank you," she said. "You don't look too bad yourself."

"Honestly, I haven't worn a suit since Kristen," Jax admitted. "She always wanted me to dress fancy."

"Guessing you don't like dressing up?" Carson eyed his pristine suit again; confident he had just purchased it for this event and this event only.

"Not even a little. If I ever get married again, which I'm still debating since the last time didn't work out so well, I'm going to show up in jeans and boots." He tugged at his collar. "I might even shower."

Carson laughed. "That will be one lucky bride."

Their conversation came to a halt when Hunter and Raegan returned to the table.

"What are you two smiling about?" Raegan asked while Hunter pulled out her chair for her.

"My future wedding," Jax said.

"Oh, great," Hunter complained. "This time, can you choose someone who isn't a traitorous wh—"

Raegan smacked Hunter's arm.

Jax grinned. "That's the goal."

"So, are you going to explain to me why you called Carson, Mr. Hoover?" Raegan pried.

"I had a meeting at her office with him," Jax explained. "Except he was busy, so she took over."

"Really?" Raegan raised her perfectly plucked eyebrows. "Why do you need to see an attorney?"

"Kristen got a new job, so I'm trying to end spousal maintenance."

Raegan glanced at Carson. "Is that possible?"

"It's possible." Carson pushed a lock of hair behind her ear, giving her attention to Jax. "To be honest spousal support is rare for cases like yours. Judge Callaghan, who was assigned to your case, is a sucker for women's sob stories in divorces. I typically don't speak ill of the judges, especially at work and with clients, hence why I didn't say anything during your consultation."

Hunter shook his head. "I didn't even know Kristen was capable of working."

"Me either," Jax fumed. "I'm still kicking myself for believing all her lies."

Raegan looked nervously at Jax. "Are you sure you want to put yourself through all of that again? Since . . . you know . . ." Raegan, Jax, and Hunter exchanged glances as though there was a secret between them. A few times those glances were pointed at Carson.

Before Jax could answer, a screech from the speakers broke up their conversation. A short, plump man standing at the podium onstage lowered the mic to his height.

"Good evening, ladies and gentlemen, and welcome to the Get Active! Youth Sports Club Charity Auction," he boomed in a baritone voice. "Thank you for joining us this Saturday evening."

Carson adjusted in her seat to get comfortable. Except she couldn't, because the tape from one of the bandages was tugging on the delicate skin on her stomach. She scooted forward a couple of inches and leaned back to allow the adhesive to lay flat. Much better.

The presentation was a little boring for her taste. But what fundraising event wasn't? As expected, recognition was given to people who boasted about the so-called good deeds they were doing. Carson believed these events were not only for raising money but for rich people to flaunt how much of it they had and how they were better than everyone else because they donated it to help the needy. Maybe the money spent on the event should go to those in need instead of pampering the rich attendees. Yet she couldn't say anything because she was there. *I'll leave a donation to make up for it*, she promised herself.

The only enjoyable part was a short video of local youth projected on a large canvas. Tiny faces with round cheeks filled the screen. Toothless smiles and giggles warmed the coldness currently encasing Carson's heart. These children were the reason why she got out of bed and put on makeup and heels. Why she had joined her friends for a night out instead of sulking on the couch.

Carson's composure shattered when a little boy with a head full of curls waved shyly at the camera. She dropped her eyes to look at something, anything else, then elected to shut her eyes all together. *Breathe.*

A gentle nudge on her shoulder got her attention. She looked up at Jax who, without using his words, questioned her countenance.

She faked a smile.

"It's time for the best part of the evening," a new speaker said, her eggplant gown glistening in the lights. "Can our eligible bachelors please come forward?"

In unison, Hunter and Jax stood and followed the other beefy firefighter clones up to the stage.

"Oh, this is going to be good," Raegan sang.

"Are you going to bid on Hunter?" Carson asked.

Raegan gave her a devious smile. "Nope."

The auctioneer continued, "We have Prescott's finest bachelors up for grabs tonight. And ladies"—she hid her mouth from the men on the stage with her hand—"they're firefighters, and we all know what that means." Then she whispered, "They're good with their hoses."

A rumble of laughter spread through the audience. Onstage, Hunter and Jax had taken their place in the middle of the row of men. Jax's hands were shoved deep into his pockets, and he was entranced by something on the stage floor. Hunter whispered a comment to the guy next to him, and they both chuckled.

"You will be bidding on a date with one of these very fine gentlemen," eggplant-dress lady continued. "Or more. I'm not here to judge. Pull out your pocketbooks, because the bidding starts now!"

The first firefighter, a blond man whose abs strained the limits of his dress shirt, stepped forward. Before the auctioneer could finish reading his bio, women in the audience began throwing out bids of two hundred, three hundred. Carson's eyebrows rose with every increment until the auctioneer announced the winner, a brunette in a skintight, thigh-length dress, at twelve hundred dollars. Apparently, these people took charity very seriously.

"Wonderful!" the auctioneer cried. "Please find a seat next to your new date. Next, bachelor number two!"

As the auction played out, the firefighters would flex or spin to try and schmooze the audience. Carson couldn't believe how much money some of the women were willing to spend for a date with a firefighter. It only proved her point about rich people flaunting their money.

Hunter's turn came up. He sashayed into the spotlight, its light drowning out his freckled skin, and frivolously paraded himself like his fellow coworkers before him as if he were saying to Raegan, "Fine. If you're making me be part of the auction, then I'm going to *be* part of the auction."

"A thirty-three-year-old Arizona native, Hunter Olson, spends his spare time using his big, strong hands to give the most sensual massages . . ."

That was when Hunter pretended to drop something on the stage and proceeded to theatrically bend over to pick it up, showing off his backside to the audience.

"One thousand!"

Carson searched for the bidder who'd spoken. Much to Raegan's visible delight, it was an elderly woman who could not have been a day younger than a hundred. Maybe even two hundred. Damn, she was old. Onstage, Hunter's eyes bugged with uncertainty, perhaps realizing the reality of his situation.

Raegan, on the other hand, cackled. "My night just got better." Then she scowled at Carson. "Don't you *dare* bid on him."

"Thirteen hundred!" a younger, more age-appropriate woman yelled. Hunter regained his composure and twirled. The little old lady shot her competitor a death glare and countered with fifteen hundred. Before Carson knew it there was a bidding war. Hunter cheered them on, soon becoming the most expensive date yet. Eventually the younger woman gave up, leaving the frail lady victorious at twenty-one hundred dollars. Her arthritic hands clapped as she celebrated her win.

Hunter stuck his tongue out at Raegan before descending the stage to meet the aged champion who enthusiastically threw her boney arms around him. One of those arms slid down and gave his butt a quick squeeze.

Tears were streaming down Raegan's face from giggling. She used her table napkin to dab under her eyes. "And that's why I love him."

The voice of the auctioneer came over the speaker again. "Our next bachelor is thirty-two-year-old, Jax Miller, a born-and-raised Texan. The highest bidder may get a chance to learn if *everything* is bigger in Texas."

Unlike Hunter, Jax didn't brandish his body. He kept his hands in his pockets, his shoulders up by his ears. A bashful smile played on his lips.

"Let's start the bidding!"

Immediately Jax locked eyes with Carson. His expression was pleading, almost forlorn. Then the connection was broken when someone cried out the first bid.

"One thousand!"

"Fifteen hundred!"

The shouting progressed. Carson observed the different women bidding on Jax. They were all lavishly attractive. She pictured him beside one of them, going out for dinner, him holding the door open, his date hanging on his arm.

Carson's spine went rigid. Was physical touch part of the arrangement? What were the limits? She couldn't remember them describing what a date with a firefighter entailed. Surely it was just platonic. It would be absurd if anyone would allow anything more than dinner. Oh, who was she kidding? They were adults and could do whatever they wanted.

Another bidder called out the next offer. Leaning back, Carson folded her arms across her chest, crossing her legs. Another bid. She rolled her eyes. These people were ridiculous. It was just a date, for crying out loud.

"Three thousand going once . . ."

Carson craned her neck to spot who might be the highest bidder; a woman squeezed into a green cocktail dress and a curtain of platinum hair. Kristen had blond hair, she recalled.

"Going twice . . ." A dramatic pause. "Sold!"

Carson flinched at the word. Jax nodded at the auctioneer and ambled down the steps toward the woman who had purchased him. The closer he got to her, the faster Carson's heart beat in her chest, and the lower her shoulders sank. The woman stood to greet him, flipping her hair behind her before giving Jax what Carson believed was an inordinately long hug.

Uncomfortable, Carson squirmed in her chair. She was overreacting, but why? Why did she care about the way green-dress' eyes twinkled at Jax or manicured hand lingered on his arm? Raegan's own husband had been auctioned off, and she was acting perfectly rational. So why did Carson's chest twinge at watching Jax take a seat next to the woman?

Just then, Jax caught her eye. He didn't seem too enthusiastic about the woman's advances either. As his eyes darted between Carson and his new date, his expression was somber.

Carson mustered a fake smile for him, wishing he would stop looking at her. Confused and flustered enough as it was, she didn't need those ocean eyes muddling her thoughts even more.

Returning her attention to the stage, Carson wondered what Luke would do if he was there. If he had been a firefighter, Raegan would have most definitely forced him into the auction just like Hunter. And Carson would have allowed it. Both wives would giggle as their husbands tried their hardest to sell their bodies. She could imagine Hunter and Luke teaming up on stage and doing a silly dance or striking absurd poses. But, unlike Raegan, Carson would bid on him. Just like in the movies, where the main character would throw out a crazy amount of money and the whole room would gasp. She would give anything to be able to bid on Luke.

Finally, the last fireman was sold off, and the ceremony finished with a final speech from Prescott's mayor. People began standing up and excitedly conversing with one another. Hunter and the feeble lady appeared at their table. Carson could detect the suffocating stench of moth balls emanating from her.

"Who are these . . . people?" rasped the old woman, giving them a disapproving leer.

"Gloria, I'd like to introduce you to my sister," Hunter said, his hand extended toward Raegan.

Carson choked on her spit. Raegan scowled at Hunter, who glowered back with a twinkle in his eye.

"I'll take good care of your brother," said Gloria. "See you next week, dear." Then, to Carson's surprise, the little old lady slapped Hunter on the butt before waddling away.

Carson strolled over to the few tables overflowing with silent auction treasures: woven blankets with Indigenous designs, season tickets for the local football team, an obscure painting of . . . she had no idea what it was. Someone had even donated a signed photograph of Elvis Presley. Luke's grandpa was a huge fan of The King of Rock and Roll. He would have loved to add another to his collection.

Eyeing a particular piece of jewelry—a copper ring embedded with circular raw turquoise that sat flush with the metal and two small Apache tear fragments bordering the main stone—she gently brushed the tip of her finger over it. According to the place card, it was her size, and she was tempted to bid on it. She balked when she saw the amount of the latest bid, five hundred dollars. But she promised she would donate money for the cause so she scribbled down a hundred dollars more than the last offer, not having much hope that she would win.

"Mr. Hoover."

Jumping at the unexpected visitor, Carson slammed her hip into the table—the same hip that she'd maimed the night before. The table rocked once before settling, its load of items safe.

"Oof." She tensed at the sharp, stinging pain and rubbed her side.

Jax was already reaching to console her. "I really need to stop hurting you. Are you okay?"

Not wanting to draw any more attention to her body, Carson dropped her own hands. "I'm fine," she said. Then she noticed that Jax was alone. "Where's your date?"

Jax's lips fell disapprovingly. "She left. But I wanted to check out this stuff before I went home."

"Oh . . . me too."

"Are Hunter and Raegan still here?" he asked, as they inspected the next item, a ride on a Zamboni at the Roadrunner Sports Complex.

"They left a few minutes ago."

"How do you know them?"

Stopping, she turned back to him. He was focused on her, seemingly uninterested in the silent auction.

"I've known Raegan since freshman year of high school," Carson said.

"We were on the same volleyball team."

"Were they already high school sweethearts when you met?"

"Not till senior year. I stole Raegan's heart first."

Jax's eyes gleamed for a moment as they moved to the last table. A few other lingering guests were huddled around a gift basket full of expensive summer sausages and Wisconsin cheeses.

"Does that mean you're from around here?" he asked.

The rough fibers of a woven blanket scratched Carson's fingertips as she stroked it. "Yes," she said. "Well, I was born in Phoenix and moved to Prescott just before high school."

Jax also reached out and rubbed his palm on the blanket. "Oh? What made you move from Prescott to Chino Valley?"

The question made Carson retract her hand. She had loved living in Prescott. Loved the trees that offered shade and the natural landscaping of the giant granite boulders. She adored the first home she and Luke had purchased. It had taken them two years to save enough money to afford the down payment. A little two-story nestled in one of the hills. It was where they were going to raise babies . . .

Glancing at the other patrons, Carson hesitated before saying, "I was in a car accident that killed my husband and . . . unborn son. I couldn't live in that house anymore."

Subconsciously, she placed a hand to her stomach, where her baby had been. The memory of seeing his silhouette on the sonogram strip for the first time popped into her mind. She had told Luke she thought their son had his nose. Luke didn't think so. Still, she had pictured birthing a miniature Luke with a head full of auric ringlets, imagining those spirals bouncing when he learned to walk.

Her chest ached knowing she never had the chance to see if he'd had

Luke's nose. Never got to kiss those baby cheeks. Never got to witness those first steps.

An emotion flashed across Jax's face, as if he had just solved a puzzle. Then he frowned.

"Shit. I'm sorry. I didn't mean to pry." His voice was tight.

"I didn't think you were," Carson assured him.

"My ma always tells me that I ask too many questions. Sometimes I don't even realize I'm doing it."

There was a clatter from across the room. The event staff scurried over to a stack of chairs that toppled over.

"It's getting late. I should get home," Carson said, looking back at Jax.

"Right, late." He peered down at the sizable titanium watch on his wrist. "Can I walk you out?"

"As long as you don't try to jump me," she joked.

"No promises."

As he escorted her outside, where only a few other vehicles were scattered about, Carson recognized Jax's truck on the opposite end of the parking lot before they had reached her own truck. Hers was newer and smaller than his. Black instead of red, gas instead of diesel, Toyota instead of Ford. Hers smelled like plastic and leather, not old dirt roads on a rainy day.

"Carson?" Jax leaned against the bed of her truck.

Before turning to him, she popped open her clutch to find her keys. "Yeah?"

Across the lot, a vehicle's headlights swept across them. Quiet, Jax stared down at the asphalt beneath their feet. Finally, his eyes met her stare.

"There's something I need to tell you."

Patiently, Carson waited for what he had to say. It was curious to watch him struggle with his thoughts, as he seemed to always be collected.

After another moment's pause, he said, "I'm really sorry about what happened to your family."

"Thank you." Carson wasn't convinced that's what he was originally planning on saying. But the sincerity in his tone made her feel comforted in knowing she had made the right choice in telling him about the accident.

Clicking the key fob, she opened the driver's door while he stood up straight and held the door open so she could climb in. He seemed poised in indecision, not ready for their conversation to end, for the night to end.

Surprisingly, so was she.

But then he said, "Goodnight, Carson." And with one last look, Jax shut her door and vanished into the night.

Chapter Six

"It's pronounced Press*kit*, not Press*cott*," Carson repeated, somewhat impatiently.

It was Friday, the last day of the week-long Western Legal Professionals Convention. Will, a blond attorney from Los Angeles, had spent all five days mispronouncing the name. When Garrett had suggested Carson head down to Scottsdale for the convention, hope sparked within her that her boss didn't consider her a lost cause. And much to her delight, the convention just happened to host multiple seminars about the business side of running a law firm.

"I told you, it's going to be impossible to remember because I had a law school instructor with the last name of Press*cott*," Will muttered.

"Well, if you're serious about transferring to Arizona, then you better pronounce the cities' names correctly," Candi, a young paralegal from Tempe, criticized from across the table.

Will and Candi had been Carson's companions for most of the week. They'd sat at the same table for the very first seminar, and they'd struck up enough of a rapport to keep sitting together.

"Welcome," the lecturer called, and the humming around the room fizzled out. "My name is Thea Rodríguez of Picacho Professional Development Specialists in Tucson, and today we're going to learn how to align your professional goals with your personal goals. Aligning these goals is important because when your personal life and your job are in harmony you are more likely to succeed in both."

The projector stationed in the middle of the room clicked on and text appeared on the front wall that said, "Personal Goals and Professional Goals."

"The first thing I want you to do," Thea continued, "is make a list of your current goals you have. Separate them into two columns: personal goals and professional goals. I'll give you about three minutes."

The scratching of pens on paper filled the room. Carson obediently drew a line down the middle of her paper. On the right side, she listed her professional ideals. She knew she wanted to be junior partner. Again, she thought about delving more into family law. The versatility of practicing on all sorts of matters could give her a fighting chance of opening her own firm—her ultimate career goal.

Before she knew it, the entire right column was filled. She stared at the other side and scowled. It was blank, just like her mind.

What life goals did she have?

She snuck a peak around the table. Will was already finished and flashed a smile at her. Candi was furiously filling out her professional column with impeccable handwriting. Noticing how the others' entire papers were filled with hopes and dreams only made Carson's frown deepen.

Did she have nothing to achieve outside of work? Writing down her personal goals shouldn't be this difficult. *Write something, for heaven's sake.*

Eyes dropping to her fidgeting fingers she followed the design on her sleeve up to her inner bicep. There was a subtle bump from a Band-Aid stanching blood from a fresh cut.

She'd been up in the early hours of the morning, sitting on the floor of her hotel room, slicing away at her skin. Her stomach knotted at the memory.

It was then she realized she did have a personal goal. Or at least she consciously thought of it for the first time: freedom.

The presenter called for everyone's attention once again. "Hopefully by now you have had a chance to determine both professional and life goals. Would anyone like to share?"

There was a brief pause before a few hands rose around the room including Candi's.

An older gentleman who Carson recognized from another class spoke. "To retire in the next three to five years. I just wasn't sure which column to put that under."

Thea laughed. "Seems like that belongs under both columns. Anyone else want to share?"

Candi raised her arm again.

"Yes?"

Grabbing her notepad off the table, Candi cleared her throat. "A professional goal of mine is to become a presiding judge."

"That would be a great feat," Thea said approvingly," I wish you the best of luck."

Candi scooted back into her chair, looking a bit smug from the attention everyone was giving her.

"Now, the goals that you have written down, are they achievable? If not, how can you adjust them?"

Carson peeked down at what she had written. One simple word. It sneered back up at her, provoking.

Was it achievable? Was it even possible? What did freedom look like?

As she thought about freedom, Jax in the black suit and bowtie he had worn to the auction a month ago came into her mind, which didn't make any sense. She chewed on her inner cheek and focused even harder on the freedom she desperately wanted.

For almost two years, Carson had been trapped in the endless cycle of cut, heal, repeat. She was tired of hurting herself, tired of the lies, tired of feeling guilty. Freedom would mean a future with no more scars, no more bleeding, and no more secrets. Which meant more possibilities.

Again, Jax's face came to mind. As a possibility? A possibility for what? A relationship? Her husband was dead, and she was daydreaming about the possibility of a relationship? Carson scolded herself. It was way too soon to think about that kind of future.

Except, what would she have to do to have a future with someone? With Jax? She would have to stop cutting herself, because that someone would eventually expect to, want to—she swallowed the giant lump that formed in her throat—see her body. And that was impossible at the moment.

Even as Carson thought it, her hand moved to lay over her arm, as if protecting the secret that lay underneath.

Could she stop? *Would* she stop?

She knew she needed to stop. If she was going to set a goal to be free—have a future with or without Jax—she absolutely had to quit what she was doing to herself.

Start small. Yes, she could start small. Something manageable like not cutting herself as often. Only allow it once a week. That was doable.

A relationship with Jax was not doable.

The seminar finished after they had dissected the "anatomy" of a goal. Carson stayed silent as everyone began filtering out of the room, buzzing about the conclusion of the convention. As she reached the elevator her name was being called from behind.

"You were out the door before I had a chance to say bye," Will said, jogging up to her, bringing a faint floral scent with him. Was that his cologne? This entire week, Carson had thought it was Candi's perfume she was smelling.

"I wanted to leave as soon as possible to beat the weekend traffic," she said.

There was a faint drop in his face. "Oh . . ."

"Was there something you needed?"

Shifting his feet, he said, "It's nothing."

"What is it?" she pressed, confused about his shyness.

Will coughed into a closed fist. "I was just wondering if you wanted to go get some dinner together before I went back to California."

"Dinner?"

"Yes, dinner. As in, a date."

The shock slapped Carson across the face. She and Will had gotten along so well the past week. They'd laughed and eaten meals together. When Will had mentioned he was interested in moving from California to Arizona, she'd encouraged him, telling him about all Arizona had to offer, especially if he moved to the Valley of the Sun.

That's where she wanted him to stay.

"I'm . . . already seeing someone," Carson lied. It was the best way she could think of to turn him down without hurting his feelings.

Will drew his chin in, making the coat of hairspray on his blond hair shimmer. "I didn't realize you had a boyfriend. You never said anything all week."

Carson could only stand there, hoping her body language kept up her facade.

"Does he live in the Prescott area too?" Will asked.

What was with the third degree? He didn't believe her. She needed to be more convincing. Then the auction popped into her brain again and she said the first thing that came to mind: "His name is Jax. And yes, he lives in Prescott." Even though she had no idea where Jax lived.

"Huh." Will seemed to finally accept her answers. "If I would have known I wouldn't have asked you out. I'm sorry. Have a safe trip." He stuck his hand out for a shake.

Carson tried to mask her cringe before shaking Will's hand. "You too."

Mercifully, the elevator dinged and the door opened, letting Carson inside to escape the awkwardness. And as the doors closed on Will's longing face, Carson silently thanked Jax for unknowingly helping her dodge a bullet.

Chapter Seven

The next day when Carson stepped through Raegan's front door, her best friend shoved an arm full of deflated balloons at her, commanding her to inflate and decorate. Carson was happy to oblige, but her lungs were even happier when she spied the helium tank sitting on the kitchen table.

"You'll never guess what happened this week at work," Raegan said, fretting over the pasta salad in the kitchen. "First, a little girl throws up all over the X-ray machine. And I mean *covers* the machine in vomit. Then the next day, another little girl bites my dental assistant."

Carson laughed over the whirring of expanding balloons.

"It's not funny," Raegan whined. "My assistant threatened to quit."

"Come on. You have to admit it is kind of hilarious."

Raegan wiped her hands on a rag before tugging down the white cover-up she wore over her mocha-brown swimsuit and adjusting her gold necklaces. "You're right. It is a little funny."

The door to the garage opened. Hunter squeezed himself and the two bags of ice he was holding through it. "This is all they had. Apparently, the whole town needed ice today." He hefted the bags onto the countertop, the ice crunching within the plastic. "Hey, Carson. Happy birthday to me, right? Have to go get the ice for my own party."

"Oh, get over yourself, and take these to the coolers on the back porch." Raegan patted his back while waving him off with her other hand.

The doorbell dinged.

"I'll get it," Carson offered, having just finished tying the last balloon.

One by one guests filtered in. Somehow Carson became the party usher, welcoming those who arrived and showing them to the backyard where the festivities were taking place.

"Food is ready," Raegan reported, entering from the backyard with an empty dish that had once held raw meat and placing it in the sink. "Go get a hot dog before the carnivores out there eat everything."

The sun was high in the sky, beating down on the party. Some guests—the carnivores—were already overfilling their plates, the paper goods bending underneath the weight. The pool was also overfilled. Water sloshed out and Carson wondered if there would be any left after the party.

Stomach rumbling, she snatched herself a plate and squeezed between two meaty men. The sliding glass door squeaked, and when she glanced up, Jax was just stepping onto the back porch. For a brief second she made eye contact with him, and the spoon full of fruit she was holding slipped from her grasp and clattered back into the plastic bowl. The newly formed smile beaming on Jax's face faded when a set of abs in only swim trunks pulled him in the opposite direction of her.

Satisfied with a hot dog and blueberries she had fished out of the pile of fruit, she searched for a space to eat. The tables were full, but it was too beautiful of a day to go back inside. Not daring to eat in the pool area for fear of being drenched, Carson chose to sit on a patch of freshly mowed grass, balancing her plate on her crossed legs. The blades poked her thighs through the bike shorts she wore, along with the spirit jersey she'd purchased during a San Diego trip with Luke the summer before the accident.

As she picked at her food, Carson tried to decipher the game being played in the pool. At least, she assumed it was a game, as there was a red ball being thrown around with shouts of victory and moans of defeat. After a minute of spectating, she concluded it wasn't the first time this game had been played.

Every once in a while, her eyes would wander to find Jax. The last two times she had snuck a peek, he'd been sitting in a small circle of friends, laughing with a plate of food in his lap. Once he caught her staring, to which she gave him a smile and a small wave. After that, she tried to avoid looking in his direction all together. Except her eyes would betray her and sneak a quick glimpse at him. And every damn time, he was sneaking a glimpse back at her.

Eventually Raegan found her, plopping herself down on the grass. "Having fun?"

"I'm enjoying the water Olympics."

"Boys."

Someone must have scored a goal, or whatever they were calling it, as the pool erupted with hollers.

"My neighbors are going to file a complaint," Raegan mumbled. "How was that legal something something convention?"

"Western Legal Professionals Convention," Carson corrected her.

"Whatever, same thing. Anything exciting happen?"

Carson could still feel the unpleasantness of her and Will's exchange, the flowery cologne and the graceless handshake. Will's hand was nothing like Jax's. His was clammy and limp, while Jax's was warm and strong.

"I got asked on a date."

Raegan's head turned so fast, Carson thought she was going to snap her neck. "What?"

"An attorney from California was there. Will. He wanted to take me out to dinner," she said, rubbing her hands up and down her bare legs.

". . . and did you go?" Raegan asked. Was there a hint of hope in her voice?

Carson shook her head. "No. I'm not ready for dating. At least, not yet." Or ever.

"Mind if I join?" Jax had appeared out of thin air, towering over them.

Raegan looked a little annoyed at him for interrupting their girl talk, but said, "Yeah. I need to go get the cake ready anyway. You can keep Carson company." Raegan lifted her hand, and Jax hoisted her up.

"Don't you need some help?" Carson asked.

"No, I got it." Then Raegan grinned wickedly. "But *don't* think our conversation is over." The gold chains around her neck clanged as she turned and strolled back to the house.

Jax took Raegan's place on the ground. He must not have worried about getting grass stains on his white shirt as he leaned back on his elbows, his long legs sprawled out in front of him, and let out an exhausted sigh.

"Long day?"

"I covered a buddy of mine's swing shift. I've been running on six hours of sleep for the past three days," Jax said.

"Hunter and Raegan have a huge, expensive bed inside."

Jax smirked. "Don't tempt me. I'm just glad I have the next four days off."

Putting her plate of a half-eaten hotdog and two blueberries on the grass, Carson unfolded her legs and leaned back on her hands, digging her fingers into the cool soil. Then, thinking about the tiny critters who made their home in the lawn, she quickly retracted them.

It had been a while since the last time she saw Jax at the auction a month ago.

Oh. The auction and the stupid green dress.

Hunter's date with Gloria turned out to be a blast. Besides her wandering hands, he'd thoroughly enjoyed spending time with the old woman.

"How was your date?" Carson asked. As soon as the words escaped her mouth, she regretted them. She did not want to know how well it went.

Except her question seemed to drain him. The smile on Jax's face faded, and his body sagged even more. He stared down at his black Vans.

"That bad?" she asked, trying to sound sympathetic. Secretly, her insides were dancing with glee.

"Worse," he said. "She was supposed to meet me at the restaurant but showed up almost an hour late. Then she was downing martini after martini. When she wasn't drinking, she was talking about either herself or her ex-husbands." He paused to rub his eyes with his forefinger and thumb.

"Classy," Carson murmured sarcastically.

"That's not all." Jax stopped rubbing his eyes. "She got so drunk she started taking her clothes off. The cab could not have picked her up soon enough."

"I'm sorry that happened to you." Carson was sorry. But only a little.

"Thanks, but I feel bad for her though," he said. "I really have the best luck with women, don't I?"

A scuffle drew their attention back to the house. Hunter was wrestling with a few of the guys, hooting as they took jabs at one another. Someone put him in a headlock, and he reciprocated by hooking his leg around theirs to trip them up.

"Are they always like that?" Carson asked.

Jax glanced back at her, looking grateful that she changed the subject.

"Yes, but they're family so you get used to it."

"You like being a firefighter?"

"I do."

"What made you decide to be one?"

Jax gave her his full attention, the scuffle forgotten. "When I was a kid, my dad was drunker than usual. He fell asleep with a lit cigarette—yes, it does actually happen—and the carpet caught fire. My oldest brother saw the flames, and by the time the fire department came the fire was completely out. We ended up having to toss the couch and curtains. It took my ma a while to scrub the black off the ceiling so we didn't have to look at it anymore.

"I can remember when the fire truck rolled up to our house. I watched all the firefighters doing their job. They let me and my three brothers sit in the engine and honk the horn. I thought it was so cool." Then a slight darkness shadowed Jax's face. "They kept us entertained while my ma talked with some other people who showed up. I later learned that it was Child Protective Services investigating the incident.

"I guess those firefighters made an impression on me, because I dedicated my life to become like them. I took the test on my nineteenth birthday."

Carson's hand, only a few inches from his on the grass, twitched in its direction. She wanted to comfort young Jax and his brothers, even his mother. It was difficult to imagine what it would be like to discover your house on fire from your own father's carelessness. A parent was supposed to protect their child from danger, not be the danger.

A hypocritical pain sliced through her chest. *A parent was supposed to protect their child. She* was supposed to protect her child.

"I can't believe your dad did that," she said. *I can't believe I did that.*

Jax rolled it off his shoulders. "Accidents happened a lot in that house."

"Oh." He didn't need to explain any further.

A whistle from Raegan alerted them that dessert was ready.

"Well, Mr. Hoover, would you like some cake?" Jax rose before her, offering his hand. He pulled Carson up, and for a second she thought he would keep holding her hand, but he dropped it, causing a minor twinge in her gut.

Everyone crowded around the extensive, concrete patio table for the celebratory birthday ritual. Raegan had placed the red velvet cake full of lit candles in the center. One of the meaty men from earlier squeezed in front of Carson, pressing her right into Jax. Jax's musky scent enveloped her, making her dizzy. It reminded her of being in his truck. Then she felt his hand on the small of her back. Apparently, Jax didn't feel the need to move as they stood crammed together. Every part of Carson that was pressed up against him pulsated with electricity.

She tried very hard to focus on singing happy birthday, but Jax's breath was hot on the top of her head, sending goosebumps down her arms.

The song ended, Hunter blew out the candles, and Raegan plastered a very happy birthday kiss on him. The table whistled and cheered. Carson glanced up at Jax and pretended to gag at her best friend's display of affection. He suppressed a laugh.

With her slice of sugar, Carson sat at the table, listening to the banter bouncing back and forth between the leftover party guests.

Tim, whom she'd learned was the captain at Station 71, had just finished telling a story about a kid who was almost beheaded by an invisible wire while riding his quad. Thankfully, the wire had snagged on the kid's helmet and ripped it, instead of his head, off his neck.

"Where did this happen?" Carson asked, stressed as she thought about all the trails she used to explore on her dirt bike.

It was Hunter who answered. "Somewhere off Senator Highway. I don't think they ever figured out who put up the wire."

"That's right," Raegan chimed in, her small face pinching with concern. "That was one of your favorite spots to go riding."

"Oh, this was like six months ago," Tim reassured them, wiping cake crumbles from his comically stereotypical mustache. "The police searched the whole area and only found that one wire. There haven't been any reports of another wire."

"Do you ride quads?" Jax asked Carson.

"I had—have a dirt bike, but I don't ride as much anymore." In fact, it had been years since Carson had mounted her bike. It currently sat in the shed, collecting dust and spider webs.

Jax's face lit up, impressed. "So do I. We should go riding sometime."

"Not down Senator Highway," Raegan quickly interjected.

"I haven't been out in forever. I'll probably crash," Carson speculated.

"Great news, Jax is a certified emergency paramedic," Hunter said slyly. "He can treat your injuries."

"Seriously, though, we should go ride," said Jax. "All of my lame Arizona friends don't own a dirt bike."

Raegan huffed. "My husband is not allowed to own or ride one of those death machines. The only reason Carson can is because I am not married to her and therefore cannot tell her what to do."

"Hey," Hunter contended.

Raegan gave a devilish smile. "You like it when I tell you what to do."

He wrapped his arms around her, giving her a squeeze. "Yeah I do."

"Gross," someone muttered.

Jax ignored the exchange. "Since I don't work tomorrow," he said to Carson. "Want to go riding?"

Carson hesitated. She would probably make a fool of herself. No, she would definitely make a fool of herself . . . again. In front of Jax.

Pinching her cheek between her teeth, her eyes darted around the table. Everyone was looking at her expectantly. Maybe she should go. It would get her out of the house and out of her head.

Then she remembered the personal goal she recently made. It would be a distraction from the other activities she could be doing, like taking a blade to her thigh and pressing—

"Why the hell not?" Carson said.

CHAPTER EIGHT

Perkinsville Road ran down the middle of Chino Valley, splitting the town in two. Jax's truck rattled when the pavement ended and the dirt road began. By the time Jax pulled off onto the shoulder and parked the truck, the terrain had transformed from flat valley to rolling hills.

After they had unloaded their dirt bikes and put on their gear, Jax yelled through his helmet, over the roar of the engines, "I'll follow you!"

Carson took off, settling into her seat, feeling stiff. Her movements were rigid as if her joints were made of wood. It took a while, but she fell back into the rhythm of controlling the machine, becoming less and less jerky.

They raced across the desert, dust pluming behind them, weaving through spiny shrubs and cacti. Their tires spit the soft sand as they wound through dried creek beds. Carson's muscles worked as they climbed berms and descended hills. She was going to be sore tomorrow.

The sun beat down on them, making it hard to believe it was early October. The monsoons had dried up over a month ago to yield to the harsh, dry Arizona heat. October was supposed to be full of changing leaves, hot chocolate, and chilly weather, not sweat, dehydration, and dried-up vegetation. Today seemed like the hottest day of the year. Carson feared for the back of her neck, exposed to the sun.

When the trail split into a fork, she pulled over to the side, nodding for Jax to go first. He ended up taking a side path that snaked down into a small canyon. Following his lead, Carson maneuvered carefully around some sharp boulders. The shrubbery gradually became greener, and the trees thickened as they approached the Verde River. Braking, Jax came to a stop just before a rock face that hung over the murky, jade water. She rode up next to him, squeezing the clutch and downshifting into neutral.

Cutting his engine, Jax flipped out the kickstand with his heel and removed his goggles, motioning for her to do the same.

"You hot?" he asked, pulling off his gloves.

"Yes," she said, taking off her own goggles.

"Want to take a dip to cool down?" He chinned toward the river, unbuckling his helmet and hooking it on one of the handlebars.

Carson's eyes bugged out of her skull. "Right now?" she squeaked. "In our gear?"

"No, in our underwear." Jax winked, teasing, as he swung his leg and dismounted his bike. Filthy from the day's ride, his hair was chaotic from sweat. There was a line of dust on his forehead where his goggles hadn't quite reached his helmet. Even more dust powdered his nose and cheeks.

Tasting dirt in her mouth and feeling the grittiness whenever she ran her tongue over her front teeth, Carson knew she was grimy too. She was hot and exhausted. Her muscles weren't as strong as they used to be. Handling the heavy machine took more of her energy than she remembered. Dipping in the river sounded so refreshing. She peered down at the water, its cool liquid beckoning to her.

Underneath Carson's riding pants and jersey were athletic shorts and a tank top. Swimming in her clothes wasn't the problem, though. There were too many scars that would be exposed. She debated with herself whether she could just hide her arms under the water behind her back. Maybe

Jax wouldn't detect anything. Immediately, she rejected the thought. He would certainly notice how weird she was being.

Shirtless, Jax was already standing on the edge of the overhang scanning the ripples in the water, his skin shimmering in sweat. When had he taken off his roost guard and jersey? She gaped at how toned his back was, compliments to his career as a firefighter.

On his right bicep was a half-sleeve tattoo. Traditional-style designs—an octopus, a skull, and a ship were intermixed with roses—climbed their way up his arm and settled on his shoulder. At one point Carson had thought about getting a tattoo, thinking it could cover the shame of her self-harm. But at the rate she was going, not only her skin would be mangled, but the beautiful artwork as well.

Her palms grew sweaty, but not from the scorching sun. Quickly she averted her gaze, realizing that she was checking him out. Seeing Jax shirtless made Carson's body react in an unfamiliar way. It was so unlike her. Why did everything seem so different and out of place when she was around him?

"Coming?" Jax was facing her again as he unclipped his boots and tossed them aside. The octopus' tentacles reached around the front and covered the right side of his chest.

Removing her helmet and gloves, Carson hopped off the bike and set them on the seat, trying to smooth down her French braids. "I think I'm just gonna stick my feet in," she said, arriving at the lip of the rock and bending over to undo her boot buckles as well.

"Oh, come on, the water's not that cold."

She guessed he was being sarcastic. The Verde River was well known for its frigid waters, even during the boiling summer.

"I'm just not dressed appropriately underneath," she lied. More like her skin was not appropriate underneath.

"Oh. We can keep going if you want."

There was an unexpected drop in her chest. She didn't want to go. At least, not yet.

"No, I want to stay." Carson plopped down on the hard rock, peeled her socks off, and let her bare feet swing close to the water's surface, nodding toward the river. "Go ahead. Jump."

"No way. You have to let yourself ease into it," Jax said, sitting down beside her.

"Wimp." She reclined back on her hands, the ground hot beneath her palms. Out in the distance she spotted the mesmerizing red rocks of Sedona.

"Says the girl not getting in," Jax grumbled.

"Hey, I have an excuse. Just do it."

"I thought my days of peer pressure were over." Jax scooted closer to the edge to dip in his toe.

Unable to help herself, Carson leaned forward and gave him a teasing push on the shoulder. He was closer to the edge than she'd realized. With a yelp, he plummeted into the water, the cold liquid splashing Carson's legs and feet. Her hands flew to her mouth as he came up, shaking the water from his hair.

"Jax! I didn't mean to push you in, I swear." Then laughter climbed its way out of her lungs.

"You think it's funny, huh?" He reached up, caught her ankle, and yanked her down.

A shriek filled the air as she plunged into a river that could only be described as glacial. The chill knocked the breath from her lungs. Rising to the surface, Carson gasped for air.

"Son of a bitch, that's cold!"

Practically howling from amusement, Jax grabbed and hauled her to him. She latched onto the same rock he was holding, kicking her numb legs.

"Still laughing?" Jax asked.

She glowered at him with chattering teeth.

"What? It was funny," he said, innocently.

"So is this." Carson slapped her hand across the top of the river, drenching his head with a wave of water.

"Hey!" Then he splashed back.

"No! It's so cold!" she yelled, turning away and shielding her face behind her arm.

The water calmed, and when Carson lowered her arm, Jax was even closer than before. The smile was gone, but his eyes were on fire. Those twin blue flames heated the cold space between them as their bodies bobbed up against the rocks. He wasn't shivering like she was. He was staring at her lips, which were probably purple. She peeked down at his mouth.

"Want to get out?" he asked.

Aching from the cold, she nodded, and they maneuvered their way over to the muddy bank and slopped up the shore to a large rock. Water seeped out as Carson wrung her braids, then the hem of her jersey. It surprised her that the water droplets didn't sizzle when they hit the ground below.

"If that doesn't cool you off, I don't know what will," Jax said, settling beside her on the stone and resting his elbows on his knees. The sun reflected off his wet skin.

The heat was already baking Carson's dark hair and jersey, but her riding pants were still soaked. The water in the thicker material was going to take longer to evaporate. Thankfully it was hot enough they wouldn't have to wait long for the both of them to dry out.

Pulling up a leg, Carson hugged it to her chest and relaxed her chin on her knee. "Thank you for inviting me," she murmured.

"I'm glad you agreed to come," Jax said.

"I really needed this."

Secretly, Carson was proud of herself. She had opted to get out of the house, away from work, away from her nightmares. Away from the collection of sharp objects that held such power over her. Was this what it looked like to be free? Then she thought of how she couldn't take off her gear to swim in the river. She wasn't free yet.

Jax was eyeing her with the same expression he'd worn in the river. He sat up as Carson raised her head. Hesitating for just a second, he gradually gripped the side of her neck, his thumb on her cheek. Was she paralyzed or mesmerized by the intensity of his eyes? Like the wings of a hummingbird, the beat of her heart sped up, and her breathing stopped as his eyes dropped to her lips. Then he slowly leaned in.

At the last moment, before their lips could touch, Carson turned her head.

"Jax," she whispered.

"I'm sorry, I didn't mean . . ." he stammered, jerking his hand away from her.

Her hammering heart seized and fell.

"No. It's not like that. It's just . . ." Carson's voice trailed off, unable to finish, and she peered down at her toes covered in dried mud, praying she hadn't offended him. "I'm sorry."

Stopping Jax from kissing her wasn't because she didn't like him. It was because she *did* like him, and that frightened her. A lot.

Was she ready to move on? Was she ready to open herself up to another person? Meeting Jax and being with him was something new, something that surprised her. But she needed to step back and evaluate what was happening. This was the first time since Luke that she had felt this way, and she wasn't sure how to handle it.

"You don't need to be sorry," Jax said, standing and ruffling his drying hair at the same time. "I shouldn't have tried to kiss you." He seemed embarrassed.

"That's not what I'm trying to say. I don't want you . . . It's not . . ." She was flustered. How was she supposed to communicate the torrent of emotions washing over her? "Nothing like this happened since my husband died. I don't want you to think it's you."

"Oh."

Gnawing on her cheek, Carson grabbed the ends of her braids and began to fidget with them, feeling as though she had ruined their day.

After a moment, Jax asked, "What was Luke like?"

The question made Carson's chest swell, and she smiled. "He was *every-thing*. Thoughtful. Genius. A bit nerdy." She laughed. "Funny. Especially when he would get together with Hunter. They were goofballs."

"How did you guys meet? Was he also an attorney?" Jax had sunk back down to sit on a rock. Not the same rock as hers, though. He was keeping his distance.

"No, he was an engineer. We went to the same college and there was a bar across the street from campus that my friends and I loved going to. One night some tool kept bothering me. I guess Luke had enough and stepped in."

It was one of Carson's favorite memories of him. She remembered right when the man grabbed her arm, another bigger, much stronger arm had grabbed his, twisting it back.

"The lady said no," Luke had said, "so I suggest you listen to her and get the hell out."

When she had followed the arm up, she was pleased to find chestnut eyes shadowed under caramel curls, looming over them.

The jerk had tried to resist, but Luke twisted his wrist harder. Finally with a huff, the offender yanked his arm away and stomped off. The situation had lasted only seconds and gone undetected by the bar's patrons as the dancing continued and the uninterrupted music bumped on.

"Are you alright?" Luke had asked, settling onto the bar stool next to hers.

"Yes, but you didn't have to do that."

"I know," he had said. "Can I buy you another drink?"

The memory always brought a smile to Carson's face because even though Luke had scared the jerk off, he was the biggest teddy bear she knew.

"How long were you married?" Jax's question pulled her out of her reverie.

"Four years. But we dated about a year before we got married," she said.

"He sounds like he was an awesome person."

"He was."

A hawk flew overhead, its shadow flashing by. Carson reached out and squeezed Jax's hand, noticing for the first time how worn the knees of his riding pants were. "Thank you . . . for asking about him."

He squeezed back. "Are you dry enough to head back to the truck now?"

Putting on the rest of her gear, Carson straddled her bike and stomped down on the kick starter. The engine sputtered but didn't start. She tried again. Nothing. Twisting the throttle, she tried a third time. The engine gave a pitiful cough.

"Damn it," she grumbled. Before Jax had picked her up, she'd pulled her bike out of the shed for a quick inspection. The engine had started just fine back at the house. Of course, in the middle of nowhere it decided to give her trouble.

"Everything okay?" Jax called over the sound of his own bike, which was rumbling just fine.

"Won't start," Carson shouted back. Using her feet, she rolled her machine forward and backward, then tried kicking it to life again. This time, the engine didn't even wheeze at her.

Jax turned his bike off and came to stand next to her. "Try it again," he said, his voice muffled by his helmet.

Nothing.

Frustrated, Carson removed her goggles. "I think my battery is officially dead."

"That's what I was thinking," Jax said.

After Carson dismounted, Jax gripped the seat to reveal the battery. An initial exploration didn't reveal anything to be wrong, like major corrosion or disintegrating wires.

"It's an old battery that hasn't been used in . . . a long time," she explained. Five years, to be specific.

For a second, Jax poked around inside the dirt bike's opening before saying, "We can go get the truck and come pick it up."

"I can wait here with my bike."

Even through his goggles, Carson could see him look pointedly at her. "I'm not leaving you here by yourself in the desert."

Snapping the seat back in place, Jax pulled the key out of the ignition and handed it to her. After shoving it deep into her pocket, Carson stepped out of the way so he could roll her bike under the shade of a nearby tree.

Once back on his machine, Jax kicked it on and scooted closer to the handlebars, gesturing for her to hop on behind him. She wavered before slipping her goggles back on and placing her hand on his shoulder for support. Swinging her leg up and over the bike, she adjusted herself until she was balanced behind him. When he took her gloved hands from his shoulders and guided them down to his waist, Carson stiffened. His hard muscles now rested under her hands, tempting her. If she raised his jersey she could feel them directly—

"Ready?" Jax called over his shoulder, snapping Carson out of her fantasy.

She gave him a thumbs up as she chided herself. It was totally normal to wrap arms around the rider in front for better balance and safety. And why were these daydreams even happening? If only she could smack herself.

Even still, during the ride back to the truck, with Jax literally in her arms, Carson thought about him and their almost-kiss. She felt stupid. He was obviously starting to like her, and she was a complete fool, possibly ruining a friendship with him.

A kiss, though? It was crazy to think about. After Luke's death she'd sworn off anything of the sort, never wanting to have her heart ripped to shreds again. Yet less than an hour ago, she'd been face-to-face with a man, centimeters from his lips.

Carson knew she owed Jax more explanation of why she'd rejected him. It was important that he knew their relationship could not go any further. She wasn't ready.

Was she?

The only reason she'd stopped him from kissing her was because she couldn't comprehend how comfortable she felt. In fact, her heart was still shriveled from when he pulled away. She shouldn't be feeling like this. How could she move on so quickly from Luke? The ambivalence of it all made her exasperated.

It didn't help that his body was pressed against hers. The touch only befuddled Carson's thoughts even more. Her brain, heart, and body were sending mixed signals to each other. Forget mixed signals—it was more like an all-out war underneath her skin, and she was the collateral damage.

When they reached the truck, Carson was happy to get off yet sad she had to let go. Yep, she definitely needed to slap herself.

In the truck, Jax blasted the air conditioner, angling the vents to point at himself and Carson, the air smelling like its signature dusty scent.

Tilting the visor down, Carson looked at herself in the little mirror. "Oh, geez. That's embarrassing."

There was dirt caked on her forehead and nose. She tried to wipe it off with her hands.

"I like my girls dirty." Jax laughed, then caught himself. "That was inappropriate. Please don't tell my ma I said that . . . Here." Reaching across her, he opened the glove box and pulled out a napkin, using a water bottle to wet it and handing it to her. Happily, she took it and attempted to remove the dirt.

"There," she said, slapping the visor closed and turning to him for his approval. "How's that?"

Jax inspected her. Carson became self-conscious; she probably resembled a train wreck. Reflexively, she smoothed her hands over her braided hair.

"I'd go out in public with you," Jax teased, then wetted his own napkin, trying to wipe off as much of the grime as he could. "Now, what about me?" There remained a smudge above his left eyebrow.

"You missed a spot," Carson said, sliding over and grabbing the damp napkin out of his hand. She bit her tongue as it took a couple of swipes to get it completely off.

It wasn't until Carson glanced down from Jax's forehead and met his gaze did she realize how close she was to him. Once again, his eyes were burning. By his expression, she knew exactly what he was thinking and wanting to do. It was the same expression he'd had right before he'd tried to kiss her by the river. But this time, he didn't make a move. The air around them thickened, the air conditioner not making any difference.

Even as she dropped her hand, Carson didn't back away. Blood raced through her veins as her gaze dipped from his eyes to his lips. Why wasn't she moving away from him? Then a crazy idea flashed into her mind. When she peered back up at his eyes, they were bright with curiosity.

Before she could talk herself out of this second chance, Carson bent in and lightly kissed him. As soon as their lips connected, Jax's body froze. Carson put a hand on his cheek, his facial hair pricking her palms, and deepened the kiss.

That was his cue. Putting a hand on the back of Carson's neck, Jax kissed her back.

Spinning. Carson's mind was spinning like the dust devils that swirled in her front yard. It was nothing like she remembered, but it felt right. It felt safe and electrifying. She expected it to feel wrong. It didn't. Kissing another man after the death of her husband should have felt wrong . . . right?

It was a short, innocent kiss. That was all Carson could handle. She could tell that Jax was waiting for the end as well, because the second she began pulling away, he instantly released her.

Slowly, she removed her hand from his face, clenching it into a fist in her lap.

"That was . . . unexpected," Jax breathed.

"It was unexpected for me too," Carson confessed, her lips still tingling from the pressure. Embarrassed, she began to scoot back to the passenger seat. As Jax stared at her curiously, she sensed he wasn't going to ask for an explanation for her erratic behavior or for more kissing or both.

Unsure of what to do at that point, Carson reached up behind her to put the seat belt on. With a chuckle, Jax shook his head, then put the truck into gear and pulled out onto the dirt road, back toward her dead dirt bike.

Chapter Nine

As soon as the blade touched Carson's arm, her phone rang, causing her to spasm and the knife to slice through her skin like butter. A curse escaped her lips, and she quickly ripped tissues one by one from the box sitting on top of her desk and pressed them firmly to her forearm.

What she should have been doing was taking advantage of an empty office to prepare a mediation brief or tackle the pile of cases on the corner of her desk. All day the blade she had stashed in her desk drawer had been flaunting its sharpness. Eventually, Carson was seduced by its tantalizing power, not having the patience to wait until she was well hidden behind the walls of her home.

The phone continued its shrills until she answered the incoming call.

"Hello?"

"Carson?"

"Jax?" Hearing his voice brought back the memory of kissing him the day before, causing tingles in her gut.

"Hey, do you have a second?" he asked.

Pulling the tissues away, she inspected her arm. Blood continued to pool and drip down her skin. A single droplet fell and splashed onto her pants, saturating the charcoal-colored fabric.

"Shit." The tingles vanished and Carson grabbed more tissues and pressed even harder, shooting pain up her arm and into her shoulder.

"Is this a bad time?"

"No. No. I just, uh, spilled something on myself." It wasn't technically a lie.

"Oh. I was calling to see if you would like to go out to dinner with me."

"Tonight?"

"If that's alright. I know it's kind of last minute."

The phone began to slip from between her cheek and shoulder. "Can you hold on a second?"

Without waiting for a reply, Carson leaned forward and let her phone fall on the desk with a thud. As the blood flow slowed, she discarded the wadded tissues and ripped out more, stacking them on her new cut. The tape dispenser zipped as she pulled a long piece of tape and wrapped it around her arm one, two, three times. It was a crude wound dressing, but it would have to do until she got home.

Shoving her arms back into her blazer, Carson ripped a few sheets of paper from her notepad and flung them into the trash. A sad effort to cover the massacre.

Before picking up the phone, she adjusted her blouse, smoothed down her hair, and straightened her spine.

"Sorry 'bout that. What did you need?" Why was her voice so high? She cleared her throat.

Jax took a second before answering. "I was hoping you would have dinner . . . with me . . . tonight." Each word he enunciated, similar to the way her colleague Dan would slow down his legal explanations when clients got blank expressions on their faces.

The reality of what had happened solidified, making Carson feel as though she'd been punched in the stomach, and her body sagged in her chair. Jax was calling to ask her to dinner, but she was focusing on her filthy habit instead.

"Yes, dinner," she said, hoping it appeared that she was listening the first time he said it.

"Yes, you'll have dinner with me tonight?" he repeated.

"No. I meant I understood."

"So, no to dinner?"

Carson smacked a palm on her forehead and let it slide down her face, not caring if it smeared her mascara. Jax was going to think she was dumb by the time their conversation ended.

"I mean I can't do dinner. I have plans."

"I see," he said slowly. "Maybe another time?"

The tingling returned. Something about being asked out on a date made her body buzz with energy. She recalled when Will wanted to go on a date with her. She had cringed then. Now, Jax asking, a smile grew on her face.

But the anticipation was quickly extinguished when she spotted something next to her heel. In her frenzy to answer the phone and stop the bleeding, the blade had fallen to the floor. As she watched, the red dots of her blood grew into a puddle, and the blade morphed into Luke, lying in a pool of his own blood.

She remembered that she shouldn't be happy.

"Maybe," she said.

They hung up, and Carson continued to glower down at the sleek, shiny steel. Then she stomped her foot on it, over and over. She wanted to stomp out her self-harm. Stomp out Luke's dead face. Stomp out the absolute shitshow of her life. This was the reason she'd been denied the promotion.

"Leave me alone!" she cried.

Defiantly, she scooped up the knife, chucked it into the trash, and marched the trash bag to the dumpster behind the office building. Satisfied, she wiped her hands together and went straight back to her office.

It wasn't a lie when she told Jax she had plans. She'd had a date with a kitchen knife. But not anymore. She had set a goal to gain freedom, and she was going to fight for it.

Jax answered on the first ring. "Hello?"

"Jax."

"Carson?"

"My plans fell through. Still want to have dinner tonight?"

As Carson walked up the ramp that led to Barry's Burgers and Shakes, she spotted Jax already sitting at a table in the middle of the dining area.

Earlier that day, on the phone, he had suggested they dine at The Lakehouse which had cozy, quiet booths, dim lighting, and a seductive color palette. Something upscale and intimate. She wasn't ready for intimate. Instead, she had proposed a more casual eatery with bright blues and whites. Barry's Burgers and Shakes' dining room was basically a large, enclosed porch; open and very public.

When Jax caught sight of Carson, he immediately stood. Blood pulsed throughout her body, making the cut on her arm throb. Except she didn't mind the pain; it gave her satisfaction, which was disturbing. Self-inflicted pain shouldn't please her the way it did, but in reality, it pacified and soothed her aching heart. The contradiction of it all gave her a headache.

Jax's hair was damp, the ends flipping this way and that way. Looking suave, he certainly didn't belong in a place that served fish sticks. As she reached the table, Carson was enveloped by the scents of soap, spices, and the invariably present dust. How was it a man could smell just like his truck?

He didn't offer her a hug, or a handshake, but he did step around the table and pull the chair out for her.

"Mr. Hoover."

"Jax."

It had been one day since they had seen each other. One day since they'd raced dirt bikes across the Arizona desert. One day since they'd kissed.

All of Carson's earlier bravado wavered. Jax probably thought she was crazy. First, she'd rejected his kiss, then kissed him not an hour later. When he'd asked her out, she'd said no. And within minutes, she'd called him back. No. Yes. Maybe. Never. Yes. No. Yes. She was going to give him whiplash.

He was clearly aware of her behavior. His cheek was twitching. Well, it was more like his lips were undecided if they wanted to smile or stay the way they were. Amused. That's what he was.

A girl with a spotted, frayed apron wrapped around her tiny waist approached their table. "What can I start you off with tonight?"

"Water, please," Carson ordered.

"I'll have water as well," Jax said.

The waitress scurried off, leaving two giant menus for them to peruse.

"How was your day off?" Carson asked as her eyes skimmed over the variety of meal options without really reading what they were. At the table beside her, a toddler started fussing because he wanted the red crayon his sibling had stolen from him. She smiled at the cute whimpers, wondering what her son would have sounded like at that age. If he were still alive, he would have been four-almost-five years old. He might even have a younger sibling to fight over a crayon with.

Jax clapped his menu shut. "Lazy. I mostly caught up on sleep."

"Nothing exciting happened?"

"Nope."

"Not even a solicitor at your door?"

"Not even a solicitor at my door."

The waitress came back with their drinks. "Have you had a chance to look over the menus?"

Jax, with his menu flat on the table and hands resting on top, looked questioningly at Carson. She'd had a chance to look over the menu, but her nerves had made her blind. She glanced back down and ordered the first thing she saw, pork tacos and jasmine rice.

When the waitress left again, Jax leaned back and crossed his arms over his chest. His black button-up shirt was tight against his biceps; his tattoo peeked out under his right sleeve. Carson knew just how firm those arms were.

"Any other filler questions you want to ask to break the ice?" he asked.

"Is it that obvious?"

"Your leg is shaking the table."

Once Carson's foot stopped bouncing, the ice inside their waters calmed. "Oh."

She didn't know what to do with her hands. First, they gripped the edge of the table. That was too tense. So she folded them on top. Too formal. Finally, she let them fall in her lap, drumming her fingers on her thighs.

Jax leaned forward and rested his forearms on top of the table. "Alright. What is your favorite animal?"

The beat of her finger drums stopped. "Serious?"

"Trust me."

Skeptical, Carson played along. "Fine. My favorite animal is a platypus."

"The duck-beaver?"

"No, the *platypus*," she said. "What is your favorite animal?"

"The octopus."

"Why an octopus?"

"Have you seen one? They're cool."

She grinned, and so did he. His plan was working.

"What is your favorite book?" he asked.

Placing an elbow on the edge of the table, Carson rested her chin in her palm. "It's a children's book. Well, a children's series about a farm dog called *Hank the Cowdog*. I loved it so much, I always had one checked out from the library." She reminisced on sneaking a flashlight into her room and squishing herself under her bed so she could read. How exciting and free it had been to learn about a dog who had unlimited access to the outdoors and friends who were there for each adventure. "I was always getting in trouble for staying up past my bedtime reading them."

More than in trouble. One time, her mom caught her reading after dark and tossed the book out the window. It had rained that night. Carson had wept for three days over the death of that book. Worse, she'd had to use her own money to replace it in the school library.

"I don't think I've read them since I was in elementary school," she said. "I wonder if you can find them anymore. It's been so long."

A throaty laugh coming from the table behind Jax distracted her.

"Are your nerves feeling any better?" Jax asked, pulling back her attention and smoothing out the scowl lines that had grown on her face.

"A little." She was still gnawing at her cheek, but she had a mission tonight. "Actually, I'm glad you called because there was something I wanted to talk to you about."

A thick, black eyebrow rose peaked with interest.

"I owe you an explanation about what happened in your truck yesterday." A rush of embarrassment heated her cheeks. *Don't kiss me. Just kidding, kiss me.*

"You don't owe me anything," he said.

Carson shook her head. "But I do." When Jax opened his mouth to protest, she lifted a hand to silence him. "I need you to listen for a minute because I need to explain myself. It's not fair for me to act one way and then act the opposite five seconds later."

"It wasn't five seconds," he countered.

She let out an excessive breath, a strand of her hair fluttered in front of her face. "I shouldn't have done what I did."

"What? Kiss me?"

"Yes."

Jax sucked on his front teeth.

"I mean, no." Again with the whiplash. "What I mean is, I told you I wasn't ready and then I did what I said I wouldn't do in the truck." The memory of her lips on his and his firm grip on the back of her neck made her shiver.

"Kissed me," he clarified.

"Yes . . . kissed you."

A huge mound of food appeared in front of her face. "I have the pork tacos for you, ma'am, and the brisket-and-chuck-blend burger for you, sir."

Crummy timing, thought Carson.

"Anything else I can get you two?" the waitress asked.

Jax didn't take his eyes off Carson. "No, thank you," he said, dismissing their server. Once she was gone, he continued, "Then why'd you kiss me if you weren't ready?"

The fluorescent lights drowned out the beautiful colors of a sunset turning into night. Carson knew that the deep burgundy sky was dulling into a slate gray. Still, she tried to see past the screens that covered the glass windows, thinking. Why had she kissed him? She had been asking herself that for the past twenty-four hours. It was impossible for her to decipher her own feelings, let alone define them to someone else.

"When I said I didn't know if I was ready, I meant that," she started slowly, her food untouched. "I honestly don't know what I am. I'm not who you think I am. This isn't me." She rubbed her forehead with her palms. The sweet, tangy scent of mango salsa filled her nose. "When you tried to kiss me by the river, it caught me off guard because I wanted you to kiss me. My husband is dead, and I wanted another man to kiss me."

Now she wished she had agreed to the other restaurant. Luke's death was too sacred to be discussed in a place like this.

"I didn't mean to make—" Jax started.

"No, you didn't do anything wrong," she interjected. "As soon as I turned away, I regretted it. I regretted it because I didn't want to ruin what we . . . I kissed you in the truck because I wanted to."

"Do you regret it?"

Jax's voice was so quiet, almost as if he were afraid of her answer. Carson had to strain to hear his question.

"Regret the kiss?" she asked.

"Do you regret kissing me?"

She picked up her fork and pushed the rice around. Steam escaped from between the white kernels. "I don't think I regret kissing you, but I don't know what I think. This is all so confusing. I'm just amazed you don't think I'm bat-shit crazy and still want to have dinner with me."

He popped a fry in his mouth before he jokingly said, "I felt bad for you."

She chuckled, and they dug into their awaiting dinner. Her corn tortillas instantly crumbled, their weak bodies unable to bear the generous serving of meat. She resorted to using her fork instead of chancing dropping food all over her lap. She could only stomach a few bites of rice and half a taco. Jax, on the other hand, devoured his entire burger and all of his fries. Only the remnants of juices and seasoning dirtied the tray's paper. She wondered if it was because of his fireman appetite or if his mother had properly taught him to always eat all of his food.

Instead of bringing up the kiss again, he asked her about trivial things. She knew he was only asking these types of questions because he was giving her space. Letting her decide if it was more than just a first date.

The first date she'd ever had was boring. A simple dinner and movie. That wasn't the boring part. First-dates were supposed to be full of nerves and giggles, but there'd been nothing.

When she and Luke had gone on their first date, it was extraordinary. Somehow, he'd managed to set up a table and candlelit dinner in a road median.

"Isn't this illegal?" she had asked.

"Hell if I know." Then Luke's eyes darted toward the passing vehicles. "If you see red and blue lights and hear sirens, we should probably run."

That night, the lawyer in her had researched loitering in road medians. She had laughed because the two of them had committed a misdemeanor.

What was this first date with Jax like? Nerves. Check. Excitement. Check. The opportunity for another date . . . Check. They hadn't even finished their first date, and she was already thinking about a second one. Was that considered a small step or one very large step? She'd have to think about that.

But what would happen after the second date? A third? Then a fourth? Date after date after date. Same trivial topics. Same humdrum meals. At what point would she allow him to take her to a more romantic restaurant?

Romantic? Absolutely not. At least not right now. No. Not ever.

"Everything alright?"

Carson blinked, trying to remoisten her eyes which had been staring relentlessly at the swamp cooler in the corner window. She squared her slouching shoulders and looked timidly at Jax. The family beside her had left and was replaced by an old couple who were slurping their soup.

"Remember when I said I wasn't ready?" she asked.

Scooting forward, Jax put his hand on top of hers. For a second, Carson thought he was going to push her sleeve up and confront her about her newest cut.

"This doesn't have to be anything more than just a friendship," he reaffirmed, although he was doing a poor job at hiding the regret in his voice.

She eyed their hands resting together on the tabletop. His touch was so hot, it burned her skin.

"That's the confusing part," she whispered. "I think I don't want this to be *just* a friendship."

There. She'd done it. She'd finally admitted to him the very foundation of her inner turmoil. The reason for her chaotic thoughts.

Carson West wanted a relationship with Jax Miller.

She interlaced her fingers with his. "I don't understand how happy I am with you. I shouldn't be happy. My family is dead, and I shouldn't be happy." Her voice broke. Her heart broke. Her walls broke.

Instead of responding, he squeezed her hand tighter. Not even trying to find the right words to say to her. All he did was touch her.

Oddly, this was exactly what she needed. For years, people tried to make her feel better with words. It was always "It's going to be okay." "You're so strong." "You're going to make it through this." Frankly, it was all bullshit. She wasn't okay. She wasn't strong. And she sure as hell was not making it through this. But she couldn't blame them for their words. What else were they supposed to say to someone who was the sole survivor of a car accident? "Your entire family died, and now you're going to suffer"?

No words were exchanged for seconds. Minutes. Long enough that the heat in her hand had subsided. Long enough that the plates were removed, and the bill was paid.

Jax's silence was becoming suspicious. Then blood flooded her neck and cheeks. *Oh no*, Carson thought. What if, after all she had confessed, he was quiet because he didn't feel the same way? But in the truck, he'd kissed her back, hadn't he? Or had it just been her imagination? It had been so many years since she had kissed someone.

Except he'd invited her out to dinner. Then again, he'd said they didn't have to be more than friends. Was that him friend-zoning her? Was she spilling her guts like a fool to someone who wasn't receptive to it all?

"You haven't said anything," she blurted.

His face scrunched. "About what?"

"About what happened in the truck. About the kiss." *Our first kiss.* "I mean I just told you I wanted to be in a relationship with you and you didn't respond."

He rested against the back of his chair, never letting go of her hand. "You haven't given me a chance to say anything." There it was again, his mouth twitching with even more mirth than before.

Her own mouth opened to argue except thinking back on all their conversations, she had interrupted him over and over again. "Oh."

"Am I allowed to talk now?"

She nodded.

"When I tried to kiss you by the river, I wasn't thinking about your accident and what happened to Luke. I was caught up in the moment. And I felt like a total asshole. When we were riding back to the truck, I knew that I needed to give you your space. Then *you* kissed me, and the way you kissed me said everything you've been trying to explain to me. I didn't ask you to dinner because I expected something from you. I asked because I like being in your company." He smirked at her. "You're pretty cool."

She blinked at his last statement. *Cool?* She was a total mess, and he thought she was cool? "Seriously?"

"The coolest."

"You might be the crazy one," she said, wrinkling her nose.

"I think you're more than just cool, Carson." Jax's deep-sea eyes caught fire, and flames spread to consume Carson's attention. "I also don't want this to be just a friendship."

Ice froze her lungs. So Carson wasn't imagining everything. Jax had feelings for her too. Suddenly, this scared her. A lot. All of her courage was gone. Disappeared. Goodbye.

She could never be with Jax. She could never be with anyone. Eventually they would want progression, and that meant exposure, mentally and physically. She could never open up to satisfy them—to satisfy Jax. And she couldn't do that to him: a relationship with no next step, never moving forward, stagnant, keeping secrets, and telling lies. Would she do that to herself?

Why were they even talking about a relationship when Carson's body and mind were so ugly? Jax deserved so much more.

Ripping her hand from his, Carson stood, the chair grating and making her ears recoil. "Please forgive me," she stammered. "I should have never done this to you."

Not waiting for a reply, she spun and rushed past the old couple, who were now sharing a piece of carrot cake, and dashed out the door. The tsunami wave that had unfolded over the past couple of days now swallowed her up, and she was drowning.

"Carson, wait!" Jax called from behind her, his footsteps thumping down the wooden ramp and into the parking lot. Before Carson could open her truck door, he caught her. "What do you mean? Done what to me?"

She whirled to find creases sitting between his eyebrows. His mouth was open, confused.

"Led you on. You don't want someone like me." Carson's words shook, distorted with shame and self-hate.

"What's going on?" Jax asked. When his hand extended out to her, she shrank away from it, cowering. "Did I say something?"

It was the pain in his voice that stopped her. Carson was already hurting him, and they hadn't even begun. "I can't give you what you want."

The lines on Jax's forehead grew larger. "How do you know what I want?"

"I know you wouldn't want this."

"If you're implying I don't want you, then you clearly don't know what I want," Jax said, his eyes narrowing.

"I come with too much baggage. Trust me, I'm not worth it." She spat the words at him like her mother had done to her.

"Baggage?" He almost laughed. No, he did laugh. "You think I wouldn't want to be with you because you have baggage? Everyone has baggage. I have baggage. I have a gold-digging ex-wife that will always fight for my money. I had a father who—who . . . I had gotten myself into some trouble. If anything, *you* shouldn't want to be with *me*."

Carson drew back, shocked that Jax thought he had baggage. That was all minuscule luggage compared to hers. A carry-on. A wallet.

Jax had no idea what she was talking about. Tempted to blurt out the real reason, Carson bit her tongue. Maybe the only way she could convince him was by showing him her mangled scars. She bit her tongue harder.

"You're jumping to conclusions," Jax said. "We just met. There doesn't have to be expectations."

She exhaled from her nose, warming the tip of it. "Eventually, you're going to have expectations and needs that I won't be able to give you."

"You're crossing a bridge that hasn't been built. It may never be built."

"It's built in my mind."

"Not in mine," he growled, his nostrils flared with irritation.

Now it was a staring contest. Carson stood strong even against his blazing blue eyes. But Jax's arms were crossed, protective. Had he grown taller? The shadows enveloped him as if he were their ruler and they were ready for his command.

Only, Carson was an attorney. Fighting battle after battle was her everyday job. Astuteness and intelligence were her weapons, sharp and ready. She was prepared to win.

Did she want to win, though? Did she want to leave, never giving Jax another thought? Her stomach tightened. She didn't want to leave.

When she went to bite her cheek, she flinched. It was raw and sore. How much gnawing had she done tonight?

"I haven't done this in a while," she finally admitted. "Since . . ."

"I know," Jax said softly.

Piece by piece, Carson's armor fell away. She was no longer ready for war. She gripped her tiny necklace charm and pulled on the chain, the cool metal pressing into her neck. "Can you be patient with me?"

"We'll just take it one step at a time and see what happens. Nothing more," he said.

Small steps.

Carson took one of those small steps toward him. Then another. The muscles in her shoulders released the tension that had been building. Defenses lowered, Jax placed his hands on her elbows. She let him bring her closer until she was in his arms. The shadows surrounded her, too, ready to shield them from any outside force. What they didn't know was that the enemy was from within.

It was a strange sensation, being in someone's arms. It wasn't as distressing as she had imagined it. His arms were the perfect size to nestle comfortably in. No matter how wrong it felt to be in another man's arms, it felt right to be in his.

One step closer to freedom.

"I feel really idiotic," Carson said, her voice was muffled from the fabric of his shirt.

Jax snorted. "Why?"

"For leaving you in the restaurant like that. I'm the asshole."

"Hey." Jax guided her chin with the knuckle of his forefinger until she was looking up at his stern face. "You're dealing with a lot right now."

"It doesn't excuse the way I behaved."

Jax shrugged. "Nobody's perfect."

Carson thought about the night he'd taken her to urgent care and what he'd said to her.

"You don't owe me anything anymore," she said.

"Owe you?"

"For hitting my head with the door. You've made it up to me, so you don't owe me anything anymore."

Jax gently kissed the crown of Carson's forehead, precisely where her only visible scar lay. "Whatever you say, Mr. Hoover."

Chapter Ten

Adrenaline surged through Carson's veins, propelling her forward as she stumbled away from the demolished car and toward Luke's dead body that lay in the middle of the intersection. Kneeling on the wet asphalt she took a moment before placing her hand on the blanket covering him. No matter how many times she had dreamed about the accident, she always, always hesitated at this moment.

With one hand she ripped back the fabric. Blood and death lay before her. Luke's eyes were open, blankly staring up at the stormy sky that swirled above them. The color of Luke's eyes stopped her screams. The brown had been replaced with blue. Sapphire blue.

Then Luke's face shifted into another's. It was now Jax, with the same scrapes and bruises. His fire uniform was torn and ripped, exposing parts of his torso. But that wasn't right. He wasn't supposed to be the one dead. He wasn't supposed to be in this dream at all. Of course Carson's subconscious would do this to her.

Except he was in the dream—no, not the dream, but at the accident. Jax had been the one who pulled her off Luke's lifeless form—

Hands grabbed her, dragging her away from Jax, who was supposed to be Luke. Carson clawed at the arms that restrained her, leaving deep canyons in their skin with her nails.

"Let me go! Luke! Wake up! Luke!" Her cries echoed around the intersection.

"Hey, hey, hey. Shhh," Jax's voice pleaded, trying to subdue her screams. "It's okay. It's okay."

Yes. This was where Jax was supposed to be, cradling her as she sobbed into his shoulder.

As she was pulled farther and farther away, Luke's body grew smaller and smaller. Eventually, Carson's arms grew heavy and tired from reaching out to him. She stopped and latched onto Jax, who was lowering her onto the awaiting stretcher, which might as well have been a coffin. Restraints were strapped across her body, yet she could only focus on Jax.

"Please," she whispered.

People bustled around them as Jax hovered over her. His hand was in hers. Grip just as desperate. It was plain on his face that this wasn't her nightmare. It was horrifically real—

The gasp violently attacked Carson's lungs when she awoke. She couldn't breathe. Air. She needed air. But she was still in the clutches of the arms that tore her away from Luke. Disoriented, she twisted and writhed until she realized she was contorted in her own blankets.

Gathering herself, she unfolded her limbs from the silks and plopped onto the floor. For whatever reason, the air seemed thinner and fresher near the carpet. But that didn't dispel the dream still playing in her head.

He had been there.

So many first responders rushed to do their jobs. Jax's job was to take care of her.

Jax had been there.

Two days ago, when they'd ridden dirt bikes down by the river, he had asked about Luke. But Carson had never said Luke's name in front of him before. How else would he know?

Because Jax had been there.

Bang. Bang. Bang.

Carson's thunderous fist against the front door broke the quiet morning of the neighborhood. The lizard on the wooden railing waiting for the warmth of the sun, scurried away. It probably would have been a smart idea to have peeked in the garage window for Jax's truck to confirm that he was home before she knocked.

After she had collected herself from the nightmare, she'd snuck into the office, riffled through the file cabinet stuffed with client folders until she found "MILLER-Jax," and tapped his address into her phone. She needed to confront him. She needed to know the truth.

If Jax really had responded to her accident, then he would have witnessed her in her most vulnerable state. Carson wasn't sure how she felt about that. It was unnerving for him to know the moment that had completely shattered her world but not say anything for the past two months, not even during dinner last night.

A Texas flag hung lazily off the front porch. Jax was from Texas, right? Hadn't the auctioneer mentioned something about Texas and big . . .

A gulp slid down Carson's throat. This had to be the right place.

Still no answer. Again, she thumped her closed fist against the door. Was he on shift? She didn't think so. It would have been better to have sent a text or called him instead of showing up to his house, slamming on the door at the crack of dawn. But she needed to talk to him in person. This wasn't something to text about.

The door swung wide open, creaking on its hinges. Jax's hair was wild and restless. He rubbed the palm of his hand against one eye, while the other was a thin slit against the morning sun.

He was also shirtless. The tattooed octopus on his shoulder greeted her good morning. His gray sweatpants were barely hugging his hips. They looked like they would fall off at any moment. Carson's vision trailed down his abs to the v-lines just below his waist. She gulped again.

"Carson?" His voice was gruff, sleepy, like he hadn't had a chance to clear his throat of snores and dreams.

"Were you there?" Carson asked, getting right to the point. No reason to waste time.

It was clear Jax didn't need an explanation, as his hand dropped from his face and he stepped aside, motioning for her to enter.

Marching past him, Carson entered his living room. A ridiculously large flat screen hung on the wall to her left. A cord like a skinny tail from the bottom was wedged into an outlet. Surprisingly, his house didn't smell like the dust she'd expected. Instead, the smell reminded her of the carpet section at Home Depot. When she turned to face him, a muddy pair of boots sat on the floor next to the front door and dozens of keys overfilled a single hook hanging on the wall.

After shutting the door, Jax moved to a graphite-colored sectional against the opposite wall of the television and sat on the edge of the cushions. His movements were slow. He hunched forward and leaned his elbows on his knees for support, as if some unseen burden was weighing him down.

"Why didn't you say anything?" Carson asked, her voice barely audible.

He waited a moment, eyes on the floor, before looking up. "I didn't recognize who you were at first. It wasn't until that night at the auction, when you told me that your husband and son were killed in a car accident, that I figured it out. It was clear you didn't recognize me either. I never felt it was right to remind you."

Remind? Carson thought about the accident every second of every day.

Though her stomach was still in knots, Carson closed the distance between them and lowered herself onto the couch. "I always wondered why you never asked questions like everyone else does. Now it makes sense. You already knew."

Jax didn't respond, breaking eye contact with her. The wooden coffee table in front of them seemed to have him in a trance. Its deep hickory stain filled the hundreds of crevasses in the blemished wood. Only two remotes and a duck-hunting magazine littered the surface.

"What are you thinking about?" he asked, after a moment.

She picked at a fuzz on her knee. When she'd left her house, she hadn't bothered changing out of her pajamas. Her ratty, plaid pants were well worn, the color faded, and she wore an oversized shirt that had been Luke's. The sleeves hung well past her fingertips. She had shoved her feet into the first pair of shoes she could find: flip-flops.

"I don't understand why it has taken me so long to recognize you," Carson finally said, sliding a hand over her unbrushed hair.

"What made you remember?"

"A dream."

"A dream?" Jax repeated.

"I dream a lot about what happened."

"So, a nightmare?"

"You could say that." Jax could never imagine the actual nightmare of those dreams.

Lifting a hand to rub his jaw, Jax breathed in once and let it out. "We were called to the scene for vehicle extraction because you were trapped in the car. When we arrived, another engine was already tending to you."

Loud drumming filled Carson's ears as he told the story, making it hard to hear him. It took her a moment to realize it was her thudding heart.

"When I first saw the car, I couldn't believe anyone was still alive," Jax continued. "When a semi-truck that large hits a car that small . . . Then I saw you. The car mangled around you. It took us twenty-seven minutes to get you out."

Then Jax grimaced. "You suddenly became alert and began running when we tried to put you on the stretcher. We didn't even get the chance to put the neck brace on you."

Internally she recoiled, thinking about why she had become alert. Again, Luke's body covered with the blue blanket haunted her mind.

"It took three grown men to pick you up," Jax whispered, deep in memory. "Finally, you clung to me. It was the first time in my career I hadn't known what to do. I felt so helpless watching what was happening before me." Blinking, he focused back on her. She had not moved, had not taken a breath. "You were so broken. Your body shouldn't have been able to move like that. We figured it was from adrenaline."

"The doctor said my brain didn't understand that I'd been hurt," Carson confirmed.

"Then when they put you in the ambulance"—he swallowed—"you started screaming about . . . about . . ."

"My baby." Carson finished for him, shocked at the ease of her words.

Again, Jax's gaze wandered to the coffee table, absentmindedly nodding. "At first, I thought you meant there was a child in the car. Then I overheard you tell the EMT you were pregnant."

That was the moment Carson's world had crumpled all around her. As soon as she was wheeled into the ambulance a shearing pain had ripped through her abdomen. It felt as though a chainsaw was cutting her in half. The EMT had promised her baby would be fine, but Carson had known she had not only lost Luke, but her son as well.

Her brain tried to digest this information as they sat in somber, contemplative silence. It was so strange to hear about the wreck from another perspective.

Chewing on her thumbnail, Carson's eyes wandered around the interior of Jax's home. A short, wood bookcase was shoved in the corner. Its shelves held DVDs, a row of wooden ducks, and a portable Bluetooth speaker. In the kitchen on her right, a loaf of bread sat near the sink, next to a nearly empty roll of paper towels. A collection of knives were mounted to the wall under a cupboard. Butcher. Chef's. Boning. Filet. Was that a cleaver? Carson wondered if Jax was a cook. What would those blades feel like against her skin . . .

"I've thought about you a lot over the years," Jax said, breaking the silence. "I wondered what had happened to you and how you were doing."

Carson pictured her mutilated body, the scars, and the years' worth of self-inflicted pain. She thought about when she'd fled the restaurant the night before, fled from their conversation.

Then she thought about Jax, knowing about her accident and how traumatic it had been for her. It made her uneasy just how much he knew.

And his excuse of not telling her because he didn't want to remind her continued to not sit well either. Deep down, Carson felt he should have said something. He should have confessed. Instead, he'd left her completely oblivious to his part in all of it.

What other secrets was he keeping? Did he know about her self-harm as well? Had he somehow pieced together her idiosyncrasies and concluded that she was cutting herself? Her stomach twisted harder and harder as her skin seemed to crawl with scorpions. It was unsettling.

Not even Raegan knew Carson's secret. She and Hunter knew Luke was killed on impact, and that Carson had miscarried on the way to the hospital. What they didn't know was that Luke had been thrown from the car and Carson had tried to run to him after being freed from the wreckage. That she had been pulled from Luke's dead body. That she takes sharp items and butchers her skin.

Now it felt like she didn't have control anymore. Jax had put a chink in her armor, and it left her overwhelmed and agitated. If Carson had known this would happen, she would have done a better job at hiding how screwed up she was.

"I think you should have told me when you remembered," Carson finally admitted as her leg bounced and bounced and bounced. "You've let me believe otherwise for almost two months."

Jax winced. "When we walked to your truck after the auction, I was trying to figure out the best way to tell you, but I just couldn't."

"Because you didn't want to remind me about the day my family died?" The bluntness of Carson's words made his shoulders sink lower, but she continued anyway. "I think about it all the time, Jax."

"I should have said something, I know. I'm not . . ." Jax leaned back against the couch, clutching fists full of hair for a second before letting his hands fall into his lap. He tilted his head back, his eyes staring at the ceiling. "I'm not good at . . ." A frown touched his face, as though he was troubled with the words in his mouth. "Conflict." Looking back at her, he continued, "Conflict isn't the right word. I have a tendency to avoid anything that is contentious. There's so much tension and stress at work,

I don't want to deal with it in my personal life too." Then he let out a single gust of air that sounded like a laugh but excluded the humor. "Why I married Kristen, I don't know, because she was very dramatic."

Sitting upright, Jax took Carson's hands and held them tightly. "I should have confessed that night. I realize that now. I was thinking about myself and my feelings. I should have been thinking about you and yours." He lifted his hand and placed it on her cheek. "I am sorry about what happened to you that day. And I'm sorry that I didn't say anything."

The intensity emanating from his eyes felt to Carson like a blanket being wrapped around her during a snowstorm. It was easy to understand his position, his sincerity, his regret. Plus, Carson was holding onto her own secrets. Who was she to get upset with him having some of his own? And if he had any suspicion about the scars on her body, the conversation would have gone completely differently.

Maybe, just maybe, Jax being at her accident would give him better insight into who she was or why she did the things that she did. Self-harm included. Finally, the frost that had taken over her body began to melt, and she could breathe again. This could be a good thing.

Leaning forward, Carson touched her forehead to his. "Thank you," she whispered.

At her words, she could feel the stress leave Jax's body. Stress that may have been cemented in his bones for weeks.

"I really am sorry, Carson."

Pulling away just enough to look at Jax's face, Carson smiled, then leaned forward once more to kiss his lips. She was interrupted by a sudden squealing buzzer.

Snatching her phone from her pocket, Carson muted the alarm with a curse. "I'm going to be late for work." As soon as she stood up, Jax tugged her back down.

"Gross, adulting. Why don't you call in, and we can finish what we started?" he teased, inching forward to steal another kiss.

A day off work sounded enticing and spending it with Jax was even more exhilarating. But she had a job to do.

"Playing hooky wouldn't look good for the promotion I'm trying to get." Carson wiggled her hand from his and headed for the front door.

"A promotion?" he asked, following suit.

"I'm attempting to become junior partner." Attempting. Trying. Wishing. Praying. Whatever it took. She wasn't going to give up.

As she gripped the door handle Jax placed his hand over hers and twisted it with her. Anywhere his skin touched made hers hum with electricity.

"That's really awesome," he said, opening the door.

"Thanks. I'm sorry I have to go." Carson stepped onto the porch. The sun had risen fully past the horizon. Birds were singing its praises.

"No worries."

"What are you doing Friday night?" she asked.

He leaned on the doorframe, filling it with his height, arms crossed over his bare chest.

"I'm on shift until five. So, don't know. What *are* we doing Friday night?"

"I'm going out to dinner with Raegan and Hunter. You should join us."

Jax flashed a grin, making her heart skip with anticipation. "Double date it is."

CHAPTER ELEVEN

Carson's boots thumped against the concrete as they weaved between the patio seating filled with guests digging into trays of wings and fries and gourmet sub sandwiches.

"Do they know I'm coming?" Jax asked.

"No. I haven't mentioned you to Raegan yet."

When Jax pulled the door open, the waft of deli meats and fresh-baked bread greeted Carson's nose: salami, rosemary, olive oil, provolone. It made her stomach rumble.

The Sandwich Shack hummed with bustling patrons and loud voices. At first glance, it appeared all the tables were full. The line to the counter snaked between the tables, making Carson wonder if they would be able to order and eat before closing.

Then she spotted Raegan sitting amongst the crowd. Her gilded hair glowed under one of the ceiling lights, as if it had been strategically placed as a spotlight just for her. Raegan waved when she spotted Carson; then her eyes, already the size of saucers, grew into dinner plates at the sight of Jax. When he slipped his hand down into Carson's, Raegan's jaw popped open, and Carson could've sworn she heard the gasp from across the restaurant.

Heat flooded Carson's body. This felt like bringing home a boy to meet the parents for the very first time. At least, that's what she imagined; her mother never cared about the boys she dated, and she hadn't had a father to bring a boy home to.

Raegan's shell-shocked face didn't change even after they had taken their seats.

"Where's Hunter?" Carson asked, trying to ignore the awkwardness swirling inside her.

Reluctantly, Raegan peeled her eyes off Jax. "Bathroom." It took a couple shakes to wipe the shock off her face. Her lips still twitched, and the wheels in her head appeared to be turning faster than normal. "Are you two—?"

Raegan's eyes bouncing between the two of them reminded Carson of a ping-pong ball being smacked between two players. It made her want to crawl under the table and hide. All of the emotions and uncertainties from before came rushing back, threatening to drag her down again. She didn't remember it being this uncomfortable when she had introduced Luke to Hunter and Raegan.

Apparently, Raegan didn't need confirmation. "Wow," she breathed. "Why didn't I think of that?"

"Is that Jax?" Hunter had come up from behind, slapping Jax on the shoulder, and took a seat. "Did you hear about this place too?"

"Hunter," Raegan murmured, patting his freckled arm.

"Huh?"

"He came with Carson." Raegan said it so delicately as if speaking too loudly would shatter the words into pieces. Still Hunter's mouth hung open and one of his eyes continued to squint. "They came together as a *couple*."

Now Hunter's eyes played ping-pong. "Wait. You two? Hell yeah," he said a little too boisterously for Carson's liking. He fist-bumped Jax, who happily complied. "Why didn't I think of that?"

"That's what I said!" Raegan affirmed.

"If you two are done, I think we should order before they run out of ingredients," Carson suggested.

"Oh, good idea," Raegan said, turning to Hunter. "I'll have the Italian chicken salad. No—"

"No croutons. I know." Hunter stood from his chair.

"What would you like, Mr. Hoover?" Jax asked.

Carson peered past him to read the menu, a huge yellow rectangle hanging just behind the order counter. Except the script was so tiny, she couldn't read the words from where she was sitting. "I'll have the same thing as Raegan."

The second the men were out of earshot, Raegan whirled on her. "Um, why didn't you tell me about you and Jax?"

A sliver of guilt wedged its way under Carson's skin, like a splinter. "I don't know. It kind of just happened," she said, shrugging one shoulder.

"You go riding dirt bikes one day, then *poof*, you're together? I'm missing something." The bangles on Raegan's wrist clanked together as she wiped a stray hair from her face.

"That's basically it." Carson peeked up at Jax, who was chatting with Hunter in the line. "We stopped to take a break from riding, and Jax fell into the river."

"He fell into the river?"

"Well, we both were in the river."

"You *both* fell into the river?"

"Can I finish?"

Grinning widely, Raegan gripped an invisible zipper between her thumb and forefinger and pulled it across her mouth. Carson leaned in closer.

"He tried to kiss me when we were drying off," she said. Raegan's cheek muscles spasmed as if she were about to burst, but she kept silent. "I pulled away before he could then later in his truck I—I kissed him."

"You kissed him?" Raegan's hand smacked the table so hard the conversations around them stopped. "Wait, wait, wait. *You* kissed him."

Mortified, Carson's face fell into her hands. "I have no idea what got into me."

"It's that chiseled body that got into you, that's what." Then Raegan slapped her hand on her mouth. "*Did* that chiseled body get into you?"

"Of course not," Carson snipped, dropping her hands. "But I shouldn't be kissing and dating and . . . and . . . I mean it's only been five years since Luke passed away."

Flustered, Carson's leg bounce was on overtime. Both cheeks were raw, probably bleeding inside. And she could no longer feel her fingertips. If only she had something sharp in her pocket. She could go into the bathroom for a quick fix.

Somewhere she'd read that people who cut carried a "toolkit" with them. Carson had thought about creating her own for moments like this, but that would have meant she accepted herself as a cutter. And she refused to do that.

A soft hand delicately touched her arm, bringing her back to the table. Back to the restaurant with the clinking of ice in cups, the munching of crisp vegetables, "Order up!" being shouted every few moments.

"It has been five years," Raegan said quietly. "Just because you start to have feelings for someone else doesn't diminish your love for Luke. There is nothing wrong with what you are doing."

Raegan's words enveloped Carson and began to soothe her aching heart. Why hadn't she come to Raegan sooner? Her best friend always listened to her and knew what to say. Sometimes her advice was unsolicited, but it was welcome, nonetheless. Carson could have saved herself a lot of inner turmoil by talking about her feelings for Jax with Raegan in the first place. For a split second, she pondered telling Raegan about her self-harm. That idea was squashed like a bug.

"Shouldn't this take time?" Carson asked.

"Not always. Give Jax a chance. He's an incredible person. You can always take it slow."

Carson played with a thread at the end of her sleeve, rolling the cotton between her fingers. *Small steps.*

"Do you want it to be serious?"

"I think it's too soon to know exactly what I want," Carson breathed. Again, the uncertainties swirled in her brain. With Jax. Without Jax. Cut. Don't cut. Live. Or don't.

"I know what I want." Raegan smiled infectiously. "I want my best friend to be happy."

"Thank you," Carson said, feeling Raegan's love. Then she snuck another glance at the guys, who were now waiting off to the side for the food. "There's something else I have to tell you."

At the tone of Carson's voice, Raegan leaned closer, as if to shield what she was about to say from the rest of the world.

"Jax responded to my accident."

Now it was Raegan who peered at Hunter and Jax. "How do you know?"

"I remembered. I guess he knew all along. Well, since the auction."

"Why didn't he say anything?"

"He said it's because *I* didn't say anything. I didn't say anything because I didn't recognize him until a couple of days ago," Carson explained.

"Oh, honey." Raegan's eyebrows bent with concern, and her eyes grew glossier. "How are you feeling?"

Carson started to fidget with her sleeve again, and her leg continued to shake. "I mean, it's a bit uncomfortable. It did bring back some memories."

"You're digesting a lot right now, aren't you?"

"You can say that again," Carson mumbled.

"Tell me what you need, and I'll do it. And Carson . . ." Raegan pulled on Carson's hand to get her attention once more, just as Hunter and Jax returned with their meals. "I hope you find peace in all of this. You deserve it."

Chapter Twelve

Carson had always hated the cold and frozen sections of the grocery store. It didn't matter how hot the day was, or how many layers she was wearing, her fingers and toes would always go numb whenever she went to purchase frozen dinners. Right now she had her fingers shoved under her armpits while Jax perused the assortment of steaks. After dinner with Hunter and Raegan, Jax had asked Carson if they could stop at the Safeway down the road because he was running low on groceries.

"I meant to ask you, are you a chef or something?" Carson asked.

He looked at her, then back to the red meat. "No. Why?"

"When I was at your house, I saw all of the knives on the wall."

Jax tossed two thick ribeyes into the cart. "I think it's important to have the right tools for each job."

"So you don't use the same knife to cube a steak and slice carrots?"

Jax gave Carson a repulsed look. "Never."

They wandered into the dessert aisle. There were so many options to choose from: double-stuffed cookies, bags of hard candy, strawberry wafers, glazed donuts, every flavor of mints.

"So, you were inspecting my house, huh? Any other assumptions?" he asked.

"I assumed you had a Dalmatian, since you're a firefighter."

"Can't. I'm allergic."

"Allergic to dogs? That sucks." It was difficult for her to imagine being unable to snuggle a puppy.

Jax grabbed a package of Oreos off the shelf. "Not just dogs. Practically any animal with hair." He put the Oreos back and chose the off-brand version instead.

"Horses?" she asked.

"Yep."

"Cats."

"Swell up like a balloon."

"What about hamsters?"

That made him think for a second. "I don't think I've ever held a hamster."

"There's a pet store up the road," Carson teased. "We can test it out."

"You want to put my life in danger?"

"I know how to dial nine-one-one." Carson winked.

Catching her by the elbow Jax pulled her toward him, pressing their bodies close together, his hand on the small of her back. "Wink for me again. That was sexy."

She laughed.

"I see you found yourself a new girl," interrupted a velvety voice.

Startled, Carson tore away from Jax.

Beady eyes adorned with fake lashes trailed up and down Carson, clearly not thrilled at what they were seeing. Hair extensions, long and full, cascaded past the woman's face. A manicured finger steadily tapped against her inner bicep. The suede boots she wore consumed most of her legs.

Carson instantly recognized the woman from Modern Locks' website while simultaneously feeling Jax's body go rigid at the sight of his ex-wife.

"Is this why you won't pay me anymore?" Kristen pouted, her bottom lip jutting out. "My lawyer will be interested to learn about your new little friend." Venom curled around each word.

Jax, who still had an arm around Carson's waist, pulled her closer to his body. "We're not having this discussion."

Carson glanced up at him shocked because she had never experienced Jax this *angry*. Animosity rippled from him in waves. The muscles in his neck were taut, his jaw ticking.

"Fine." Brushing off Jax's bitterness, Kristen picked at a piece of lint on her arm. "You know how I live, Jax." Carson flinched at his name on her tongue. "I need the income. Maybe we can lower the amount to something more manageable."

The grip on Carson's waist grew firmer. "I said, we are *not* talking about this," Jax spat.

As if she were the one being attacked, Kristen lifted her palms. "We'll just wait to see what the judge says. I won once. I can win again."

Carson's jaw unhinged, and Jax didn't justify the words with a response. Apparently Kristen wasn't expecting one, because she gave one last fleeting glare at Carson, then strode past them as if this had been an ordinary encounter.

Jax was an indignant statue: tense and scowling. Carson could only imagine what he was thinking and feeling, what he had gone through being married to that woman. Then he had to relive it month after month after month, every time he had to write those damned checks.

The stone cracked, and Jax's sullen mask melted away, though his eyebrows stayed furrowed. A curse slipped from his lips, before his shoulders sagged even more, the burden of his circumstances too heavy for him to carry.

"Will us being together affect my chances of ending spousal support?" he asked apprehensively.

"No," Carson assured him. "It won't."

The tension alleviated from Jax's body, but only a little. He cupped her face with his hand. "I hope she didn't offend you."

Carson kissed his palm. "Not at all. I'm more worried about you."

The corner of his lips barely lifted. "I'm used to it."

While Jax put away his groceries, Carson sat at the edge of the kitchen counter, her feet dangling inches from the floor. Ever since seeing Kristen at the grocery store, Jax had been quiet. Very quiet. In fact, his forehead was still creased. The lines had apparently made themselves as permanent as his tattoo.

It seemed he was taking his frustrations out on the purchased food. The milk jug thudded as he dropped it in the fridge. He tossed the box of protein bars in a cabinet with a little more force than Carson thought necessary. Not to mention the poor apples that were dumped into a wire basket, bruising their fragile skin.

"Do you want to talk about it?" she asked timidly.

Her fingers squeezed the edge of the counter when the pantry door slammed shut. Opposite her, Jax rested against the stove, arms crossed.

"What is there to talk about? It's not like I can do anything."

"That's not true. You *are* doing something. Your trial is only a couple of weeks away. And I know the new judge assigned to your case. He's extremely fair."

Jax ran a hand down his face. "I don't know, Carson. The only reason I'm taking her back to court is because my brother Billy talked me into it. It may be easier to pay her the money and be left alone."

The defeat hung in the air between them, a dense fog not even the brightest lighthouse could cut through.

"Not when you now have a fighting chance," Carson argued.

"You saw what happened at the store," Jax said, swinging his arm out. "It's only going to get worse. It's not worth the fight."

This wasn't the first time Carson had heard this. Many of her clients had said the same thing. While many times that was true, some cases were worth the fight. She was strategic in choosing which legal battles she was willing to go to war over. Based on the facts she knew, and especially after meeting Kristen in person, Jax's case was a sparring match Carson would enter the ring for.

Still, she decided not to speak, feeling as though it wasn't her place to say anything more. She hadn't been there during the divorce. She hadn't experienced the dynamic between Kristen and Jax, the rise and fall of their relationship, or the twelve months' worth of checks to an ex-spouse.

Interlacing his fingers behind his head, Jax looked up at the ceiling for a few seconds, then placed his palms on the counter behind him. "I don't want to go through all of that again. I can't go through it again." He dropped his gaze to the porcelain-tile floor, his next words were raspy as if it pained him to speak. "I don't know if I have the strength."

Voice trailing off, he didn't look at her. Carson could only guess the emotions inside him: pain and embarrassment. It made her sick that he might feel that way. He looked vanquished, as though it took everything he had just to stand there. His usual laid-back demeanor was depleted and empty.

"Why don't you think you have the strength?" Carson asked.

The question stirred him. He switched the foot he was leaning on. Then switched back, scratching a cheek. The soft sound of fingernails on his close-cropped facial hair was loud in the quiet kitchen.

"Kristen cheated the whole year we were married. I'm still trying to fig-ure out why she even married me when she wasn't planning to be faithful. The only reason I can come up with is because she liked the idea of being married to a firefighter. Then, come to find out, she cheated the whole six years we were together."

Carson had no idea what any of this had to do with his strength to go back to court, but she didn't interrupt.

"When I think back on it, there were plenty of signs, but I trusted her. I believed in our relationship. I trusted our wedding vows. I was stupid enough to believe her lies. Ignorant enough to stay with her. It wasn't until her affairs were right in front of me that I finally faced the truth. I mean, you can't really ignore coming home from work to your wife screwing another man in your bed."

Anger boiled inside Carson. She bit her tongue in an attempt to keep still and let him continue.

Pushing himself off the counter, Jax came to stand next to her, staring at the melamine cupboards in front of them.

"It was humiliating, living the life of the credulous husband. The divorce was awful. She fought over every little thing. I finally gave up and let her have it all. I walked away with nothing. She walked away with everything. And I didn't handle it very well." The tone of his voice shifted to something darker. "I drank. I drank *a lot*. So much that I almost lost my job. I hid it from my ma and brothers for as long as I could. You know, since my dad had been an alcoholic. How was I supposed to tell my ma that I was becoming an alcoholic just like him?" Jax's breath caught on the last word. "I spent my whole life trying not to be like my father, and I ended up embodying his worst quality. I didn't speak with my family for months, which ended up breaking my ma's heart anyway."

Finally, Jax looked at her. His face was desperate. Desperate for help, for relief, for his own nightmares to end. Carson knew the feeling.

"When I say I don't think I have the strength to go through it all again," Jax said, "what I mean is I don't want to fall back into bad habits. It was ugly, Carson. I was ugly. I was a complete dick to everyone, and I don't want you to ever see that part of me. If I go through with the trial and lose, I'm afraid it'll happen again."

Carson wondered, the night of the auction, if this was the reason Raegan had asked Jax if he was sure he wanted to go to court again.

She placed her fingers on his forearm. The muscle was tight with helplessness, and Carson felt helpless as well, not knowing what to do. If only she could protect him.

At her touch, she could feel Jax's body soften. He pivoted until he was standing right in front of Carson, and she took him into her arms. He buried his face into her neck and his arms were tight around her chest. She didn't mind that his embrace caused one of her fresh cuts to smart.

Only, Jax's honesty fermented her guilt. It sliced Carson open and bled her shame all over them. Why couldn't she be honest with him? Why couldn't she stop her own bad habits? Why couldn't she put her life back together just as he had and move forward?

Her contrition was more constrictive than his arms, because she was keeping secrets from him. Every day, every smile, every touch was layered in falsehood. It was as though every second spent together was a lie.

Lies

upon

lines

upon

lies.

Carson was a liar. She was no better than Kristen.

Chapter Thirteen

The next week, Carson did something she never thought she could ever do: make an appointment with a therapist.

For a place meant to help people with their mental health, the building was depressing. Square with sharp corners and stucco the color of rice paper was smeared all over the exterior. It reminded her of a box, beige and boring. A single glass door with vinyl lettering read Granite Dells Center. Carson rolled her eyes at the brown awning that hung over the door, disproportionate to the building. Whoever the plodding architect was obviously hadn't cared or had an eye for style.

It wasn't the stodgy architecture that stopped her from entering, though. Apprehension. That was the reason why she had been standing in the parking lot staring at the building for the past thirty minutes.

The night Jax confided in her about his toxic relationship with alcohol, Carson knew her world with Jax and her world with bleeding skin could never mesh. Before, she could cut, then live her life perfectly normal. Her self-harm had become so natural that for two years, since she had started self-harming, she had balanced the two lifestyles perfectly: odious, then composed.

Now Carson dreaded any opportunity to self-harm because she was starting to understand the consequences. The once small, gray cloud that had hung over her, easily ignored, now thundered like the great monsoons of the western desert. Clapping bolts of lightning struck around her while torrents of falling, hurricane-like rain threatened to drown her. The almighty storm loomed above Carson, threatening to expose her hideousness to Jax. To Raegan and Hunter. To the world.

Even more exhausting was the cycle of trying to stop but miserably failing. Why couldn't Carson just quit? What she thought was a simple demand of herself seemed to be against the laws of nature itself. Hot tears would roll down her cheeks whenever she implored herself to stop.

To. Just. Stop.

Those attempts always ended with new additions to her body.

If only Carson could slice all the way through her skin, through the muscle and bone, and cut her hands off completely, she could finally find relief.

The guilt of her self-harm continued to fester, eating away at her from the inside out. She felt as despicable on the inside as she looked on the outside. Before, it hadn't mattered as much that she was self-destructing. Now, the thought of losing Jax because she cut herself was excruciatingly unbearable.

She had to do something.

A middle-aged woman stepped out of the office. Carson went taut for a second, thinking it was the therapist, looking for her, wondering why she was late to her appointment. The lady strolled into the parking lot and slipped into a silver Subaru. Faded *Save the Dells* and *I love my dog!* stickers sat crooked on the back bumper.

Carson stood there for another minute. Then five. Then ten. Some people went in. More people went out. The door was locked. The parking lot lamps flickered on. The sun grew tired of waiting for her and fell behind

Granite Mountain.

Yet she didn't move. She didn't know why she couldn't move. Carson peered down to see if her feet had fused to the pavement. They hadn't. This was all her. Why wouldn't she go in? So many why's. She started to grow weary from asking herself why all the time.

Finally, she gave up. But before she reversed out of her spot, Carson promised herself she would try again.

Chapter Fourteen

The ponderosa pines' emerald needles rustled in the breeze, still green even in mid-October. Although, the forest floor was covered in fallen yellow needles. If this year's monsoons had been generous, the ground would bear more saplings. Still, some were pushing through the lack of moisture and Carson silently cheered for them, hoping the baby trees would grow as big as their ancestors.

"We need another rainstorm. It feels too dry this year," Carson said.

"I wonder if we're going into another drought." Jax wiped his hands together, ridding them of peanut dust, and took a swig of water. Carson drank as well, swishing the electrolyte-infused liquid around in her mouth, remoistening her tongue from the hot air.

They relaxed in the bed of his truck, leaning against the back of the cab. This ride hadn't been as grueling as the first time they'd gone out. They'd taken a scenic trail through Thumb Butte's forests. Luckily, no unseen wire had been strewn up to behead them.

Their dirt bikes rested just beyond the tailgate. The difference in size was almost comical. Carson's looked like a children's motorcycle compared to Jax's beast of a machine.

Taking another chug of water, Carson thought about her attempt to go to counseling the day before. It was pathetic. Maybe if therapists held their sessions in beautiful forests like this one, she'd be more willing to go.

"Did Luke ride dirt bikes?" Jax asked, drawing her attention back to him.

"No," she said, cracking a smile. "He tried to get into it, but couldn't."

"When did you start riding then?"

"When I was a teenager. I taught myself how to ride."

"Your parents didn't care?"

Shaking her head, she said, "It was just my mom and I. And she didn't care what I did. As long as I paid my portion of the rent, she didn't ask questions."

Disgust flashed across Jax's face. "She made you pay rent?"

"It was better than sleeping in a car," Carson said, unconcerned.

"Do you still talk to her?" His blue eyes grew in size, abashed at his question. "Dammit. I asked you an insensitive question. If my ma was here, she would smack me."

The thought of Jax's mother smacking him for something he said made Carson grin. "It wasn't insensitive," she assured him. "And no, I don't talk to her. As soon as I turned seventeen, she was gone."

"Oh." It was clear that hundreds of questions were sitting on the tip of his tongue, trying to escape his lips. Carson indulged him.

"I was an accident. She was young and . . . exploring. Never did figure out which guy was my father. It wasn't easy for her to raise a baby on her own."

Jax pressed his lips into a thin line, displeased. Hoping to relieve him of his worry, Carson digressed. "What about you? When did you get your first dirt bike?"

The flat line of Jax's lips curved up, creating slight lines on the outside of his eyes. Carson could see memories filling his mind. "I think I was eight when my brother Beau found a little Honda 50cc. We had no idea where he found it." Then he leaned closer to her as if telling her a secret. "He probably stole it. The four of us boys took turns racing it around our front yard."

She couldn't help but match the grin that grew on his face. "Do your brothers still ride?"

"All but my youngest brother, Wyatt. When I was still living in Texas, Beau, Billy, and I would go all the time. I really miss it. I miss them."

"It sounds like you have a close relationship with them," she said.

Jax's face grew serious. No, not serious; humble. "I do." He spoke those words with reverence, as if he knew how blessed he was to have his family.

A bird whistled for its mate somewhere above, and the branches wrestled as another breeze blew in. Jax was picking at the water bottle's label with his thumbnail when Carson spotted a tear in his jersey, near his shoulder. With the sewing kit at home, she could stitch it back together.

"I hope you get the chance to meet them one day," he said, quietly.

The colors around Carson grew more vibrant. "Me too."

Jax met her gaze, eyes trailing up and down her face. Then in unison, they shifted. He sat the bottle of water down and turned while Carson straightened her back. Reaching his hand up behind her head, he pulled her in to kiss her lips.

Instantly, Carson caught fire. The flames engulfed them, swallowed them whole. The sensation was tender and sweet. It was yearning and need. It was fire and ice.

She wanted more. Needed more. Like a cactus craving the sun.

Jax was happy to oblige because soon Carson was straddling his lap, gripping the back of his neck and head and running her fingers through his shaggy hair. At first his hands were firm on her thighs, but as they continued to kiss, his grip slowly made its way to her hips. The few healing cuts where his not-so-gentle hands touched whined in protest. She tried to ignore them.

Then his hands started to slide up her sides. That was harder to ignore. Would he feel her uneven skin under her riding jersey? She pushed those thoughts out of her mind and focused on him instead. His mouth tasted like peanuts; salty, just like the sweat on his skin. As he trailed his nose up and down her throat, she breathed in his dusty hair.

Jax's fingers were dangerously close to finding the edge of her jersey, Carson writhed with discomfort, causing him to pull away. She looked into his eyes. So much fire. So much ice. Again, she pushed her fear down and found his lips once more.

How she wanted to be touched. To feel his hands on her bare skin. What would it feel like for her ugly skin to be caressed and loved with his pure hands?

It was going too far. Carson was losing control. Suddenly all she could focus on was the placement of Jax's hands. They were on her ribcage, sliding back down to her hips. What would happen if his hand slipped up her shirt and—

"I—I can't." Carson gasped, pulling away.

They were both panting hard, apparently having forgotten how to breathe. She took advantage of his lack of oxygen and slid off his lap. Jax didn't complain, sitting up to cross his legs and rest his forearms on his knees.

"Yeah, that was . . ." he rasped.

He didn't understand why she'd stopped. To be honest, if her scars weren't holding her back, Carson would have continued. Probably to the point of getting a high five from Raegan. Letting the flames thaw, she pulled on the bottom of her jersey to readjust it for maximum coverage.

It was getting dark. How long had they been kissing? One of Jax's hands raked through his hair before he looked at her. Something he saw amused him.

"What?" Now Carson ran her hands through her own hair. Was there a twig? Did she have peanuts in her teeth?

"I think I gave you a hickey," he said.

In the heat of the moment, Carson hadn't noticed what he was doing. Her hand shot to where his mouth had been on her neck seconds ago. "Is there really a hickey?" she squeaked.

Jax moved her fingers out of the way to inspect the area and let out a small whistle. "Definitely a hickey."

"Shit." Carson grabbed her neck again, trying to hide it. It was already hard enough having to hide her scars.

Jax grinned impishly. "I'm not even sorry."

Then her eyes grew wide. "I have a status conference at the courthouse tomorrow."

"Still not sorry."

CHAPTER FIFTEEN

With every slice of the blade, Carson trembled with regret, but her hand continued to slash away at the skin on her upper forearm. One, two, three swipes. The blood began to seep out. She was only vaguely aware of the massacre before her, perfect for All Hallow's Eve.

Hunched on the floor of her bathroom, with a razor blade pinched between her fingers, she saw red splatters of blood all around her. The pain was burning, an intense fire on her skin. The blood was hot, like lava. She loved it. Desired it. Yearned for it.

Attraction.

Like a long pull of a cigarette after a stressful day, Carson leaned her head back and let the pain envelope her. The room pulsated with euphoric energy as her blood dripped onto the floor.

Drip.

Drip.

Drip.

She was weightless. Just as the clouds in the sky. Floating and free.

Gravity took over when she noticed the time on the clock hanging just above the bathtub. Jax would be arriving any second.

"Shit!"

How long had she been in this stupor? Flicking the bloody blade from her fingers, Carson jerked away as if it had just bitten her. She hissed at the new pain in her arm, no longer a pleasurable ache.

Repulsion.

Almost ripping the rod from the wall, she yanked a towel off the rack and pressed it to her arm with as much pressure as she could. Lifting her wrist to her shoulder, she was able to hold the towel in place while she hurriedly shoved the razor into a drawer, hiding it beneath the makeup clutter, and wiped up the blood with another rag.

Sprinting into the laundry room, Carson threw the two towels into the washing machine, not caring there was freshly washed clothes still in there, waiting to be transferred to the dryer. She activated the rinse-and-spin cycle to wash away the remaining evidence.

The bleeding didn't stop. Dashing back into her bathroom, she knocked every item out from the cupboard under the sink to find her first-aid kit. Just as she was cleaning the excess blood from her skin, there was a knock on the door. Her heart lurched into her throat, choking her.

"One second!" Carson yelled, her voice was shaking with panic. She needed to get herself under control.

There was no time to properly bandage her arm. Slapping on a large Band-Aid, she shoved everything back in the cupboard and pulled down her sleeves. It would have to do until she could sneak back into her bathroom and apply a more substantive dressing.

Before opening the door, she took in three deep breaths to calm her frazzled nerves. Air in. Air out. She could do this.

Jax was waiting patiently for her on the porch with a plastic grocery bag hanging from his hand. Against the desert backdrop, he looked handsome in a black polo and gray slacks. Carson grinned at his choice of shoes—Vans—wondering what her boss, his attorney, Garrett, had thought about them in the courtroom.

"Sorry, I meant to unlock the door for you," Carson lied, stepping to the side to let him in. She wasn't sorry at all about the door being locked. As if to show she wasn't hiding anything, she pointed to the flowerpot on the edge of the porch. "There's a spare key under there."

Confirming she was losing her touch, her voice continued to quiver, unable to go from one world to another.

Giving only a glance at the flora, Jax stepped up, gave her a peck on the lips—could he taste the lies there?—and walked into the kitchen. The bag's contents spilled out when he set it on the counter. A variety of sprinkles, frostings, and cookie dough. Decorating cookies to celebrate Halloween wasn't her thing, but she'd agreed anyway when he'd suggested it.

"So?" Carson pressed.

Jax's eyes flashed a brilliant aqua before a giant grin split his face in half.

"Does that mean you won?" she guessed.

His smile grew impossibly bigger. "I won."

Carson's squeal echoed in the kitchen, and she flung herself into his arms, mindful of her injury. Jax had to step back to brace for impact. For a second, Carson forgot all about her sins, leaving them in the bathroom.

"I told you you had a chance. I knew it." She kissed him, elated for his victory and relieved for his freedom from his ex-wife. For the first time, she appreciated the length of his hair as she could grip his inky mane between her fingers to better pull him closer to her.

Unexpectedly, Jax hoisted her up and sat her on the kitchen island. When his hands dropped down to her waist, she strategically guided them away from her scars and placed them on her neck.

Desperate to know what happened, Carson broke away from his lips. "Tell me everything."

"It was going pretty much the same as the first trial we had," he began. "Then, when Kristen was on the stand, she said she quit her job."

"She quit her job?"

"To claim disability."

"*What?*" Carson said, voice rising with surprise.

"It was the first time we had heard about it. She alleged that being a hairdresser did something to her wrist."

"But she only worked at the salon for a few months."

Jax gave Carson a pointed look.

"The judge caught that, didn't he?"

Nodding, he said, "If only you had been there. The look on Kristen's face when the judge ruled that I didn't have to pay her anymore."

"I know," Carson said, kissing the top of his hands. "But it was better for everyone if I stayed completely out of your case. The judge knows me, and it would not have looked good if I was sitting in the back as the girlfriend."

"I know, I know," Jax said. "I agree with you and Mr. Hoover on that. But still—"

"But *still*, you won, and we should celebrate." Carson pushed him out of the way so she could slip off the counter to preheat the oven.

Jax peered out the French windows that took up the entire living room wall. Beyond the glass, nothing but dirt and curly grama grass rolled like gilded waves for miles and miles. "Do you get trick-or-treaters?" he asked.

"Not since I've lived here."

"You have a nice place," he said, glancing around the kitchen and living room.

Carson had forgotten this was his first time inside her house, as she had been deliberate in keeping him at a distance. "Thank you. I bought it as a fixer-upper. After the accident, I had a lot of free time on my hands, so I found myself a project."

Jax joined Carson by the oven and wrapped her in a hug. "It looks wonderful," he said, before kissing the crown of her forehead.

"This is so lame," Carson whined, while attempting to make a witch's hat with the violet sprinkles.

Jax leaned over to inspect her work. "What's lame is that cookie of yours."

Mouth popping open, Carson shot him a glare. "How *dare* you diss my cookie," she said.

He shrugged. "I'm just saying, my two nephews have decorated cookies better than you, and they're five."

Glancing down at his treat—a blob of sugar paste and bat-shaped sprinkles—Carson pressed her finger right in the middle of it.

"Hey!" he yipped.

The mischievous look spreading across his face cut her giggling short. In the corner of her eye, she caught him dipping his finger in the lime-green frosting.

"No!" Carson shrieked, twisting off the stool, but she was too slow, and he caught her arm before she could escape.

He grabbed the wrong arm.

As Jax's fingers dug into her fresh cuts, Carson cried out in pain, the debilitating stinging shooting up and down her arm. It felt like a lightning strike.

"What's wrong? What happened?" he asked, all playfulness gone, dropping her arm. Then he noticed the blood seeping through the fabric of her shirt.

"You're bleeding," he said.

Before she could pull away, Jax snatched her arm and yanked up her sleeve. Instantly, she ripped it back and shielded it behind her body. But, it was too late.

"Carson . . . give me your arm."

A flurry of curses filled her mind. Wiping the frosting from his finger, Jax took a step closer to her, and she took a step back.

"Give. Me. Your. Arm. Now."

When Carson didn't move, didn't budge an inch, he reached around to grab her arm himself. She didn't resist. What was the point of hiding anymore?

Carefully, Jax stretched her arm straight and gripped the edge of her sleeve. Slowly, *slowly*, he pushed the fabric up. When he noticed the lines didn't stop at the Band-Aid he pushed her sleeve even higher, higher, higher up her arm.

He had unveiled her deepest secret.

Her disgraceful habit.

Her drug.

It was as though a ton of bricks had come crashing down from the ceiling, the weight of the moment crushing her. Every fiber of Carson's being wanted to run and hide under a rock where nobody could find her. She was appalled at herself, appalled that Jax had found out. Would it make it worse if she pulled away and sprinted out the door?

She wanted to vomit. Heave out the horror of this moment. Because of her selfishness, Jax had escaped from one problematic woman only to gain another.

His silence was screaming in her ears, but she didn't dare look up at his face, afraid of what she would see. Anger. Disgust. Disappointment. *Repulsion.* The same emotions she was feeling for herself.

After a minute or an eternity, she didn't know which, Jax slid his hands down to hers.

"Where's your first-aid kit?" he asked.

As Carson led him to her bathroom, he never let go of her hands. Not even when he bent down to retrieve the box of medical supplies.

Neither spoke while he cleaned and dressed her wounds with skill gleaned from years of first-aid training. Even after he had finished, Carson's body continued to quiver.

This was it. It was over.

To her surprise, Jax pulled her close and wrapped his arms firmly around her. She didn't dare speak, dare move. Was he giving her one last goodbye?

How could she have let this happen? Let him see the part of her that she hated the most. For years, Carson had been so meticulous in making sure no one ever found out.

She had grown too comfortable.

She had become sloppy.

Eventually, her body ceased shaking. That was when he let her go and lifted her chin.

"Why?"

It was a simple question, but with a complicated answer. Carson tried to look away but Jax's grip was firm.

"Why?" he asked again.

Her mouth opened. Closed. Opened again. "I'm so sorry," was all she could say.

"That didn't answer my question."

This time, Jax let her go when she tried to pull away and she buried her face into her hands, her stomach sinking even lower. How does one explain to another the reason they cut themselves?

"Please tell me," he insisted quietly.

She dropped her hands but didn't answer him. Her voice was lost in her humiliation.

"Do you cut because of Luke and your baby?"

Carson's mind spun. The room spun. Everything was spinning.

"I understand if you want to leave." Her voice was monotone, like a robot.

He sighed, his eyes looking at something behind her.

"I didn't mean for you to see," she whispered.

"Does anyone else know?" he asked, focusing back on her.

She shook her head. This had to stop. She needed to stop.

"Are there more?"

"More scars?"

"Yes, more scars."

She stared at him for a long time, thinking about the white lines that littered parts of her body. Her cheek started to grow numb as she chewed and chewed and chewed.

Defeated, she nodded.

"May I?" Jax asked.

Strength withering away, she grunted permission.

Lifting her other arm, Jax shifted the sleeve to examine it. Line after line. Crosshatch after crosshatch. Like a series of railroad tracks.

Then he stepped back to gently lift the fabric of her shirt and expose her stomach. He sucked in a breath through his teeth.

As he continued to lift her shirt higher to view her ribcage, Carson closed her eyes. What did it all look like to him? Dozens of faded white, pink, and red scars scattered on her torso mixed with fresh ones. A few of them Jax traced with his finger, the thicker lines that had caused the most damage. His touch sent a ripple of goosebumps down her body.

"Please don't leave me," Carson pleaded as a single tear dropped down her cheek. Surely he would want to leave, because who would want to be with someone like her?

Dropping her shirt, Jax placed his big hands on either side of her neck. She grabbed his wrists as much for support as to keep him there. He wiped Carson's tear away with his thumb.

"I won't," he said.

Then he pulled her in for another embrace. Carson's heart swelled, filling her chest cavity with so many emotions. Shock, because he hadn't run at the first sight of her hideousness. Embarrassment that he'd found out. Relief that she no longer carried this secret on her own. Then guilt, for forcing this burden on another.

She peered up at his face, and he pressed his lips on her forehead, on the scar that hadn't been caused by her.

"Are you mad at me?" Carson asked, weakly.

The question made Jax take a breath and uncurl his arms to look directly at her. "No, I'm not mad. I'm horrified that you feel the need to hurt yourself." He grabbed one of her arms, eyes trailing up and down the scars. Carson's insides twisted; she wasn't used to being so exposed. "I feel awful that I didn't notice it sooner so I could help you sooner." He rubbed his thumb under one of the white lines.

She put her hand on top of his. "Please don't say that. This isn't your fault."

"Then let me help you through this," he begged. "You're going to get help. You understand that, right?"

Feeling like she was beyond help, she faltered.

"You can't keep doing this to yourself anymore."

Now Carson really hesitated. "I don't know if I can stop."

As though he understood what she meant, he pondered on her statement before asking, "What can I do to help?"

"I don't know. I don't even know where to begin." Carson stepped back until she was leaning on the bathroom sink.

"Have you tried talking to someone? Like your doctor or anyone?"

"I tried." She looked at Jax, then down at her bare feet. "After you told me about your drinking, I made an appointment with a therapist. I thought if you could stop drinking, I could stop cutting. I never ended up going, though." She recalled the blah-building and its blah-colors.

"Why?"

Her shoulders bounced up and down. "I don't know. I guess I'm not convinced it will help."

"Then it might be a good place to start."

Carson stood in a hallway of mirrors. Her naked body reflected back at her in hundreds of different angles. Her ivory skin was bright, beautiful, scarless. Taking a step toward the nearest reflection, she reached out to touch the cold silver. When she drew closer, three scars formed on her abdomen. They were thick and ugly, making her look disfigured.

She hated them. Hated what they were. Hated what they meant.

A blade appeared in her hand. She knew what she had to do to never have to look at those three scars again—

It was difficult to open her eyes because her head was so heavy, as if all the strength had been sucked out of her as she slept. Carson didn't know when she'd eventually fallen asleep. After Jax had discovered the lines all over her body, he'd sat her on the couch, wrapped her in a blanket, and placed a plate of cookies in her lap. Together, they'd eaten their sweets and watched *Beetlejuice*. That was all she could remember.

Finally, her eyelids fluttered open. The ceiling fan's monotonous, rotating blades filled her vision. She was in her room. Her fingers crept along her bedding. Empty.

It took every muscle she had to sit up, patting down the lumps of her comforter and frowning. Where was Jax? Her heart, which was already at the bottom of her ribcage, sank into her stomach. Did he leave?

Tiptoeing down the hall to the living room, Carson's footsteps were as quiet as a desert mouse. A human-shaped lump was sprawled out on her couch, which was much longer than what the sofa had to offer. Her favorite fuzzy blanket was trying its best to cover Jax's huge frame. Though there was no pillow to cushion his head, and he was still wearing the clothes from the day before, and his feet hung over the end of the armrest, he looked peaceful. Carson wondered if Jax's firefighter experience had taught him to sleep under any condition.

Pivoting on her foot, she stalked back to her bathroom. Judging by the early morning sunlight streaming through the windows, she had enough time to shower before work—to wash away the shame of the night before.

No reflection looked back at her as she brushed her teeth, the steam having fogged up the mirror. Good. She didn't need a reminder of her dream. As she stripped off her shirt, Carson noted the bandage that continued to hug her arm, reminding her of Jax's tender touches.

She let out a frustrated sigh. What had she done?

There was a light knock on the door. Scooping up her shirt, Carson slipped it on before opening it.

Jax took a step back, as though he hadn't expected it to open so quickly. "I didn't know you were . . ." His eyes flicked to the running water behind her and back again. "I wanted to make sure you were doing alright."

The memory of his patience and understanding the night before solidified. Carson nuzzled up to him, wanting to feel it all again. Gladly he took her into his arms.

"I'm fine," she breathed into his chest. And she was. Having her secret exposed gave her a glimmer of hope. Now that Jax knew, all those possibilities she had refused to dream about before filled her mind. They made her stomach tingle with excitement. Could she start this new life with him? Could they have a future together?

Then she realized something that had been forming in her very soul, from the very moment they met, waiting for the right moment to appear.

Carson pulled away to look into Jax's face.

"I love you, Jax Miller."

His eyes caught fire, and once again Carson was engulfed in his flames. "I love you too, Carson West."

Then Jax gripped her face and kissed her. *Hard*. She wound her arms around his neck, pulling herself closer to his body. Before she knew it, she was sitting on the bathroom sink, knocking over the soap dispenser and perfumes. It didn't matter, because she was too busy thinking about the way her body was pinned between the mirror and his lips, which were greedy against hers.

Something was different in the way he was kissing her, as if every kiss before this moment had been on her terms. Now it was Jax's turn. He was in control, and he was hungry. He leaned on the foggy mirror, leaving a handprint, as his other hand slid up her thigh and crept under her shirt, higher and higher.

Instinct screamed at Carson to recoil from his touch. Her marred skin was forbidden territory. Only this time, she allowed his fingers to trespass.

As Jax's kisses migrated down her neck, she panted for air, working her own fingers into his long locks. Then he was back at her mouth, which gave her the opportunity to take his bottom lip between her teeth and bite it.

Jax snarled and scooped her up, marching them out of the bathroom, shower forgotten. They fell onto her unkempt bed. The motion made her arm sting. Carson ignored it, because her body yearned for him, her skin burning where he touched her.

She needed more.

In one smooth motion they rolled until she was on top, straddling his hips. She quickly unbuttoned his pants before he sat up and ripped his shirt off, the fabric landing somewhere on the carpet.

A wave of vulnerability washed over her, causing her to hesitate before pulling off her own shirt. This was it. Her hideousness was completely out in the open. Once her shirt was removed, the air felt cold against her bare skin, puckering the scars.

Jax's eyes raked over her. Then he took her arm, the one without the bandage, and began kissing the scars all the way up until he reached her shoulder. Little by little, Carson's insecurity vanished every time his lips touched a line. Then he snaked his arms around her, sliding his coarse hands against her bumpy skin until his fingers were laced in her hair.

Without warning, he clutched a handful of it and yanked her head back. Carson let out a gasp. With more of her neck exposed, Jax's lips trailed down her sternum and back up. Gently, his lower lip glided across her collarbone.

"I love you," Jax whispered, causing the hair on her neck to rise. "I love you," he repeated over and over with a kiss at the end of each one. He spoke those three words as if he had been holding them back this whole time. Eventually, his mouth found hers again.

Carson was late to work.

CHAPTER SIXTEEN

"I understand this is your first time seeking counseling."

Carson's leg stopped bouncing, though she continued to fiddle with her keys, pressing the tips of her fingers into the grooves, leaving impressions. Nerves had cut off her vocal cords, so she nodded. When presenting in the courtroom in front of a judge or jury, she was fearless. But sitting in a private room with someone whose sole job is to listen and help? Terrifying.

It had been two weeks since Jax discovered Carson's secret. Now she was sitting on a therapist's sofa next to Jax.

The therapist, Dr. Whitlock—though he'd offered for Carson and Jax to call him Dave—leaned back, the deep-mocha leather of his chair whining. "What brings you here today?"

His black goatee moved as he spoke, the whiskers bending with the motion of his lips. The clanging of Carson's keys began to annoy her, so she dropped them by her side and shoved her hands between her thighs before glancing at Jax.

"I cut myself." No point in beating around the bush, though the words felt like mud in her mouth. Carson wished she had a hose to wash away the dirt.

"Thank you for sharing with me. That must have been difficult," Dave said. "I'm interested in hearing about what leads you to self-harm."

"I don't know. Maybe because my husband and son died in a car accident."

"I can only imagine how hard that was for you."

"Well, it was five years ago," Carson said dismissively.

Dave's head tilted to one side. "You say that as if five years is a long time. As though their deaths shouldn't be difficult anymore."

Carson's eyes dropped to inspect the patterns in the carpet, a kaleidoscope of brown and black. Compared to the Granite Dells Center, she liked the darker earth tones this office had to offer. It reminded her of the forest. In fact, the light scent of trees, like pine needles after a rainstorm, floated around the room.

"Did the accident trigger the start of your self-harm?" Dave asked.

"Not necessarily," she said, her hair lightly hitting her cheeks when she shook her head. "Well, I guess, since I have never cut myself before the accident."

"I'd like to know what you mean by 'not necessarily'."

Those three scars appeared in Carson's mind. So did her abhorrence.

After a quick glance at Jax, glad he agreed to go with her to her first session, she explained. "I was pregnant at the time of the accident. I needed surgery which left scars on my stomach. After three years I didn't want to look at them anymore."

"I'm so sorry that happened to you," Dave said, his face becoming softer, more round.

"Thank you," Carson said.

"Your mind and body have been through a lot. I can only imagine what you are feeling."

A waterfall feature covered the entire wall behind the therapist. The water descended and bubbled in the little pool at the bottom. It was a nice, calming touch.

"Sometimes," Carson murmured, "when I hurt myself, I don't feel anything at all, like I'm in a trance. I can't control it. Other times, I'm conscious of what I'm doing, and it's almost satisfying. Which is crazy, because obviously it's wrong."

"When someone harms themselves, their body releases endorphins, which are happy hormones, to the brain," Dave said, uncrossing his legs. "Are you on any medications?"

Carson stiffened, suddenly wary. "No, and I don't want to be."

"May I ask why not?"

Carson's body turned to liquid, horrified at the direction the conversation had gone. The shaking in her hands migrated up to her arms. She balled them into fists on her lap, feeling stupid for not realizing that this specific subject would come up, especially with Jax sitting next to her. For a moment she contemplated lying, but quickly rejected the thought. She was done lying.

"Carson?"

Her attention snapped back to Dave. "I don't have a good relationship with medications," she said. That hadn't been a good enough explanation, as Dave continued to stare at her expectantly. Carson adjusted in her seat, chewed her cheek for a second, then spoke. "About a year after the accident, I found my leftover painkillers. I took every single one with an entire bottle of vodka."

"You attempted to end your life by overdosing?" Dave asked.

Hearing her actions spoken out loud made Carson's soul leave her body. Meekly, she looked at Jax. His eyes held so much pain.

Looking back at Dave, she gave a tiny nod.

"Have you tried again since?" Dave gently pressed.

"No, I haven't."

"I'm very glad to hear that." He paused for a second, analyzing her. Carson became even more nervous, wondering if this was the part Dave declares her crazy and puts her into a straitjacket. But all he said was, "I can see you're very uncomfortable being here."

Again, Carson made her leg stop twitching and shrugged.

"Tell me about that," Dave continued.

"I don't know if therapy will fix my problems," Carson said, somewhat resolute. "I have nothing against therapy or therapists. I don't think it's a resource for me, though. I think that ultimately it is up to me to change. I shouldn't rely on drugs or a therapist to change me."

Dave tapped his pudgy finger against his chin. "You are correct, Carson. It is ultimately up to you to change. But sometimes people need a little help along the way. It seems that you are willing to give therapy a try. After a few weeks, you may determine that therapy is the tool you need to get better. Or you may choose to find another path.

"For now, I think it's important to get a handle on your self-harm. Let's talk about a safety plan."

By the time Jax's truck pulled into her driveway later that evening, Carson was lounging on the couch. She was exhausted, mentally and physically. Who knew going to therapy would be just as demanding as riding a dirt bike for hours on end?

Jax's headlights disappeared as he pulled around back. They had left the counseling office at the same time. She had already driven home, changed, and put a frozen pizza in the oven. Where had he gone?

Within seconds, the side door opened, and Jax's footsteps thudded through the kitchen. She sat up off the couch, about to ask him where he went, when the words got lost in her throat. Jax approached her with a large bouquet of flowers: ivory roses with splashes of baby's breath, a stark contrast to the black tissue paper they were swaddled in.

"Oh, Jax, I love these," Carson cooed, pressing her nose into the petals. They smelled better than the pizza currently cooking.

"Congratulations on surviving your first session of therapy."

She laughed before stretching on her toes to give him a peck on the lips.

"I am *so* proud of you," he said gruffly.

"I'm proud of myself too. Though I feel like I just got my ass kicked."

"I can only imagine what that was like for you. Thank you for being so honest and willing to try."

"It wasn't easy," she whispered.

Jax kissed her forehead. "I know."

When Carson moved to put the roses in water, Jax snatched her arm. "Where the hell do you think you're going, Mr. Hoover?" he said, before leaning down and kissing her lips with so much vigor it caught her off guard. His hands found their way to her back, sliding under her shirt.

"The flowers," Carson mumbled against his lips, concerned that his eagerness would damage their fragile bodies.

"I'll buy you new ones," Jax growled, now kissing her chin line.

His kisses and roving hands made Carson's blood pulse throughout her body. "Let me at least set these down," she said.

After an annoyed huff, Jax smashed his lips back onto hers. Before she could complain again, he took the bouquet from her, slid his hand down to her thigh, and lifted her up. She tried to gasp, but he wouldn't let her lips leave his. Afraid he was going to drop her, she hooked her ankles around his waist.

With the bundle of roses in one hand and Carson in the other, Jax walked into the kitchen. He sat the flowers on the counter, then spun her around. A cabinet opened, and glass clinked. They spun again. Carson heard the rush of the sink faucet filling a container and stems settling into a vase. He did all of this while kissing her.

It was moments like this that Carson appreciated his career choice. Years of training to naturally carry a person while having to do other impossible tasks made kissing him that much more enjoyable.

Now he was taking her somewhere. She didn't care where. Her mind was wrapped around the way his tongue mingled with hers. How his breath tasted of fresh peppermint, like the flavor of gum always resting in the cupholder of his truck. How the hat he wore was in the way of her fingers trying to run through his hair. Grabbing the bill, she tossed it aside blindly.

Soon, Jax lowered himself onto Carson's bed. Now she was in his lap with her legs on either side of him. She wanted to be closer to him. Needed to be closer to him. There was too much fabric. Breaking their kiss, she ripped her shirt off over her head and threw it on the floor. His hands slid up and down her back leaving fire in their wake.

"There's food in the oven," she warned, remembering the pizza.

"Then we better be fast."

Then he lay back, taking her with him, and rolled until he was on top, continuing to kiss down her chest. Deliberately, Jax's lips became less forceful and more delicate until he was only pushing them on specific parts of her abdomen. With a quick glance, Carson saw he was inspecting her torso. Every few seconds, he would kiss a random spot on her stomach. Her heart squeezed when she realized he was kissing her scars. The distress on his face was clear as he digested each and every one of the lines scattered all over her ribcage, stomach, and hips.

Eventually, Jax lifted his eyes and made contact with her. Carson pushed herself up to rest on her elbows, also analyzing her disfigured body. The scars no longer gave her ambivalent pleasure like it did once before.

One of his fingers traced the lines on her waist, causing her skin to erupt in goosebumps.

"Do you think you'll ever wish you didn't have these anymore?" he asked, his voice subdued.

"No," she admitted after thinking for a second.

He cocked his head at her answer, his hair spilling over to the side.

"I mean, it would be nice to be able to wear whatever I want without the whole world seeing what I've done. But I don't know if I would want them completely gone. I guess I see them as a reminder."

Jax nodded absentmindedly at her explanation. She could only imagine what he was thinking. Did he wish they were gone?

"Can I ask you a question?" she asked.

He stopped tracing the lines on her stomach, his eyes catching hers.

"Does today change things between us? I mean, knowing that I tried to . . ." Still, Carson couldn't say the words.

"What do you mean?"

"I don't know," she breathed. "I feel like it could all be too much for you at some point. It's a lot to handle."

Jax's eyes turned to slits. "You've got to give me more credit than that, Carson," he said, miffed, before lifting himself into a sitting position on the side of the bed.

Also sitting up, she folded her legs in front of her. "I know, but—"

"But, what? You don't think I can handle it? You do realize what I do for a living."

"That is kind of my point." Carson thought back to the morning he'd explained why he didn't tell her about being at her accident. "You told me you didn't want to deal with conflict at home because you have so much stress at work."

He rolled his neck. "That's not—I'm not saying it's going to be easy. You just have to believe that I love you enough to be by your side, no matter how difficult it gets. Please don't keep things from me because you don't think I can handle them."

Needles poked Carson's body, and she imagined the three scars on her abdomen laughing at her. She was supposed to take small steps, not spill her guts out all at once. The self-harm and suicide attempt should be enough for now. Would Jax be able to handle the reason she began hacking at her skin in the first place?

The day she'd first taken a sharp object to her body played in her mind. It was eerily similar to her dream the other night. Nearly two years ago, she'd been standing fully naked in front of her bathroom mirror, having just left the shower. The car accident had done more than kill her family. It had also taken her ability to get pregnant.

The hysterectomy scars were hideous, a constant reminder of what she'd lost and what she couldn't have. For three years, she had to look at the most disgraceful part of herself. That morning she finally decided to do something about it. Except she hadn't stopped on her stomach. The pain felt too nice, too sweet. The cutting began to spread like a disease across her body.

Carson's surgery scars continue to mock her as she considered how to respond to Jax's request. Apparently cutting her stomach up hadn't silenced them, it had only hid them. How was she supposed to tell Jax she couldn't bear his children?

Not yet. One step at a time. *I will tell him*, she promised herself, *just not tonight.*

Finally, she nodded once.

"I spoke with my ma today" Jax said, changing the subject. "She wants to meet you."

"Really?" Carson perked up, relieved that the conversation had changed direction.

"I'm flying back home for Christmas. I was wondering if you'd like to come with me. My brother's wife Marlo is about to have a baby, so we'll get to snuggle a newborn."

"I'd love that," Carson said. How she would have loved to have held her own newborn. Then her body hummed with apprehension. She wrapped her arms around herself. "I hope they'll like me."

Eyes twinkling, Jax caught her wrists and lifted them above her head, forcing her back onto the bed to finish what they had started. Letting his tongue explore hers for a minute, his lips eventually moved up her chin.

Breath tickling the delicate skin of Carson's ear, Jax whispered, "If they have any brains, they will."

CHAPTER SEVENTEEN

Carson's son tugged on her hand, pulling her closer to the park. Mirroring his excitement, she picked up her pace. All week he had been begging her to go. The sandy curls on his head sprung as he skipped in front of her and Luke, giggling with anticipation.

The playground was just across the street, its swings and slide urging them forward. Unable to wait any longer, her son dashed toward the equipment.

"Wait!" Carson called out to him. "Look out for traffic."

Then she turned to Luke to roll her eyes, but Luke wasn't looking at her or their son. His eyes had glazed over, dark clouds reflecting off his pupils.

"Mommy?"

Carson turned. Her son was standing in the middle of the road. When she tried to yell, her voice caught in her throat. She couldn't speak. Looking back at Luke for help, he had disappeared. Whipping her head around, she found both of them staring at her from the road.

Then it was there. The cherry-red semi-truck. It barreled down the street toward Luke and their son. Carson tried to cry out, but her warnings never made it out of her mouth, her lips having been glued shut. Her feet were fused to the asphalt. Tugging. Tugging. Tugging. Her legs wouldn't move.

The truck approached at full speed, its horn blaring, getting louder and louder until it was right behind them, inches from their bodies—

Gasping for breath, Carson bolted upright from her bed, disturbing her dark, silent room.

I can't breathe. I can't breathe.

She stumbled out of her bedroom and into her bathroom, tripped over to the window, and wrenched it open. The fall air stung her face.

I still can't breathe.

She slammed her fists against the screen until it crumpled out of the frame. Only when Carson stuck her head into the dark night did she finally suck in a cold breath. Hanging out the window, she let the breeze cool the hot blood pumping throughout her body until she could finally collapse to the tile floor.

Pain pierced her chest as her heart shredded inside. Anguish swirled around her, its cold hands caressing her body. Willing the awful nightmare of her husband and son to vanish, Carson squeezed her eyes so hard that white spots appeared.

Make it stop. Make it stop.

Ripping open a drawer, she rummaged for anything sharp enough, flinging the contents onto the floor. Nothing. She moved to the next drawer and the next and the next. The blade was comforting in her hand once she found it. She pressed it to her skin several times, anticipating the soothing pain of the puncture.

Shivering and encircled in the mess she had created searching for the razor blade, Carson lay curled in the middle of the bathroom floor. Somewhere a door slammed shut followed by hurried footsteps down the hall.

"Carson?"

That voice sounded familiar. It was warm to her ears.

"Carson," the voice repeated, sounding just like Jax. How was he here?

Then he must have spotted the disassembled shaving razors next to her, because she heard him kick something from out of her reach and kneel down beside her. A hand touched her arm.

"You're freezing."

Too weak from the battle raging inside her, Carson didn't respond. She kept her eyes shut, afraid that if she opened them, she would see Luke's dead face and not Jax.

There was a shuffle. A window slammed loudly. The water knob squeaked as Jax turned on the bath. He scooped her up into his arms and carefully set her in the tub. Pulling her knees to her chest, Carson rested her heavy head on them. The warm water made her feet prickle.

Brushing the hair out of her face, Jax stroked the top of her head. After a moment, she felt him lift her shirt. Then he grabbed an arm, turning it over, and did the same to her other arm. He was searching for new cuts.

"I didn't do it." Her voice was muffled between her legs.

"What?"

She cleared her throat though it didn't do any good. "I didn't do it."

Over the rush of the running water, she could hear his sigh of relief. Jax must have been satisfied with how full the tub was, because he turned off the water. They sat in silence while he stroked the top of her hair, calming her, making her feel safe.

"Are you ready to get out?" he asked after a few minutes.

Nodding weakly against her knees, Carson let him help her step out of the tub, her soaking pajamas drenching the floor. Piece by piece he stripped her of her dripping clothes then pulled off his sweatshirt, putting it over her head and threading her arms through the sleeves. There was a whiff of dust on the fabric. The jacket practically swallowed her whole. It was warm from his body, like being in the protection of his embrace.

Then she was in Jax's arms as he carried her to her bed and lay her in the middle. Carson heard him kick off his shoes to climb in with her. He wasn't going to let her go as he tucked his arm under her head, letting it rest on his chest.

"Thank you," Carson managed to croak.

Jax grasped her hand that was resting on his stomach, squeezing harder than normal. "I'm just so glad you called."

Carson could feel his heartbeat pick up its pace. Confused, she asked, "I called you?"

"You don't remember?"

She recalled the dream and waking up. Except she thought she had gone straight into the bathroom to open the window because she needed fresh air. Then she'd looked in the drawers for something . . .

A shudder shook her body. "No, I don't."

"You did," Jax said. "I picked up, but you didn't say anything. When you didn't answer me calling your name, I rushed over here, hoping I wasn't too late." He hugged her tighter to his body, his tone changing into something she hadn't heard from him before: fear.

"I didn't do it," Carson repeated. Then it hit her. She hadn't done it. Hadn't used an object to hurt herself. Hadn't caused herself pain or damaged her body. She'd been very close, even pressing the blade to her skin without puncturing it, but she. Hadn't. Done. It. For the first time in two years, she hadn't hurt herself.

Attraction.

What was even more inspiring was that she had come away unscathed by *herself*. No one had been there to stop her. She'd done it all on her own. This gave her a shred of confidence that she did have what it took to end her self-harm. She wasn't just doing it for Jax. Somewhere deep within her, she had the strength to stop herself *for* herself. Even with her lingering nightmares, Carson didn't have a single scratch on her body.

Dave, her therapist, would be so proud. Raegan, if she knew, would be smiling ear-to-ear.

"I know, baby. I know. I'm so proud of you," Jax said, kissing the top of her head. Then, after a couple of seconds, he asked, "Do you want to talk about it?"

Carson's gut reaction was to say no. But she was feeling strong. If she could stop herself from cutting she could talk to Jax.

Teeth grazing the inside of her cheek she started, "I have this dream."

"The dream about the accident?"

"No, it's a different one. Luke is there and so is . . . he." Her voice caught.

"He?"

"The baby I was pregnant with, but he's not a baby anymore. He's the age he would be today if he were still alive." She stared at the ceiling, illuminated by the bathroom light that cascaded into the room. "In the dream, I have this history with them. My baby's born and Luke and I are parents. Most of the time we're taking him to the park. The dream always ends with . . ." Squirming, Carson tried to find the additional strength to speak the nightmare out loud. "The semi is there, and I can never reach them fast enough. I'm always too late to save them." Tears pricked her eyes.

"So you woke up from this dream and went into the bathroom," Jax stated. "You do know that their deaths weren't your fault, right?"

Jax was repeating what Dave had explained to her during her second counseling session. Evidently she had been suffering from survivor's guilt. The guilt that she survived and her baby didn't. But Carson had been his mother. It had been her job to be his caregiver, his protector, and she'd failed. It had been her responsibility to guard the little human inside her. Instead, she had forsaken her baby.

"I was supposed to protect him," she murmured.

"You did protect him. But you couldn't have controlled what happened that day."

"I know. I can't help but think about it though."

"I can understand that."

As they lay there, Carson began to feel closer to normal. She could feel her toes, her feet, her legs. Hands and arms, one curled underneath her and the other across Jax's chest. The expansion of her lungs as she breathed. Although it felt as though there was a boulder on her chest.

"What time is it?" Carson asked.

"I'm not sure. You called around two." Jax dug his hand into his pocket to pull out his phone, shifting Carson's weight in the process. He squinted against the bright digital light. "It's three."

"Thank you for coming all the way out here in the middle of the night. I'm feeling better now. You can go home and get some sleep."

Tossing his phone on the night stand he rolled on his side to nestle down into the sheets and wrapped his arms around her. "Don't be ludicrous, Mr. Hoover. I'm staying."

Instead of objecting, Carson lifted her head and kissed his prickly chin. "Is it alright if I fall asleep now?"

"Sleep. You need it."

After nuzzling her body into Jax, Carson closed her eyes. With all her energy drained and a smile on her face, she was fast asleep within seconds.

CHAPTER EIGHTEEN

J ax was standing on his front porch when Carson rolled into the driveway. It was too cold of a night to be outside. The weatherman had been
warning the public for days about a cold front that would hit Thanksgiving
Day. Even with the heater on full blast and a thick sweater, Carson wished
she had put on fuzzier socks and a beanie.

The drizzle of rain didn't deter him from ambling around to the passenger side as soon as her truck stopped. He let the icy droplets land on
his face, wetting his hair. If it were Carson, she'd be dashing to get into the
warm cab.

Jax slipped inside, his build squeezing into Carson's smaller pickup.
Maybe that was why he'd purchased a diesel equipped with more spacious
seating.

"Hey," Carson said, turning down the radio as a new song began. It was
a Christmas carol that had no right to be playing on Thanksgiving.

"Hi." The tip of Jax's nose was red. He wasn't even wearing a jacket, just
a gray long-sleeved flannel that definitely wasn't thick enough to battle the
weather.

"You're not cold?" Carson asked.

Looking down at himself, he barely lifted his shoulders. "Not really."

Although Jax's body was beside her, she could tell his mind was somewhere else entirely.

Hundreds of scenarios flashed in Carson's mind. Was it Kristen? Was she planning to continue her fight for money? Or had something happened to one of his family members? His sister-in-law just had her baby. Had he finally had enough of Carson's problems and decided to break up with her?

"Everything okay?" Her question was timid, afraid that she might scare him off.

Closing his eyes, Jax leaned his head back. Even in the dim light, Carson could have sworn she saw the color drain from his face.

"Hey, what's going on?" She reached over and grabbed his freezing hand. As soon as she touched him, he put his other hand on top of hers. Hopefully Carson's fingers were hot enough to warm his.

Jax chose silence for a little longer, squeezing his eyes shut. His breathing was slow, methodical.

"Talk to me, Jax."

Eyes fluttering open, he looked down at his lap.

"Did something happen at work today?" she asked.

Jax let out a long breath. "We got a call for DV."

"DV?"

"Domestic violence."

"Do you want to talk about it?" Carson rubbed her thumb against his hand in an attempt to encourage him.

"The husband went into a drunken rage. We were treating the wife's injuries, trying to persuade her to go to the hospital. But she couldn't because she had children." Jax had to swallow before he could continue. "Then four little boys came down the stairs."

It only took a second for his words to register what that meant to him. *Oh.*

Finally, Jax looked at her, eyes wet with history. "I saw myself. I saw my family. That was my ma who was black and blue." He buried his face in his hands, and his shoulders began to shake as his whispered sobs filled the silent night air.

"I'm so sorry, Jax," Carson said, her own sobs threatening to clog her throat.

How she wished she could take away his pain. Make him forget the horrors of his childhood. She reached up to touch his shoulders, an attempt to soothe him. At her touch, Jax unraveled and rolled into her, and Carson stretched her arms around him in the small of the front seat.

She held him tight. Held the little boy who watched his mother beaten by his father. In that moment, she was grateful for the childhood she'd had, because it was nothing compared to his. At the end of the day, no matter how terrible her mother was, Carson had never felt unsafe in her own home.

The minutes ticked on, and Jax didn't let go, even after his sniffles stopped and his breathing evened out. Carson could only imagine what he was processing, the demons he was fighting. Hoping to give him some sort of solace her hand slid up and down his back.

"We should probably go before Raegan serves our heads for dinner," Jax said, his breath hot against her neck.

"I don't mind eating a cold turkey."

Jax pulled away and rubbed the sadness from his eyes. "Yeah, but I mind eating cold mashed potatoes and gravy." After straightening in his seat he zipped the seatbelt into place.

"You sure? We don't have to go tonight. We can always rain check," Carson offered. Last year, she'd rescheduled Thanksgiving dinner with Raegan and Hunter. Instead of carving the turkey, she'd stayed home and carved her body.

Jax's smile couldn't hide his crushed spirit. "I'm sure," he said. Then he reached up and cupped her face. "Thank you."

"You guys made it just in time. Hunter just finished the turkey," Raegan said, hanging her apron on a hook attached to the pantry door, her shoes providing her the extra inches she needed to reach it.

Unlike Raegan, who wore a silver-shimmering dress and stilettos, Carson sported only boots, jeans, and a sweater. Having to wear skirts and heels all week for work, she didn't feel the need to wear them on her days off, even on Thanksgiving.

The dinner tasted just as delicious as it smelled. Buttered rolls, savory gravy and salted mashed potatoes, candied carrots, and seasoned stuffing made the meal a feast fit for a king.

After most of the food had disappeared into freshly full stomachs, Raegan placed a decadent chocolate pie on the table while Hunter pushed the assortment of dishes out of the way to make room. Carson felt like the table, not sure if she had enough space in her to fit more food, but the airy whipped topping looked heavenly.

If it weren't for pie, Luke and Carson would not have celebrated the day of gratitude. Luke was also an only child, so family get-togethers were few and far between. And Carson had never really learned to cook, her mom never having taught her anything more than pouring milk into a bowl full of cereal or boiling a pot of water. But every year, Luke would come home with a giant pie—blueberry or key-lime or pecan or cherry—and no matter how full they were, they stuffed their faces with dessert.

Smiling, she thought of how Luke would always say, "There's always room for pie," and happily took the piece that Raegan dished out to her.

"So I have something to say," Raegan announced, pushing the chocolate cream around her plate with her fork. She snuck an uncertain glance at Carson, then at Hunter, who gave her an encouraging nod.

Jax was shoveling the dessert into his mouth which reminded Carson a bit of Luke. The lit candles on the table flickered with anticipation, waiting for Raegan's announcement. Raegan set down her fork and folded her hands on the table. Again, another uncertain look thrown Carson's way.

It wasn't until Jax also put down his fork, his piece having disappeared, and everyone around the table was looking expectantly at Raegan did she finally speak.

"I'm pregnant." The words came out as if Raegan were getting something off her chest. Her eyes flicked again to Carson, apprehension shadowing them.

Her heart soaring with delight, Carson's mouth popped open in surprise. Only now did she realize that Hunter was the only person at the table with a Blue Moon in front of him.

Instantly, she visualized Raegan having a little girl with long blond hair and rolls for days. Or a baby boy with auburn hair and kisses of freckles spread across his skin, just like Hunter. Then Carson imagined buying cute little clothes with tiny designs on them and the little shoes she loved to coo over when she spotted them at the store.

That was why, when Raegan kept staring neurotically at her, Carson went from feeling delighted to perplexed. Why didn't Raegan seem happy about her pregnancy?

Jax didn't notice Raegan's nervous demeanor. "Are you guys serious?

That's awesome. Congratulations!" he said.

"When did you find out?" Carson asked.

"This morning." Raegan shook off her apprehension. "I've been under the weather all week, thinking it was a stomach bug. But as I was putting two and two together, I took a test to confirm it. Both our parents know, but we are going to wait until after the first trimester to tell everyone else."

"Look at you getting all knocked up," Carson teased. "I can't wait to see you with a big belly."

Hunter reached over and put a hand on Raegan's neck, and she melted at his touch. "Me either. You're going to be so sexy."

"Are you excited to be a dad?" Jax asked.

"Definitely. I'm hoping for a boy so I can coach his T-ball games," Hunter said, dropping his hand from Raegan's shoulder to pick up his fork and dig into his pie.

Raegan habitually patted Hunter's arm. "Girls play T-ball too," she gently reminded him.

"I don't know whether or not I would want a boy or a girl," Jax mused. "I can see the advantages of both." Then he chuckled. "I can see the *dis*advantages of both."

Raegan's eyes flicked to Carson, whose insides liquified and puddled at the base of her feet. The guilt of keeping her infertility a secret from Jax made the chocolate in her mouth no longer taste sweet.

"I can only imagine having a mini-Raegan running around," Hunter said. "My poor wallet will suffer even more if she's anything like her mother."

"Oh, stop," Raegan chided.

Ignoring her, he continued, "I don't know if I could play tea party, though."

"You know that if your little daughter came up asking you to play tea party with her, you'd do it in a heartbeat," Carson said.

Hunter pursed his lips in thought. "Yeah, you're right."

Having finished dessert and the table cleared of the empty, dirty dishes, the men migrated to the garage while Carson and Raegan found themselves in Raegan's closet, going through her assortment of clothes. The closet was big enough to have a lounge chair for Carson to occupy while Raegan rifled through her apparel. She had just finished inspecting the stretch of a leopard print shirt, holding it up to her belly, before hanging it back up.

"How are you doing?" she asked.

Carson stopped rubbing her fingers over the velvet fabric of the chair's arm. "What do you mean?"

Raegan gave her an exasperated sigh as though it was obvious. "I meant how are you doing about me being pregnant?"

"Um, freaking excited. Duh," she said.

Carson could see the relief wash over Raegan. "Really? You're not upset?"

"Why would I be upset?"

Raegan instinctually placed a hand on her stomach. "Because of your situation."

Understanding hit Carson, and her heart swelled with emotion. "Oh, Raegan. That's me, not you. Please don't think I am sad about you getting pregnant. Because I'm not . . . at all."

"Hunter and I debated telling you today or waiting," Raegan said. "We didn't want you to feel—"

Carson cut her off. "I am so elated to be an aunt. Well, a metaphorical aunt." Then she stood and walked over to Raegan. "Don't you worry about me. I'm fine."

Raegan's lips lifted. "Okay."

They turned their attention to the hanging rack of pants.

"Does Jax know?" Raegan asked quietly, her voice barely over a whisper.

Carson's smile faded. "No. Not yet."

CHAPTER NINETEEN

Relapse. That's all it was. Plenty of people did it. Carson tried to reassure herself as she wiped the blood from the hollow of her shoulder before pulling her shirt back down.

Standing in her laundry room, she faced the open junk drawer. A hefty wood screw lay on the small counter, watching her foolishly try to convince herself that what she had done was fine.

Lying in bed, Carson's mind had been a blender, swirling with stressors. An opposing attorney was berating her for advising against their settlement proposal. A client was refusing to pay their bill because they didn't like the outcome of their case. Garrett, her boss, was pushing her harder to become the best attorney she could be, in hopes of earning the junior partner position. Through it all, Carson longed to hold her husband one last time. Or even to hold her baby for the first time. And she still sought the courage to tell Jax about her inability to have children.

Then a thought had popped into her brain, silencing its whirring blades. It had been so long since she had done anything. She was allowed to treat herself, right? One time couldn't be that bad.

Attraction.

Like an eel, she had slithered out of her bed into the dark hall to find a dull object. Something that couldn't do a lot of damage, because then it would be okay. A screw was completely different from a knife. A screw was more acceptable. Surprisingly, a sharp screw could inflict a lot of damage when pressed hard enough into flesh.

As Carson stared down at the screw, the realization of what she had done sunk in.

Repulsion.

She ran out of the laundry room, back down the hall, and into her bathroom, not bothering with any lights. This wasn't the first time she'd vomited in the toilet in the dark.

Kneeling in front of the porcelain, her sickness complete, Carson strained to hear if Jax stirred from the flush. It was silent except for the ticking of the clock on the wall.

I have to tell him. I have to tell him . . . right now.

With weak knees, Carson walked into her room like a person marching to their death. She might as well be dead, as her hands and feet were numb. She wasn't even sure if she had a heart anymore, because nothing seemed to beat in her rib cage.

Gingerly, she sat on the bed, careful not to disturb Jax, though she was surprised that the ringing in her own ears didn't wake him up. Gripping his shoulder, Carson shook it. He didn't wake. She shook it again. This time he stirred.

"Jax?" Her voice wasn't her own. Too low. Too shaky.

Finally, Jax sat up trying to find her in the dark. "What is it? What's wrong?" His voice was thick with sleep.

"I hurt myself," she said flatly.

"What?"

"I hurt myself," she said again, louder this time. She didn't blame him for not understanding, with her voice quivering so much.

There was a pause as the realization of what she'd said dawned on him.

Then the tears sprang from her eyes, and Carson began to sob into her hands. Behind her fingers a soft light switched on: the nightstand lamp.

"Where?" Jax asked, all sleep gone. His voice was so sharp, too sharp for her ears. When he forcefully snagged one of Carson's arms, she dipped her face trying to hide her shame.

"Not my arms."

"Where," he demanded again, not asking this time.

Carson pointed to her left shoulder, then placed both of her palms back on her face. Jax tugged the collar of her T-shirt to expose what she had done.

"With what?" he asked.

So much agony. So much anguish.

"A screw."

"A *screw*?" he hissed, horrified. Probably thinking what someone had to do to cause that much damage with a screw.

The sobs continued. And she was hot. It was stifling in the room even though it was late fall outside.

"Why didn't you wake me up?"

"I don't know," Carson sputtered. That would have been such a simple solution, but in the intensity of the moment, it hadn't occurred to her.

Then she felt Jax's arms wrap around her. She shoved them away. "No!" she cried, her breath hitching. "Damn it, Jax, I don't deserve your sympathy."

Stunned, he stared at her.

"Stop being so nice to me," she pleaded.

Jax gave her a look like a patient parent would give to their screaming child as they waited for the tantrum to finish. "Do you want me to be mean to you?" he asked, still aggravatingly calm.

"Yes!" She was loud again, knowing she was being hysterical but not caring. "Stop being so weak. Recognize that I messed up. I failed us. I failed *you*. Stand up for yourself for once and stop letting women walk all over you. Kristen did it, and now you're letting me do it."

Jax flinched as though Carson had just smacked him across the face, and instantly she regretted her words.

Except sadly, somewhere deep within her, she felt it necessary to say something, *anything* to get him to acknowledge the severity of her actions. She was tired of his undying patience, because she believed if she were to continue to self-harm, he would continue to be forgiving and let her.

What he seemed not to understand was that self-harm didn't just affect her; it impacted him as well. Jax was absorbing how Carson treated herself. How was he supposed to go to bed at night, go to work, or hang out with his friends when she could hurt herself at any moment? The toll would slowly build up until Jax himself would snap.

"I do think what you are doing is wrong," he said softly, the pain in his voice very clear. "I also think being mean to you will not help the situation."

Carson took the hem of her shirt to wipe the tears from her face. "Then why can't I stop?" she begged.

"You are stopping," he reminded her. "How many times have you told me that you wanted to and didn't do it?"

There had been a day, while Jax was on shift, Carson sent him a message. He'd suggested leaving the house to escape the solitude, which she did by taking a cold ride on her dirt bike. One morning she'd taken Dave's advice and, instead of using a razor to mark her arms, used a pen to scribble dozens of illustrations all over her skin. She recalled the bemused expression on Jax's face when he came home from work and saw her little art project.

The tears finally stopped. Her breakdown had peaked, plateaued, and now sloped downward. The trauma of giving in and hurting herself finally subsided enough that the fog in her head dissipated.

Clearing the frog in her throat, Carson said, "I just don't understand how you can be so patient with me all the damn time. Not only patient, but so accepting that I cut mys—"

"Don't you *ever* think I accept you cutting yourself. Ever," Jax said, his words saturated in bitterness. "I have, however, accepted the reason you did it." His use of past tense wasn't lost on her.

"Yes, but everyone has had someone in their life die and are completely normal." Carson raised her voice again, frustrated. "Why can't I just get over it? My family died five years ago, and I'm acting like it just happened. It's been *five years*!"

Groaning, she dropped her head into her hands. Why couldn't she just let their deaths go? It was exhausting holding on. The self-harm was exhausting. *She* was exhausted.

Raising her head, Carson looked at Jax. "Don't forgive me for tonight. I don't deserve your forgiveness," she muttered.

His body turned to stone. "Are you sorry for taking a screw to your shoulder and shredding your skin?"

So blunt.

"Yes."

It was the truth. Carson was sorry. Not only for breaking a promise to Jax, but for breaking a promise to herself. And she hated the way she currently felt. She had never felt like this before and never wanted to feel like this ever again.

"Then that's good enough for me," he said before switching the light off and rolling over to go back to bed.

CHAPTER TWENTY

A ll day, Jax didn't text or call, putting Carson on edge.

Trying to make herself feel better, she told herself that he was just busy during his shift and couldn't be on his phone. Though she knew that wasn't true. He was angry and hurt. She wouldn't want to talk to herself either.

Sitting at the conference table surrounded by law books, Carson and Noah were in the trenches of preparing her for her first ever family law case: a child custody dispute. After the consultation with Jax, Carson had expressed to Garrett her interest in family law which, to her surprise, led to him assigning her this case. For the past three hours, she and Noah had been reviewing Arizona's Rules of Family Law Procedure.

When her phone buzzed with an incoming text, Carson practically threw her pen to snatch it, hoping the message was from Jax.

"Woah. You missing your man?" Noah teased.

"It's none of your business," she snapped, frustrated because it was Raegan sending Carson a link to a baby registry.

"I was just asking," Noah said, lifting his hands defensively.

"I'm sorry. I had a rough night. I'm exhausted, and I guess it's finally getting to me." Maybe Carson should have brought in her lavender candle while they worked.

"Is everything fine between you and Jax?" Noah's tone suggested that he had already brushed off Carson's attitude with him. For moments like this, she appreciated Noah's personality. He was never ruffled when it came to other people's distress, which was a handy quality to have when working at a law firm. When emotions would inevitably run high, Noah would let them roll off his shoulders.

Carson tilted the chair back, dropping her hands into her lap. "I just did something that made him disappointed in me." The ache in her shoulder burned a little hotter.

"Oh." Noah sounded surprised that she would offer this intimate detail of her relationship. "Did you guys get into a fight?"

"Yes and no," she said. "More like I overreacted and said some things I shouldn't have." Her words had been so malicious.

"Is he mad at you?" Noah asked, pushing his glasses up with a single finger.

"No, I don't think so. Frustrated if anything. Hurt, definitely. And he has every right to be."

Noah was silent for a moment, which was unusual for him. "Whatever it is, beg for his forgiveness," he suggested. "You guys are endgame."

"Endgame?" she repeated, cocking her head.

"Youth slang for meant to be together. Look it up."

"Endgame," Carson parroted once more, dropping her gaze down to her feet under the table. Her purple-polished toes peeked out of her heels.

Apparently, Noah felt satisfied with her candor, because he didn't pry anymore. They continued to build their case for another hour, then put away the books on the shelves. Carson was a mixture of excitement and concern. Excited to be given this career opportunity. Concerned because she didn't want to let her new client, Jacob, and her boss down.

As Carson made her way down the hall, back to her office, Garrett called her name. Taking three steps backward she stood in his office doorway. She eyed the highlighters and sticky notes that had graffitied the law books sprawled on his desk.

Garrett pulled off his reading glasses and laid them on top of his yellow notepad. "I just got off the phone with Mr. and Mrs. Snyder. I guess you made quite the impression with them."

This surprised her. The Snyders were one of her most difficult clients. Abrupt attitudes. Short tempers. A total disregard for how the legal system worked. Not to mention their constant complaints about their monthly bill.

"Oh, wow," Carson said, unbunching her eyebrows. "I'm happy to hear that."

"I know they weren't the perfect clients, but you were able to work with them and get them to settle." He picked up his glasses again, but before putting them on, he said, "Keep that up, and I may consider junior partner sooner than I'd originally thought."

At least I'm doing something right, Carson thought. "Thank you, sir. I'll do my best."

"Have a good rest of your day," he said, slipping his glasses back on and dismissing her.

Garrett's words buzzed in Carson's ears as she walked into her office, wanting so badly to absorb and enjoy them and to be proud of herself for her hard work in her career. But the pain in her shoulder stole all her enthusiasm.

All she wanted to do was call Jax and tell him the good news. Show him that she was doing something right. Yet her iniquity continued to eat at her, like a school of piranhas swarming and biting and biting and biting. The things she had said to him horrified her.

Picking up her phone, Carson dialed Jax's number.

"Am I allowed to stop by the station?" she asked when he answered.

He was silent for a second, maybe considering if he wanted to see her or not. "Yes, but if we get a call I would have to leave."

Grabbing her computer mouse, she began closing out of programs. "That's fine. I'll see you soon, okay?"

"Sure."

Station 71 sat on the corner of an intersection on the south side of Prescott. Built in the eighties, the muted-crimson brick building was exactly what Carson thought a firehouse would look like as she pulled into the parking lot.

Just as she was about to head to the front entrance, Jax appeared around the corner, causing her heart to thrum in her chest. The air was chilly, but she was sweating. She wished she had something to put her hair up.

"Hi," she said, stopping a couple feet from him. The afternoon sun's rays clearly showed the chagrin still evident on his face, even highlighting a few new lines that hadn't been there before. In any other circumstance, she would be ogling how his uniform hugged his body. His crossed arms distorted the patches on the navy-blue button-up, and his scowl was hard to ignore. She hated that the scowl was her fault.

The moment reminded Carson about the time her fourth-grade teacher broke a porcelain plate on the floor. Then the class tried to glue it all back together. Despite their efforts, the plate still had cracks and missing pieces. Right now, Jax was the plate: cracked with missing pieces.

"How's your shoulder?" he asked.

"It's fine," Carson said, ignoring the pain. Then, unable to hold in her apology any longer, she added, "I'm so sorry for what I said to you last night. It was unfair and uncalled for. You've been nothing but patient and supportive, and I really appreciate it." She bit her cheek, then continued. "And I'm sorry that I broke my promise to you. I want to ask for your forgiveness and try again. Even if I have to handcuff myself to the bed at night, I'm willing to do anything. You can trust me."

"Can I?"

His response stung, and she asked herself the same question: Could she legitimately promise she would never hurt herself again? Except seeing him now, so despondent, was awful. She never wanted to experience this again.

"You're right, but I really am trying. That you can trust me on."

A horn honked, and Jax looked out at the intersection, then back at her. "You called me weak."

Even though his words felt like a gut punch and she wanted to hunch over from the pain, Carson kept her posture straight, just like the flagpole erected in front of the firehouse. To keep from crying, she bit her tongue. This was her fault. She didn't deserve to cry.

"I did, and I'm sorry. I feel horrible."

"If this is going to work between us, you can't talk to me like that," he said.

"I know, and I agree." She unclenched her fists.

Jax let her response hang in the air between them.

"Good," he finally said. Then his arms fell to his sides, and he let out a sigh, nodding to the area behind him. "Would you like to see inside?"

Carson followed him behind the building to a set of rolling bay doors. A fire engine was inside, its brilliant red paint the focal point of the garage. On the side was a sizable gold *71*, tagging it to this station. It had been years, back when she was a teenager, since she had been this close to a fire engine. She'd forgotten about the abundance of tools, buttons, latches, and compartments they were equipped with.

Two other firefighters occupied the garage. One she recognized from Hunter's birthday party months ago. What was his name? Tom? Tim? Yes, Tim. The guy who'd told her about the wire almost beheading a kid. He held a clipboard in his hand, counting equipment on the ground in front of him. The other person she couldn't see because they were hidden behind one of the engine's compartment doors.

"Well, hey there," Tim greeted before slipping the clipboard onto a hook just behind him. "It's Carson, right? From Hunter's birthday party."

"Yes," she confirmed. "Good to see you again."

There was a slamming of metal behind them. Turning to look, the man walking up to her made Tim look like a regular person. Instead of a navy T-shirt with matching work pants, he wore a freshly pressed, white button-up with a long black necktie. In order to maintain eye contact, Carson had to tilt her head up. The man was bald but had the thickest handlebar-mustache she had ever seen and a set of matching eyebrows. He was the very definition of a stereotypical firefighter.

"Chief, this is Carson. Carson, this is Battalion Chief Bardot," Jax introduced them.

When she lifted her hand to shake the chief's, it swallowed hers whole. "It's very nice meeting you, Chief."

"You are as beautiful as Jax described you," the chief said in a baritone voice that could shake the earth. "If Tim hadn't met you, we'd believe Jax made you up." He flashed a toothy smile.

"I'm happy to hear that Jax only says good things about me behind my back," she said, even though she didn't deserve it.

"We wouldn't let him say anything else," Tim assured her.

"I'm very happy to finally meet Miller's lady," the chief said, "but I apologize, as I must get back to something." With one last smile he headed toward a door that led into the main building.

"Did Jax tell you I'm retiring?" Tim asked.

"No, he didn't."

"Yep, next year." Tim slapped Jax on the shoulder. "Trying to get this guy to replace me as captain."

"I told them I'd think about it," Jax said. "Now, Cap', if you'll excuse us, I'd like to show her the rest of this place."

"Nice seeing you again, Captain," Carson called over her shoulder as Jax pulled her toward the same door the chief disappeared through.

The door led into a hallway with concrete walls littered with papers, pictures, and bulletin boards. Jax identified certain doors as they passed: the battalion chief's office, a utility closet, the facilities, and a training room. The hallway opened into the front administrative area with a meager fire-memorabilia museum shoved in one corner.

They passed under an archway into what Jax called the dorms: a small room with a mediocre kitchen and television. Two doors on the back wall were labeled *Bunks* and *Showers*. Carson half expected it to smell like sweat. Instead, it smelled like a citrus wall plugin.

"Welcome to my home away from home," Jax said, spreading his arm out toward the room.

Carson nodded appreciatively. "It's a lot smaller than I imagined."

"There's only five crew members here at a time," he explained. "We don't need that much space."

Stepping over to the couch, Carson placed her hand on the soft fabric, turning to him. As if studying her reaction to his living quarters Jax watched her carefully.

"Garrett brought up junior partner today," she said.

"Really? Is he going to promote you?"

She shook her head. "No. At least not yet. But he said he's going to start thinking about it again."

"That's amazing. I'm really proud of you."

The look of disappointment on his face from last night flashed in her mind. She shuddered. "Thank you . . . but can I ask you a question?"

He nodded.

"Do you want to replace Tim as Captain?"

Closing the distance between them, Jax's eyes grazed over Carson's face. "I do," he admitted.

"Then why haven't you accepted?"

The stubble crunched against Jax's hand when he reached up to rub his chin, hesitating before answering. "I just want to make sure it's the right future."

"Right future? Why wouldn't it be?"

He paused for a second, then shrugged. "Because I was hoping it wouldn't be just my own future."

It took a second before Carson realized the meaning behind his words. He was implying *their* future. Her heart did a flip-flop.

"Oh. You're not sure whether to take it or not because of me?"

"It's a big commitment, and by the time Cap' retires we don't know where we'll be," he said before adding nonchalantly, "At least I know where I want us to be."

Before Carson could clarify his statement, a series of deafening bells echoed throughout the entire station. Her eardrums protested against their shrieks. Light fixtures began flashing between red and orange, signaling an active emergency. Jax immediately straightened, transforming into a first responder right before her eyes.

"I've gotta go. You can leave through the front entrance." He leaned in to peck her on the lips, but before their lips touched, he whispered, "And if anyone is going to handcuff you to the bed, it's going to be me."

In a happy stupor, Carson watched as her firefighter disappeared under the archway.

Chapter Twenty-One

T ires screeched as the plane hit the airstrip, jostling its passengers. The tablet sitting on the leg of the man next to Carson slipped off his lap and hit the floor with a thud. He grumbled under his breath.

Jax placed a hand on her fingers, hammering on her knees. "Don't be nervous."

"Easy for you to say," Carson muttered. "You don't have to meet my family."

Not only was she meeting Jax's family for the first time, she was also the first girl he'd brought home after the tragedy of his ex-wife. Would they compare her to Kristen? Of course they would. Would she get along with his brothers? Hopefully. What would his mother think of her? Was Carson good enough for her son? She was trying to be.

What would they think about her cutting her skin?

The moment they stepped outside the William P. Hobby airport and into the passenger pickup area, Carson's whole body became sticky, as if the air had become tangible and she could reach a finger out and touch it. She had never been to a place this humid. Sometimes, after a good monsoon, Arizona's dry air would feel less . . . dry. Here in Texas, it was stifling. Claustrophobic.

A maroon minivan was waiting for them. Before they reached it, the side door flew open.

"Uncle Jax! Uncle Jax!"

Flaming red hair came spilling out of the car as two little boys dashed and jumped into Jax's open arms, knocking over his suitcase.

"Hey, guys!" he rejoiced, wrapping them into a big bear hug.

"Be careful, boys," a woman called, stepping out of the passenger seat. Her auburn hair was pulled into a ponytail, frizzy flyaways framing her face. Carson wished she had a hair tie so she could get her damp hair off her sticky neck.

A man rounded the hood of the van, and she had to do a double take. It was Jax, or at least his twin. Clone, perhaps? He was just as tall, maybe even taller. If it weren't for the cropped hair, shaved face, and visible crow's feet on the edge of his eyes, Carson would have thought they were the same person.

"You must be Carson. I'm Billy," he said. Even his voice was the same! He gave her a big hug before the woman came up to claim her own hug.

"I'm Marlo, Billy's wife," she said. Now that she was closer, Carson noticed that behind Marlo's clear-framed glasses was a sprinkle of freckles, dotting her nose and cheeks. "And this is Henry and Hayden." She gestured at the twins who were currently latched onto Jax's legs. "We are so happy to have you for Christmas."

"Yeah, Jax wouldn't shut up about you. Now we'll get to see what the fuss is all about," Billy teased.

"Good to see you too," Jax said, giving his older brother a hug.

"I hope I live up to the hype." Carson laughed, then continued to chew her cheek because it wasn't entirely a joke.

They all squished into the van. Carson had to avoid stepping on an action figure, and when she sat down, she fished three LEGO bricks from underneath her and put them in a cup holder.

As Billy zippered back into traffic, Jax asked, "Where's Elizabeth?"

From the front seat, Marlo leaned her head back to answer. "We left her with your mother, so we had enough room in the van. We were going to leave the boys too, but they insisted on coming."

"Yeah, Uncle Jax, we wanted to see you first," one of them said.

"Oh yeah?" Jax reached his arm behind to tickle them and their giggles filled the back of the car.

"Guess what, Uncle Jax? We learned how to ride our bikes!" the other said.

"You did?"

"Now we can ride a dirt bike just like you and Daddy," the first one exclaimed, melting Carson's heart.

"So, Carson," Marlo continued, ignoring the excess noise, "have you been to Texas before?"

"No, I haven't."

"How are you liking the humidity?" Billy asked, using the rear-view mirror to look at her.

"Definitely nothing like Arizona."

"At least you're not visiting during the summer," Jax said. "This is nothing compared to August."

The city of Houston flew by. Tall skyscrapers jutted out of the earth with freeways and streets winding every which way, as if the labyrinth of exits and on-ramps was the only thing keeping the city together. The roads Billy was taking or which direction they were going was mind-boggling. It hurt Carson's brain as they zig-zagged from one highway or feeder road to the next. It all made sense when she noticed a toll sign.

Eventually, the infrastructure began to dissipate. The dull colors of concrete and steel were replaced with earthy tones. She was surprised at how green Texas was for winter. She'd have to ask if Houston ever saw snow.

They left the busy highways behind and ended up on the tree-shrouded streets of Magnolia. Every once in a while, Carson would see a store or a building. She thought about how, in Arizona, she could see a town from miles away, but in this part of Texas it seemed everything was concealed by trees and more trees.

Billy turned off the main road onto a skinny two-lane that wound through a lush forest. Was it considered a forest or just foliage? Carson didn't know. It was so different compared to the Arizona desert. Then came an unpaved road where the vegetation lessened, and a brick home appeared.

There was no driveway other than the gravel road that ended in the front yard. A compact gold sedan and a decrepit truck were parked between a shed and the house.

Carson bit her bottom lip, excited. This was where Jax had grown up. Just like him, it was quaint and easy-going.

The twins were out of their seats before the van came to a full stop. They climbed over Jax's lap, yanked open the door, and hopped onto the ground before taking off behind the house. A light breeze stirred the petrichor-scented air around them.

"You have one hour until dinner!" Marlo yelled after them.

"I got your bags. Y'all go on in," Billy offered, only adding to the southern experience.

Jax led Carson to the wraparound porch that featured a swing, a dozen potted plants, and small concrete statues of woodland creatures. One of them, a tortoise, was grinning at her as they stepped through the screen door into a front entry.

"Is that you, Jax?" called a mature voice from another room.

"It's me, Ma."

A matronly woman appeared at the end of the hall, wiping her hands on an apron that hung on her round waist. The wooden floorboards creaked as she waddled toward them, her short arms reaching for her son. Jax had to bend down a fair amount to hug her.

"Oh, it is so good to see you," she sighed in his ear, then pulled away to pat his cheeks and turned toward Carson.

"Ma, this is Carson," Jax said, his voice airy as if he was just as nervous as Carson. "And this is my Ma, Shirley."

"How lovely it is to finally meet you. Jax has told me so much about you," Shirley said before throwing her arms around Carson.

The hug was warm. Sincere. A true mother's embrace; something Carson had never experienced. One time a classmate had made fun of her old, ratty shoes. When she had gotten home from school, seeking solace, her mother had scooted to the other side of the couch and instructed Carson to cry in her room.

"I'm so happy to finally meet you too," Carson told her. Shirley smelled like vanilla, baked bread, and honey. Unlike her mother, who'd reeked of cigarettes and cheap wine. Would it be weird if she asked Shirley to never let go?

The front door squeaked open, and Billy and Marlo shuffled in with all the luggage.

"Go ahead and take those on up for them, Billy," Shirley said, turning back to Carson. "I've made up beds for the both of you in Jax's old room."

"How'd Elizabeth do?" Marlo asked.

Shirley nodded to the bassinet in the living room just beyond the front entry. "She slept the entire time. Didn't even make a noise."

Marlo waved them on. "Come meet her."

Carson followed everyone to the bassinet, which was covered in frills and bows. Marlo reached in and pulled out a tiny baby, so tiny that Carson thought she was a doll. Her little arms reached high above her small head, tinted with black hair, while her legs and feet curled up in the signature newborn scrunch.

Marlo snuck in a few kisses on Elizabeth's itty-bitty cheeks before handing her over to Jax, his hands swallowing her whole. Tenderly, he cradled the infant, automatically bouncing her up and down. With one last wiggle, Elizabeth settled into his arms, falling back asleep.

"She's so little," Jax said, not taking his eyes off the baby.

"That's what all the nurses said at the hospital. They kept asking if we were sure she wasn't born early," said Marlo.

Carson stood close to Jax, tugging down the bubblegum pink pajamas that had bunched up and covered Elizabeth's face. "She is so beautiful, Marlo."

"I don't think she looks anything like a Miller, except the hair. The rest is Marlo's genes," Shirley said, and Carson silently agreed.

"Thank goodness she takes after Marlo," someone said from behind them. "Otherwise she would have inherited Billy's big head."

Everyone turned. A giant of a man came thudding down the stairs, looming over everyone in the room. As he got closer, Carson could see the resemblance to the other brothers, the piercing blue eyes and hard jawline. But he had chestnut hair, like Shirley's, that touched his shoulders. His shoulders were so wide, Carson was curious if he could fit through doorways without having to turn sideways. And he was thick with muscle, but natural muscle, like a rhinoceros. That was it. He reminded her of a rhinoceros.

"This is my oldest brother, Beau." Jax, still bouncing the sleeping baby, nodded to the rhinoceros.

Before Carson could say hello, Beau took her into his heavily tattooed arms and gave her a hug that squeezed the air out of her lungs. "So you're the girl that my baby brother has deceived into liking him," he said in his throaty voice. Then he examined her up and down. "You're too good-looking for my brother. How much is he paying you?"

Carson snorted. "Not enough."

He grinned crookedly, thanks to a vertical scar on his upper lip which Carson presumed was from a corrected cleft-lip. Glancing back at Jax, he jutted his thumb at her. "I like her."

A tiny whimper called everyone's attention as Elizabeth began to fuss.

"She's probably hungry," Marlo said, reaching to take her from Jax.

"Wyatt and Emily should be back any moment, and then we'll be ready to eat supper," Shirley announced, making her way back to the kitchen. "I bet you two are starving after traveling all day."

Shirley was hunched over the oven, her graying hair pinned up and out of her face, pulling out what looked like a chicken pot pie with mitted hands. Marlo was juggling Elizabeth in one arm while stirring ice and lemon slices around in a glass pitcher; the liquid inside was the color of dark caramel. Out the window, Carson could see Henry and Hayden running in circles with foam swords in their hands. Watching the boys play make-believe without a care in the world made her smile.

It didn't feel right standing there while everyone else bustled around, so she asked, "Is there anything I can do to help?"

Shirley sat the large pie on the stove top and removed her oven mitts. "Oh, thank you dear, but everything is already taken care of."

"I have a job for you," Marlo said, holding out the baby. "Can you hold her while I round up the boys?"

"Of course." Carson gladly accepted Elizabeth and cradled her to her chest. Pressing her cheek to the top of Elizabeth's head she breathed in, forgetting about the newborn baby smell. It was clean like soaps and lotions. Instinctually she patted the baby's diaper.

Would her baby boy have been born just as small? She guessed he would have been long for a newborn, as Carson and Luke were both taller than average. Or maybe he would have been a chunk, barely fitting into newborn sizes. Her lips drooped, not being able to know the answers. Yet holding Elizabeth seemed to be healing a part of her soul. The mother within her had been waiting five long years to hold a baby, and now she could.

Shirley painted the pie's crust with butter, then took it to the dining room as Carson stood in the kitchen rocking Elizabeth back and forth. Wanting to do at least something, she grabbed the pitcher of iced tea with one hand, walked into the dining area, and sat it next to a bowl full of salad on the table.

Shirley leaned through an archway that led to the front living room. "Dinner is ready."

One by one, the family shuffled in. The twins zoomed past Carson and hopped into their chairs with Marlo behind them. A guy, who reminded Carson of a younger version of Beau, only his brown hair was shorter and styled with gel and his lips free of scars, came in from the living room. So did a young girl with rosy cheeks and golden-brown hair. Carson guessed they were Jax's younger brother Wyatt and his fiancée, Emily. They took their seats, not noticing her standing off to the side.

Jax came in last and found Carson with Elizabeth fast asleep on her chest. His eyes fell to the baby and back up to her. A corner of his lips pulled to one side, in a smile.

A tugging in Carson's heart reminded her of the final truth she had been harboring from him. The time was coming nearer to finally tell him about her infertility. She could feel it.

"I can take her so you can eat," Billy offered, interrupting her thoughts.

"I don't mind," Carson insisted.

Billy smiled with understanding and sat down.

It seemed only appropriate that the family said grace before they dug in. Because that's what people in the south did, right? Carson hadn't grown up religious. Other than using His name when she was upset, Carson's mother never mentioned God. Carson eyed the large metal cross on the wall before closing her eyes for the prayer and again breathing in Elizabeth's scent.

"Jax, did you introduce your brother to Carson?" Shirley asked after they had said amen.

Jax shook his head, having just taken a huge bite of chicken filling.

Shirley's lips bunched together for a second, disapproving. "Wyatt is the youngest of my boys. And Emily is his beautiful fiancée. They're currently going to the University of Memphis."

"Why Tennessee?" Carson asked.

"It's where I'm from," Emily explained. Her voice reminded Carson of the mice from *Cinderella*, small and squeaky.

"We're studying business accounting," Wyatt said. "U of M is a nationally ranked school with a higher-than-average percentage to graduate and find a career in your area of study." The way he spoke reminded Carson of an almanac.

A roll flew across the table and bounced off the far wall.

"Boys," Billy scolded, cutting off the twins' giggling.

"I want to know how the two of you met," Marlo interjected, pointing her fork at Jax and Carson.

"At a softball tournament. I knocked her out with a door," Jax said.

"You knocked her out?" Beau echoed.

Carson rolled her eyes. "Jax likes to embellish. All he did was open the door, and I was on the other side. I did not lose consciousness at any point in time."

"But he did hit you with a door?" Billy pressed.

"I was in one of the locker rooms, running late. I threw open the door, and it slammed right into her," Jax elaborated. "It hit her hard enough that it split her head open."

Shirley choked on her food. "Jax Henry Miller, I have taught you better."

"It was a complete accident. I was totally fine," Carson added hastily.

"She had to get stitches," Jax continued, moving Carson's hair out of the way to look at her scar. Then he lowered his hand so his thumb could lightly stroke her cheek. "I still feel awful about it."

"You should," Beau quipped.

Jax dropped his hand onto the table. "We kept seeing each other at different events after that. Then I learned she had a dirt bike, so we went out riding, and the rest is history."

Beau's ears perked up. "You ride dirt bikes? I like you even more now."

After dinner, Carson followed Jax up the stairs, passing more crosses and mismatched photographs hanging on the wall. She made a mental note to study every single picture before she left to learn more about his family history.

Their luggage was placed in the center of a small room, and two twin beds had been shoved in opposite corners. How Jax had ever fit in a bed that size, Carson didn't know. Old treasures were sitting on the dresser and hanging from the walls: blue ribbons, a piggy bank, a Magic 8 Ball, a poster of Jeremy McGrath. She inched closer to a picture frame displaying a young boy in a green uniform, posing with a soccer ball. The boy looked nothing like Jax.

"That's Wyatt," he said. "We shared this room."

Carson grinned. "I want to see baby Jax."

He moved closer and wrapped his arms around her from behind. "I burned all of them. I was an alien baby with a deformed head."

Carson only had one picture of herself as a baby, dressed in white ruffles and a bonnet, looking as if she'd lived on a farm before Arizona was declared a state. The photo was small and square, wrinkle lines and bent edges giving it character. Imagining Jax as a baby, Carson couldn't believe he was ugly. For a split second, she wondered what their baby would look like. Quickly she stomped on the idea, angry that she had let her mind wonder. It was all the baby talk and holding newborns screwing with her head.

"You okay?" he asked.

Loosening her muscles, she turned around. "Of course. How can I not be when I'm in Jax Miller's childhood room?" Then she narrowed her eyes at him. "I'm not going to find magazines under the mattress, am I?"

Jax smirked. "No, that was Beau."

A faint giggle came behind the closet door. Jax put a finger to his lips and took two steps to his right. There was another giggle. Then using that same hand he counted down from three with his fingers before he threw one of the doors open.

"Gotcha!"

Screams filled the room as Hayden and Henry scrambled out from the closet, trying to escape. Jax was faster and captured them with ferocious tickles. The boys squealed and laughed until Jax finally released them, and they darted out the door.

When Carson had finished brushing her teeth and said goodnight to Shirley, she was back in the room, closing the door behind her. Jax was already in one of the beds leaning up against the wall, fiddling with his watch. He was shirtless, wearing only gym shorts. His tattoo was a dark mass on his shoulder. Did it ever get cold enough in Texas to wear sweats?

Pulling out her own pajamas, Carson quickly slipped them on—wondering if she would get too hot in her long-sleeved shirt—before sitting on Jax's bed. She could hear Elizabeth's wails through the walls. Someone was walking down the stairs. Probably Billy, getting a bottle for his daughter.

Tossing his watch on the nightstand, Jax flicked off the lamp, extinguishing the last bit of light in the room. Then he scooted behind her, pushed her hair to the side, and pressed his lips to her neck.

"You surviving?" he asked, his hot breath tickling her left ear.

"What do you mean?"

"I thought you'd be overwhelmed with my big family."

Carson bent back to look at him. "Not at all. It feels like a family."

He snorted. "*Feels* like a family?"

"It's exactly how I imagined a family would be," she said, facing forward again. "Like what I see in the movies."

Squeezing her a little tighter, Jax gave her neck another kiss. "The movies, huh?"

"This whole place is a movie," Carson teased, thinking about the big city turned small town. The gravel road to a little house tucked into the trees. A family saying grace at the dinner table and having Christmas together.

"Are you ready for bed now?" he asked.

When Carson nodded, Jax sat back, hauling her with him by the waist. The bed was cramped, but she snuggled into him as he pressed his body against her back, encasing her in his arms. By now her eyes had adjusted to the dark room, and she could see the shape of the dresser.

"I'm glad you were able to come with me," he said.

"Me too. I really do like your family."

"Even Beau?" he asked, skeptical.

"Even Beau."

"Give it a couple days," he yawned, voice deepening with sleep.

She could tell he was on the edge of slumber, ready to fall asleep in the blink of an eye. A couple of minutes passed, and Carson herself was starting to get sleepy, tired from the day of traveling. She listened to Jax's slow, even breaths.

To her surprise, he spoke again. "I liked the way you looked holding Elizabeth."

A dagger stabbed Carson's heart, and the room darkened, the walls converging on her. She kept quiet, and when Jax didn't say anything else, she began to question if he said those words on purpose or in his dreams.

Chapter Twenty-Two

Carson's head hit the window, her limbs flying up then crashing back down. She was strapped to a seat, feeling weightless one second, then feeling all of earth's gravity the next. Over and over her body slammed into the door, slammed into the seat, lurched forward, then smacked the center console. It felt as though she were a tumbleweed being thrown around by the wind. Every hit, every smack, every crunch hurt. Her neck, insides, back, all gripped by searing agony—

"Uncle Jax, wake up! Santa came!"

Carson, with her head under the pillow, wiggled out of the way, trying to avoid being crushed by the two boys, who were now jumping on the tiny bed. The springs creaked unnaturally under the weight of four bodies.

"There's presents," Hayden said.

"Santa brought them," Henry tagged on.

"Santa?" Jax croaked, still half-asleep.

"Yeah!" the twins shouted.

"Hurry up and come downstairs to see," Hayden begged.

The twins then sprung off the bed, trampling through the hall and pounding down the stairs.

Carson unearthed herself from the bedding. Jax was leaning over, checking the time on his phone. Darkness lingered beyond the window, the sun not having woken up yet.

"Jax?" she mumbled into the pillow.

He rolled back toward her. "Yes, Mr. Hoover?"

"Santa came," she said.

Letting out a chuckle, Jax moved Carson's hair out of her face, and she blinked up at him.

"How'd you sleep?" he asked.

"I dreamed about the accident again."

"I'm sorry. What can I do to help?"

Lifting herself until she was propped on her elbows, Carson said, "I'll be alright. It's part of me now."

Jax's lips pressed into a thin line. Her continuing nightmares were difficult for him. In one counseling session, Dave had explained that recurring nightmares were common for Carson's situation, and she would probably have them for a very long time.

"We better get down there before the boys come back," she warned.

By the time Carson and Jax made it downstairs and into the living room, Shirley, Beau, Billy, and Marlo were lounging on the furniture. Henry and Hayden were bouncing on their knees next to the lit tree, excitedly pointing at the pile of colorful presents.

"Merry Christmas," Shirley said, rocking Elizabeth in the recliner.

"Merry Christmas, Ma," Jax greeted back, leaning over to kiss his mother on the forehead.

Beau was lying across the love seat, scrolling on his phone. He peered up at everyone, then at the stairs. "Emily must be giving Wyatt his Christmas present early."

"Beau, don't be distasteful. Especially in front of our guest," Shirley reprimanded.

Carson dropped the grin on her face. Beau's comment reminded her of something Raegan would say. *Those two would get along*, she mused.

Minutes later, Emily and Wyatt joined them. Emily was already in a floral dress and ankle-boots with makeup neatly painted on her round face, her russet hair perfectly curled. Wyatt was wearing one of those pullover sweaters with a horse stitched on the front and loafers that Carson had seen her boss, Garrett, wear.

A bit self-conscious, Carson fidgeted with her shirt. She was still in her pajamas, not having bothered to put on makeup. Maybe she could have brushed a layer of mascara on; after all, she'd just met these people. Then she noticed that everyone else was also in their lounging clothes. Shirley's hair seemed flatter than yesterday, and Marlo's frizz was twisted on top of her head. Neither had makeup on.

"Glad you could finally join us," Beau muttered, moving so Wyatt and Emily could sit next to him.

There was no rhythm or reason to the way the Miller family opened gifts on Christmas morning. Boxes and bags were passed around. Crinkled wrapping paper began piling up all over the room. Shirley had put together a stocking for everyone, including Carson. Hers was filled with chocolates and lotion, lip-gloss and a candle, candy canes and nail polish.

Shirley was happily emptying a stocking into her lap when Jax leaned over and whispered, "Each year we take turns doing one for her. This year was Marlo and Billy's turn."

Hayden and Henry gasped when they shredded the wrapping off a huge box. Santa had brought them a Hot Wheels mega track set, and they begged their parents to open it immediately. Billy and Marlo shared a kiss over a diamond necklace. Emily had gotten Wyatt a new laptop, sleek and shiny. Beau was grinning crookedly over a new pair of leather gloves for smoking meats, shoving his giant hands into them. Jax was impressed when Carson got up to grab a large cube-shaped box from under the tree and sat it on his lap.

"Open it," she urged, settling on the floor in front of him.

When he opened the box, his eyes grew wide.

"I noticed yours were a little worn down," Carson said as Jax lifted a riding jersey from the box. It was silver and black, with hard shapes and lines and hints of lime green striped throughout. Flashy, but subtle. Then he pulled out a matching helmet. And matching riding pants. Then boots. Carson hoped that her discreetly rummaging through his stuff in order to find out his sizes had paid off.

"How the hell did you fit all this in your suitcase?" he asked, pulling the helmet out of its protective sleeve.

"Christmas magic," she fibbed, winking. The magic was Carson using her detective skills to find Shirley's address, then shipping the gift to the house with a note explaining what the package was.

"That is so cool, Uncle Jax!" Henry hopped up onto his lap, pushing the box to the side. "Can I try it on?"

"Of course, buddy," he said, slipping the helmet over Henry's crop of hair like he was extinguishing a flame.

The helmet was ginormous compared to Henry's tiny body, reminding Carson of a bobblehead. Henry giggled then pulled it off and bounced back to his new toys.

"Beau, can you get that red box with the white bow next to you?" Jax asked, setting his gift off to the side.

Beau's eyes swept around him before picking up and handing the box to Carson. It was surprisingly heavy relative to its size. She lifted it to give to Jax.

He shook his head. "It's for you."

Biting her lower lip, Carson ripped off the paper, uncovering a box set of thin books. "Is this . . ." Her voice trailed off.

"Pull them out," he said, resting his elbows on his knees.

With a delicate touch, she slipped one of the children's books out and timidly turned it over. On the cover, her old friend, *Hank the Cowdog*, wagged his tail at her. She pulled out another, then another, remembering each story, each adventure.

The corners of her eyes pricked with tears. "You remembered," she murmured, holding the books to her chest.

"Get a room already," Beau muttered.

"What did he get you that's making you give him googly eyes?" Billy demanded.

Gripping the books tighter to her body, Carson's neck flushed with embarrassment. "It's just an old children's book I loved as a kid. I mentioned it to him when we first met, and he remembered."

"How sweet," Shirley crooned, patting Elizabeth's back.

A tear escaped, and Carson used the end of her shirtsleeve to soak it up. "I don't know why it's making me cry. I feel stupid."

"Don't feel stupid, honey. It's romantic, and it makes me want to cry too," Marlo said.

"Same," said Emily.

Carson looked down at the books again. Maybe she could read them to the twins before she left. Sniffing, she looked back at Jax. "Thank you."

Now it was his turn to wink.

Her body melted into the couch. She was home. Like she was a part of a family. All her doubts and concerns had melted away here in the living room, surrounded by wonderful, kind people. People who welcomed her with open arms. She was grateful to be there.

Something within Carson was piecing back together. Maybe it was the way Billy adoringly looked at Marlo, the mother of his children. Or how Emily's smile stretched from gold earring-to-gold earring every time Wyatt spoke. Or how Beau's booming laugh was infectious and filled the room. Maybe it was because Carson could see the Christmas lights twinkle in the twins' eyes as they raced their toy cars with gusto. It could have been watching Shirley, who showed her what it was like to have a mother pour out nothing but love for her children and grandchildren.

Carson didn't want to waste it. Not a single moment.

For the rest of Christmas Day, she was determined to experience it all. When Hayden and Henry showed her and Jax how they'd learned to ride their bikes, she cheered the loudest. Her arms were elbow deep in dinner, helping Shirley prepare the Christmas feast consisting of roast and string bean casserole and a garden salad. In order for Billy and Marlo to sneak away for a quiet moment, she offered to watch Elizabeth. She sought Emily's and Wyatt's advice on business accounting, explaining that she wanted to eventually open her own firm. By the afternoon, she had a business plan started. At one point, she had a lengthy conversation with Beau. He went on and on about famous supercross athletes, spewing off statistics and asking if she'd watched that year's final race, even taking her out to the shed to show off his dirt bike.

By the time dinner arrived, Carson felt accomplished. Peering around the table, she absorbed everyone's energy and listened to the conversation over the scraping of utensils against the plates.

"Jax, you remember Liza from middle school? She just had a baby," Shirley announced.

"With that idiot boyfriend of hers," Beau mumbled around a mouth full of food.

"That reminds me. My friend Hunter and his wife are expecting their first baby," Jax said.

Shirley's face lit up, and she placed a hand on her chest. "You're kidding! That's so wonderful."

"Is Hunter the same guy you worked with when you moved to Arizona?" Wyatt asked.

Jax nodded.

"Mom, can we please be excused from the table?" Hayden pleaded.

"Let me see those plates," Marlo said. Both the boys lifted their dirty dishes with scraps of food left on them. "Good enough for me. Go play till it's time to load the dishwasher."

Carson looked down at her plate. She'd eaten all her salad, but hadn't started on the roast.

Billy leaned around Marlo. "Didn't you want like fourteen kids or something, Jax?" he asked.

Jax sat back in his chair, putting his arm behind Carson. "I only ever said I wanted a bunch of kids," he clarified.

Carson gripped her knees, trying to keep her leg from shaking with shame.

"Thank heavens you didn't have any with Kristen," Wyatt murmured. Grunts of agreement came from around the table.

"How many kids do you want, Carson?" Marlo asked, refilling her glass with the lemonade pitcher.

Carson's eyes flitted around the table while everyone patiently waited for her answer. Giving up, she let her leg bounce. "Oh, uh, I don't think I want any," she lied.

"You don't want any kids?" Beau challenged, one eye squinting at her.

She shrugged, shaking her head. "Um, I mean . . . uh . . . I just—"

Beau cut her off before she could finish. "What? Why don't you want any kids?"

"Ease off, Beau," Jax snarled.

"It was an innocent question," Beau said, defensively, his massive shoulders shrugged high by his ears as if he'd merely asked about the weather.

In all fairness to Beau, it was a simple question, and they weren't strangers. He was the brother of Jax, whom Carson was perfectly fine spending the rest of her life with. The people around her—Marlo, Billy, Shirley, Wyatt, Emily, Beau—could all be her family, too, one day. They were having a discussion about children, and Beau was curious to know why Carson didn't want any. She felt safe and comfortable with them. She was confident they would protect her as much as she would protect them.

If the past few months had taught her anything, it was to be open and honest with the people she loved. At least that was what she and Dave had been working on: opening up, being honest, trusting others. Even if there were consequences, good or bad. And after the wonderful day she'd had, Carson felt strong. Courageous. She could finally tell Jax this one last secret with the support of his family around them. Dave would be so proud of her.

She unclenched her teeth from her cheek, and her leg calmed. "Actually, I can't get pregnant," she finally admitted, proud of the huge step she was taking. "I was in a car accident that killed my husband and unborn son. It also took away my ability to have children."

Time stood still. Or at least that's what it felt like. Not a single muscle moved. Forks were suspended between plates and open mouths. It was so quiet Carson could almost hear everyone's heartbeat. Hers was pounding in her ears, making them ache. Muffled sounds of a cartoon show came from the living room. Was anyone even breathing? She realized that she wasn't breathing and exhaled.

That triggered everyone else. Uncertainty flashed across Beau's face, his mouth slack. Forks were lowered back to the table. All eyes landed on her. Then they darted between her and Jax. Then between Jax and Beau.

Carson peeped at Jax who was glaring down at his plate. Oh, he didn't look happy at all. The muscle in his jaw was twitching, and the two lines between his dark eyebrows made an appearance. Her insides puddled. Was he upset because she was infertile? It sure looked like it.

"Nice, Beau," Wyatt spat.

"Way to be an ass," Billy mumbled.

"No, please," Carson pleaded. "It's really okay. You guys were going to learn about it at some point anyway."

"Beau could have been more tactful about it though," Billy argued, as though his brother wasn't sitting at the table with them.

"Carson." It was Shirley who spoke. "We are so sorry to hear about your family." Then her eyes glanced at Jax behind her. "Jax, why don't you and Carson excuse yourselves from dinner. I'll bring a piece of cobbler to y'all out on the front porch."

Without a word Jax pushed his chair back and stood up, giving one more scowl toward his older brother.

Beau hunched forward, looking smaller than normal. "I'm really sorry," he said solemnly.

"Please don't be sorry," Carson assured him. "I apologize if I ruined Christmas dinner."

Before she stood up, Marlo caught her hand and squeezed. "Nothing is ruined. Thank you for being comfortable enough to share with us."

Carson sat on her hands, using her foot to push the porch swing back and forth. It was the first time since arriving in the Lone Star State that she'd felt cold. Now she wished she'd snagged the throw blanket from the back of the couch before going outside. One of the concrete statues, an armadillo with a cowboy hat on its head, had its beady eyes trained on her. She imagined it slinging an old revolver at her.

Jax was pacing back and forth, his hands on his hips. Then he stopped to lean over the railing and stare down at the bushes. Finally, he stood straight and folded his arms, looking out into the dark. The Christmas lights colored his dark hair with reds, greens, blues, and yellows.

"Can we talk about it?" she offered, hesitantly.

He whirled around, his hair spilling across his forehead. "I'm using all my self-discipline right now to not go in and punch my brother in the face."

"Don't be ridiculous, Jax."

His hand motioned to the front door. "He just made you tell everyone about Luke and your son. You were forced to reveal that in front of everyone."

"He didn't make me do anything," Carson said, a little annoyed.

Jax's head fell to the side as if saying, *Yeah, right.*

"Really," she insisted. "Everyone was talking about having kids, and I was asked a question. It was something I needed to tell you anyway, but I never knew how to bring it up. Beau gave me the opportunity."

"That's the other thing, Carson," Jax said, his voice rough with frustration. "You didn't tell me. *Me.* I had to hear it along with everyone else."

Carson's rocking came to an abrupt halt. Dave had warned her about consequences.

"You got upset with me when I hid the fact that I was at your accident," he continued. "Now, you've done it to me. Do you know how that makes me feel?" The anger and hurt was evident on his face and in his voice.

"I didn't mean to hide it from you," Carson said, the words spilling from her mouth. "I didn't know how to tell you that I couldn't bear your children."

Those words made his eyes catch fire the way they always did when he was full of emotion. Except this time they appeared black instead of blue. Harsh instead of soft.

"I don't give a damn about that," Jax growled. "What if I'm unable to have kids myself? What I'm upset about is you not telling me. We've been together for months. We've shared the same bed. We've been through so much together. Hell, we're talking about our *future* together."

Consequences.

Carson had messed up. Never had Jax been this animated before, this agitated over the things she had said and done. Not even about Beau or Kristen. If only she could pull the Christmas lights down and wrap them around her neck.

Blowing out air, Jax sat down beside her, the swing protesting from the added weight. "You continue to not trust me. Like you think I'm this terrible person who can't support you while you work through your past. I've told you my secrets, Carson. I deserve the same from you."

A faint memory floated in her mind. During their first official date, as she sat in the middle of Barry's Burgers and Shakes, she had wondered what a relationship full of secrets would look like. This. This was what it looked like.

"I don't think you're a horrible person. Actually, I think the exact opposite." Then Carson chose her next words deliberately. "I don't want you to give up being a dad for me. I knew the moment you found out you would be okay with not having children of your own. But I can't do that to you. I see the way you play with the twins and how you hold Elizabeth as if she is your own. I watched your face light up when Raegan said she was pregnant. You want children."

Even though Jax's nostrils flared, he didn't speak. Carson was right and he knew it.

"Of course I want—*wanted* children," Jax finally groaned. "I've wanted a lot of things in my life that I haven't gotten. But what I really want is you. A life with you. Even if that future doesn't involve children."

That statement should have filled Carson with joy. Instead, his words festered and turned rotten. Just as she had expected, he hadn't even hesitated. He should have been pulling back, confused and unsure. He should have been telling her that he needed time to think about it.

Maybe Jax could accept not having any children of his own. But that was a decision he couldn't make on the spot. And Carson wasn't going to stand in the way.

CHAPTER TWENTY-THREE

Like a rattlesnake about to strike, Carson eyed Jax's every movement as he hefted their luggage from the back of his truck and onto his driveway, having flown back home that morning. The frigid Prescott air bit at her skin, as if warning her against what she was about to do.

It wasn't until Jax was on the steps of his front porch did he realize Carson wasn't following him. She stood next to her truck which she had left at his house before leaving for Texas. Slowly, he set his suitcase down and took a step toward her. It was his first sign of distress. His natural prey instinct was kicking in, Carson knew.

Steadying her body, she curled her arms around herself. Coiling.

"I can't keep doing this," she stammered. How was she supposed to be convincing when she was shaking so hard? "I mean, I can't keep doing this to you." It was a lame first strike. She planted her feet and tried again. "It's over between us."

Incredulously, Jax's mouth twitched as though she were joking, and he crossed his arms in front of his chest. There were no shadows for him to wield this time, but his stature was daunting enough.

"Are you trying to break up with me?" he asked.

Carson nodded, giving her cheek a few bites.

"Is this about last night?"

"Yes. And every night since we met. I can't let you keep sacrificing for me."

Exasperated, Jax threw up his hands and dropped them back down. The smack off his palms against his jeans was like a shotgun blast. "I told you I accepted it. I told you I would rather have you." His voice was sharp, like a sword trying to cut the head off a snake.

"But I don't accept that for you," she said.

Marching across the gravel driveway, Jax placed his hands on Carson's shoulders. Could he tell how much she was trembling?

"Do you really think this is the answer?" he asked. "Breaking up with me because you can't have children? Because that's bullshit."

"This *is* the answer. I need to let you go so you can decide between me or the life you wanted."

His hands dropped from her shoulders. Strike.

"Is that what you think? A life without you is a life I want?"

Setting her jaw, Carson lifted her chin. "It's what I know."

"So, that's it? We're finished because of a decision you made for me? After everything we've been through, you're done. Just like that." Jax's voice was husky, starting to break. Carson's prey was giving up the fight.

"It's over."

"What if I don't accept your decision?" he spat, a little more fight left in him. She couldn't tell if the steam coming from his mouth was from anger or from the frosty air.

"You're going to have to, because we are done," Carson snapped back.

Eyes blazing, Jax glared down at her, lips pressed so thin. She wished his eyes would warm her like they used to. Now they only made her shiver. Was he finally realizing she was being serious? That he wasn't going to convince her otherwise? A puff of clouds roamed over the sun, darkening his features.

Then the lines on his forehead smoothed and the clouds were gone. "I wanted to marry you," he whispered.

She wilted at his words, wanting to shrivel up and be buried underneath the ground where she stood. "Don't tell me that."

"Why?" he snarled. "Because it makes you feel bad? What about me? Huh, Carson? What about *my* feelings? Don't I get a say in this?"

"That's exactly my point!" she yelled back. "Your feelings are blinding you from what I'm taking from you. I don't want to be another Kristen." Another strike, causing his nostrils to flare, steam pouring from them. "You can't look me in the eye and tell me you don't want children because that would be a lie," she continued. "You would be lying to yourself and lying to me."

She was the hypocritical liar. She lied about her self-harm. She lied about her infertility.

"You decided within one night to not have kids of your own," she said. "You need time to think about all this. Away from me. Let me give you that space to make this decision. That's the only fair thing to do." Even though Carson desperately wanted to reach out and hold him, she balled her hands into fists and locked them at her side.

The sharp angle of Jax's stiff shoulders rounded out, loosening. Another cloud draped over the sun. After a moment, he huffed. "If that's what you want."

Then, with one last look, Jax turned on his heel and marched into his home, his luggage and Carson left behind.

Through splintered breaths Carson drove home in a haze of distress. As soon as she reached the safety of her kitchen she crumpled to the ground, sobs ripping up her throat. She wanted to make herself as small as possible.

Jax had given Carson his heart. Trusted her to keep it safe and take care of it. Instead, she'd torn it to shreds and offered it back to him like a sick joke.

The hate she felt toward herself was indescribable. How could she have let their relationship get this far? If she had just listened to herself in the first place, he would have never gotten hurt. She should have fought harder to keep him away from her, to keep him safe.

"I had to do it. I had to do it," she kept muttering to herself.

Anger and misery shook Carson's body, her house, her whole world. Maybe it would shake so hard that it would collapse on top of her and bury her forever underneath the rubble. Maybe then she wouldn't hurt another person she loved.

When she had created life within herself, she had destroyed it. Then she'd created love between her and Jax with the same result.

She was a creator and a destroyer.

For hours, Carson lay in a heap on the cool hardwood floor. Her tears finally dried, and she could no longer smell the dusty wood. A sunbeam broke through the window and smacked her on the cheek. Squinting, she jerked away from its light, rolling into a sitting position, and peered up into the kitchen. It was her kitchen, but it looked unfamiliar to her.

On top of the counter was the knife block staring back at her. The perfectly sharp edges sitting inside the wood beckoned her forward.

Attraction.

Allured by its call, Carson rose.

One week later . . .

CHAPTER TWENTY-FOUR

C *lick. Click. Pause. Click. Click. Click. Click. Click.*

Carson's fingers flew across the keyboard, her strategy for the upcoming child custody trial flowing out of her. She couldn't type fast enough to keep up with her thoughts.

Funnily enough, the breakthrough she needed to lock in her case had come to her in a dream. She'd been sitting next to Luke on their sofa with their baby fast asleep in her arms. Arms that were clear of any scars. In her dream, all she could focus on was the couch. It was so cozy and soft. Even though *Psych* flashed on the television, she wasn't laughing because the couch was everything.

A grin spread across Carson's face as she saved her document and sent it to the printer. Work done, she was ready to head home for the weekend. Maybe she would celebrate with a bowl of mint chocolate chip ice cream. Now that she had thought of it, she was definitely going to indulge. She deserved it.

The paper was hot, freshly printed. She let it warm her fingers before it cooled. The crunch of the three-hole punch was harmonic, before she inserted her work into a notebook.

"I was thinking."

Spinning, Carson found Garrett relaxing his tall body against the work-room wall. "I don't know if it's because it's the new year, or if I'm still in the Christmas-giving spirit, but I have a proposal."

Confused because she had no clue what he was talking about, Carson set her notebook on the countertop and asked, "What's your proposal?"

"Instead of jumping headfirst into a partnership, what are your thoughts on a mentorship? I'd be your mentor for six months. Once that is complete, we can start the process of promoting you to junior partner."

Carson matched his smile, which was almost blinding against his dark skin.

"I think that is a very reasonable proposal," she said, struggling to keep her tone even and professional. "I accept."

Untucking his hands from his suit pant pockets, Garrett pushed off the wall. "We start on Monday."

A red diesel truck was parked in Carson's driveway as she circled to the back of her house, the cold rocks turning under her tires. The headlights of her vehicle swept across someone leaning against the bed of the truck. The butterflies in Carson's stomach, dormant over the past week, perked up when she recognized it was Jax.

Why was he here? Had he left something and come to retrieve it? Did something happen? The questions continued to build in Carson's mind as she cut the engine and slid out of the seat.

As she closed the distance between them, her heels clicked on the con-crete. Jax didn't move from his spot, keeping his hands deep in his Carhartt jacket pockets. The porch light cast its yellowish hue on them both.

Cold and defensive, Jax's eyes glowed like two aqua rhinestones. They were fierce. They were frightening. The closer Carson got, the more they narrowed, until she stopped a few feet from him.

Even in the dim lighting, Carson detected the guarded expression on his face. What little composure she'd gathered crumbled. It shattered her to see him so . . . hostile.

Finally, he looked directly at her. Before he would set her on fire. Now she turned to granite. When he didn't say anything, she did, but all she could muster was, "Hi."

He gave her a once-over. "Hi," he snipped, sharp and bitter.

"What are you doing here?"

He sucked on his teeth for a moment before answering. "I just wanted to check in on you and make sure you weren't . . ." He hesitated, glancing down at her arms for a moment. "That you weren't doing anything to yourself. I figured the breakup could have triggered you."

For the first time in over a week, warmth enveloped Carson.

"I haven't done anything," she answered proudly.

That day when the kitchen knives had drawn her in, she'd tossed the entire block in the front yard, grabbed a pen and paper, and began to draw. Endless loops. Scribbles of trees. Flower after flower after flower until the temptation subsided, transforming her attraction into repulsion. She had used the entire spiral notebook.

His demeanor broke, and for a split-second relief flashed across his face. But only a second before the guarded Jax was back. He cleared his throat. "Good. I'm glad to hear that. I assume you still have nightmares?"

She winced and nodded.

Silently he accepted her answer. A slight breeze blew in, causing her hair to tickle her numb cheeks. Carson's legs were bare in a skirt and heels. Her bones began shaking from the cold.

Jax must have noticed her wobbling knees or heard the chatter of her teeth, because he pushed off his truck. "Better get inside before you freeze," he said, opening his door.

"Jax?" She took a step closer to him, smelling the familiar scent of his truck. How she missed it.

Turning, Jax looked down at her.

"Thank you."

A corner of his mouth twitched, fighting a smile. He gave Carson one last glance before climbing back into his truck and driving away.

Her briefcase thumped when it hit the floor. It tipped over, causing the contents to spill onto the carpet. Carson was too busy reliving Jax's visit in her mind to notice. The amount of courage it had taken for him to set aside his pride to make sure she wasn't slicing her skin was a wake-up call.

Groaning, Carson fell back onto her bed, the comforter puffing with air. From the moment she had met Jax, he had been nothing but kind, patient, and giving. She could stay up all night listing every one of his positive attributes. Thinking back, she remembered when she had first spoken with Raegan about him. The morning after getting stitches, Raegan had said that Jax was the nicest person she would ever meet. And, for the few short months they were together, he had lived up to that.

Carson knew what she had given up. Because of her distrust, she had lost the only man who understood her. He knew how to fight for her but also knew how to let her fight her own battles. Jax had brought rain to her drought. Because of him, she could feel the beat of her heart, hear the birds serenade her in the mornings. The green of the cacti was so much more vibrant than before. For the first time in a long time, she had noticed the flaming orange rocks of the Granite Dells.

The love Carson had for Jax hadn't just happened. It had started as a spark until it grew into a burning fire within her. Like a diamond harvested from the depths of the earth's deepest mantle, her love could only form under extreme conditions.

Because she'd withheld her secrets from Jax, because she'd kept them for so long, Carson had ruined their relationship. First Luke, then her child, then Jax. What other relationships was she going to lose by her own hand?

Was Carson hiding her self-harm from her best friend going to ruin that relationship too? Would Raegan be upset with her and no longer want to be her friend because Carson didn't know how to open up and trust others?

No. She refused to be the reason she lost even more people in her life.

Jax had shown her that, even butchered and sterile, she could still find love, *be* loved. It was now time to trust that others could also love her.

It was time to tell Raegan.

CHAPTER TWENTY-FIVE

C arson counted the ticks coming from the clock on the wall. Seventy. Seventy-one. Seventy-two. Seventy-three. Seventy-four. Seventy-five.

"Okay, the suspense is killing me. What do you have to tell us?" Raegan urged.

"Your silence is making me nervous," Hunter added.

Nothing could compare to how nervous Carson was for what she was about to do. It had taken her two weeks to build up enough courage to finally tell Hunter and Raegan about her self-harm. Her cheek was so raw, she had resorted to biting her tongue. Then, remembering how Dave had told her to control that habit, she released her tongue and clenched her teeth together, taking in deep breaths. Too bad she didn't have a piece of gum to chew on.

And how could her hands produce so much sweat? She kept trying to rub them dry on her pants, but the polyester material wasn't as absorbent as she needed it to be. Maybe she should have brought a handkerchief, because she could feel more sweat slide down her neck.

Hunter and Raegan sat on their couch in front of her, waiting expectantly. It felt almost formal. Carson was propped on the ottoman while Raegan sat on the edge of the cushion, back straight and still in her scrubs, having just come home from work. Hunter was slouched, arm on the back of the couch, in a T-shirt and shorts.

The waft of lasagna baking in the oven made Carson's stomach rumble. She hadn't eaten all day, sick with anxiety.

Nothing came out when she opened her mouth to speak, as shame had a hand around her throat. The nerves poked and pinched up and down her body.

One hundred one. One hundred two. One hundred three.

Two sets of eyes continued to stare at her, both confused and shadowed with worry.

Just say it. You can do it. You practiced this in therapy. It's one step closer to recovery. You can do it. It's so simple. Carson's silent monologue continued in her mind even as Raegan scooted a little closer to her.

"What's wrong?"

The shame gripped Carson's throat more tightly, and her eyes welled with tears. She didn't try to stop them from spilling over.

"Oh, honey what is it?" Raegan reached out and touched her knee. "Please tell us." Even Hunter was uncertain about what was happening before him—a grown woman having a breakdown in his living room. His eyes kept glancing at Raegan, as if she were going to explain everything to him, but Raegan appeared just as confused.

"I—I . . ." Carson hiccupped. Wow. She had no idea it would be this hard. Why hadn't Dave told her it would be this hard?

Apparently, words weren't going to work. So Carson resorted to the next best thing.

Gripping the zipper on her jacket, she pulled down. It wasn't until she slipped her jacket off and began rolling the sleeves of her turtleneck sweater up her arm—revealing line after line after line—that realization dawned on their faces before quickly turning from bewilderment to shock, then grief. Then they were staring at her. Not at her arms, but at her.

Raegan stood and plopped next to her on the ottoman. "How long have you been doing this?" she whispered.

Carson hiccupped again, then cleared her throat. "Two years. I just couldn't look at my scars from the surgery."

Without hesitation, Raegan picked up Carson's arm and touched her scars. Her delicate fingers, so different from Jax's, felt like feathers tickling her skin. Carson held her breath as she watched her friend digest what she was seeing.

"Are you still doing it?" Hunter asked, now upright on the edge of his seat, his first responder mode triggered. Raegan's head snapped up, fear encasing her features.

"No. *No*. I stopped a couple of months back," she assured them, wiping away the last remaining tears from her cheek. "I've been going to therapy and working really hard to not relapse." She cringed remembering that night between her and a screw.

"A couple of months. That means . . . did Jax know?" Raegan asked. Carson knew her friend was trying to piece everything together. She could see it in the way Raegan's perfect brows bent slightly out of shape. How her lips had the faintest twitch.

Three weeks ago, Raegan had worn the same expression on her face. When Carson had come home from Texas, she'd received a text from Raegan asking how her trip went. Carson's response had been simple: *We broke up.* Within half an hour, Raegan had walked through her front door and rushed to her side.

"What happened? Did his family do something?"

"No." Carson cleared the tears from her throat. "His family was amaz-

ing."

"Did Jax do something?"

She shook her head. "I had to tell him that I couldn't have kids."

Raegan flinched, her lips twitching with rage. "So, he broke up with you? Because you can't have children?" she hissed.

"No, I broke up with him!" Carson wailed, falling back into Raegan's hold.

Raegan then stroked her hair. "I don't understand. Why did you break up with him?"

"Because he wants children, and I can't give that to him. How can I not give him everything he wants?"

"But what did he say?" Raegan urged.

When Carson pulled away again, she saw the spot where her tears had soaked Raegan's pink scrubs. "He said that he was fine with not having kids of his own or being a dad. But Raegan, you should have seen the way he was with his niece and nephews. You should have seen the way he looked at me when I would hold the baby or play with the boys. He wants kids. And I won't let him give that up for me."

Raegan's brows bent, and her lips fluttered. She was probably thinking it over, trying to understand. That was when Carson explained she was trying to give Jax time away from her so he could make that big of a decision, on his own.

"If that's what you think was the right thing to do, then I support you," Raegan finally said.

Now, Carson felt a wave of gratitude for what Jax had been for her, and answered Raegan's question, "Yes, he knew. He found out and helped me start my recovery."

"And you've been okay since the breakup?" Raegan asked.

"Surprisingly, yes. My therapist has given me a lot of healthy alternatives to hurting myself." She tried to smile but failed.

"Oh, Carson." Raegan flung her arms around her and squeezed.

"I'm so sorry I didn't tell you sooner," Carson said. "I was embarrassed and mortified—"

Raegan pulled back, shushing her. "Don't be sorry. All that matters is that you're doing better and getting the help you need."

"Really? You're not mad?"

Raegan frowned, offended. "Of course not. I'm just happy that you trusted us enough to tell us now."

Something shifted inside Carson, like a dense fog clearing from a dark road. Clouds dispersed to reveal the sun in the form of her friends—no, her family. They were her family. Always had been. And for the first time, she recognized it.

"Yeah, Carson," Hunter said, puffing his chest like a protective older brother. "I bet it took a lot of courage to tell us. We're going to help you get through it. Whatever it takes."

Chapter Twenty-Six

People are going to notice.

The lady in the aisle over there, she definitely noticed. Is that old man staring? The Kohl's employee was totally staring as she restocked the rack.

Carson tugged on her sleeves, trying to pull them down further. Which was useless because they stopped just below her elbow. Short enough to show five scars—she'd counted them over and over until she was blue in the face. They felt like beacons for everyone in the store. She might as well have taken her shirt off, stood on the checkout counter, and yelled, "Hey everyone! Look at me and what I've done to my body."

Standing in the middle of the baby section of Kohl's, one of the few department stores in the area, Raegan grabbed Carson's hand and pulled it from her sleeve. "Nobody is looking," she said. "I promise you. And even if they did look, who cares? It's part of your life."

It was Carson's first public appearance wearing something other than sleeves that reached her wrists. Now that she had told her friends about her self-harm, Dave had challenged Carson to be comfortable in her own body. Which didn't make a lot of sense, since her body was what had started this whole self-harming thing in the first place. However, she made a promise to herself to take those small tedious steps to recovery.

Today's step was exposing her mangled skin to the public, but not in a tank top or short-sleeve shirt. Not yet. Thankfully, summer was far enough away for Carson to build up the courage to wear that kind of apparel . . . maybe. Today, she was taking Dave's challenge with three-quarter sleeves.

Small steps.

Carson took in three deep breaths, then started chewing her wad of gum, even though all the flavor was gone. "You're right. It's just so awkward and humiliating all at the same time."

"I can only imagine," Raegan sympathized, before picking up a maroon baby dress full of ruffles and sequins. "But I have never been more proud to be your friend."

Afraid that she would start bawling if she spoke and make an even bigger beacon of herself, Carson smiled, grateful for the unconditional support from her friend. Raegan smiled too before returning her attention to the red dress. Carson caught sight of a tiny pair of denim overalls and began admiring them when her phone buzzed. She tossed the overalls into the black mesh basket and grabbed her phone.

"Who are you texting?" Raegan asked.

"Will."

"Will?"

Carson finished her response and hit send before moving onto another rack of baby apparel. "We met at that legal convention I went to last year, remember?" she explained. "He's the lawyer out of California. He's back in town and wants to visit tonight. I thought I told you about him?"

Raegan leaned on the display next to her and put a hand on her stomach. Even though she wasn't showing yet, Carson understood the natural instinct to cradle, even when the baby was the size of a bagel bite.

"Isn't this the same guy that asked you out?" she asked, recalling their conversation from Hunter's birthday party.

Carson rolled her eyes. "Yes, but we're just meeting up as friends."

Raegan sniffed, then said, "Have you spoken to Jax lately?"

"No." She frowned. Really it felt like her whole body frowned.

"I heard he got promoted to captain."

"Really?" Carson said. "I knew the position was opening up. I'm happy he took it."

Raegan pushed off the display and started fingering through a rack of onesies. "Make sure you text me about your"—she formed air quotes with her fingers—"*non-date* tonight."

The horse skull's glowing green eyes stared menacingly down at Carson from above the bar entrance. She wasn't sure if the skull was meant to be rugged and bold, like the thousands of cowboys that had passed underneath it, or scary and intimidating. Maybe it was guarding the entrance to the bar.

Standing—more like shivering, it was so damn cold—outside Mustang Saloon in the dark, she waited for Will. Smoke-filled bars with sloshing alcohol and pulsing music were no longer her scene, but Will had wanted the authentic Prescott experience.

Pulling up her scarf to cover her nose, Carson nestled into the crocheted yarn. One more minute and she'd wait for him inside.

"Carson!"

Will was walking up the sidewalk, avoiding a group of tourists fervently photographing the famous Whiskey Row. He looked so out of place wearing a woolen trench coat, striped scarf, and were those leather gloves? His shoes were too shiny for the desert, missing dirt and goatheads stuck to the bottom. They would have been more appropriate in the streets of New York, not a small rodeo town. When he got closer, Carson recognized the smell of flowers, maybe peonies. It was stronger than the last time she saw him. It was dainty, and nothing like the way Jax smelled.

"You made it," Carson said, relieved that she could now get out of the cold.

"Just barely," he huffed. "I couldn't find a parking spot."

"Even in the parking garage?"

"There's a parking garage?"

Carson pointed at the bar behind her. "It's just on the other side."

"Of course there's a parking garage," Will muttered.

Leading the way, Carson pushed open the heavy wooden doors. Her nose crinkled at the bitter smell of alcohol, and she choked down a gag. Lights danced and swirled like the few folks who were swinging to the raucous, thumping music. Why bars played music so loud that guests couldn't hear themselves think, Carson would never understand. The bartender didn't seem to have a problem with the music's volume as they ordered their drinks and chose one of the tall tables near the bar.

"Why do they call it Whiskey Row?" Will asked after taking a long pull from his mug.

"Huh?" The music, the buzzing conversations, the clinking of glasses. All too loud.

He repeated himself.

"Oh. I guess back in the early nineteen hundreds, a fire burned down a majority of the buildings. They rebuilt it with a bunch of bars, and, I think, at one point there were about forty saloons," Carson explained, pulling off her jacket and scarf. Her sleeves were long and safe. Nobody on this planet could persuade her to show her scars in front of Will.

"That seems excessive," he said.

She lifted her Shirley Temple. "Welcome to the wild west." Then she added, "You could say downtown Prescott is cursed. Fires are always happening here."

Will took another drink while his eyes raked over the bar. Something caught Carson's eye in the corner. A large Maltese cross was printed on the back of someone's shirt. She squinted in the dim lighting. The guy standing next to the shirt looked familiar. Had she seen him before?

Shaking her head, she sipped her soda and asked, "What brings you into Prescott?"

"I took a job in Scottsdale and moved in last weekend."

"Really? What firm?"

"Caddel & Madden. Do you know about them?"

"No, but there are a ton of firms in the Phoenix area . . ." Her voice trailed off as a shorter man with a mustache walked through the entrance. He looked an awful lot like Tim, Jax's old captain. She cleared her throat. "How do you like Arizona so far?"

"The Phoenix area reminds me of California, but here"—Will's eyes darted once again around the saloon—"is nothing like L.A."

"It's definitely a unique place," she agreed.

The song booming in the air switched from a new, upbeat tune to an old classic. Around them there were grunts of approval as the twang of Toby Keith floated about the bar.

"What about you? Did you ever become junior partner?"

Sagging into her chair, Carson chewed on her lip before speaking. "Not yet, but I'm doing a mentorship with my boss." Her finger touched the droplet of condensation on her glass before it could reach the tabletop.

"You don't seem too excited about that."

"I am," she said, tossing her hair behind her shoulder. "It wasn't what I'd originally planned." More like the last five years hadn't been what she'd planned. "I'm not complaining, though. My boss could have turned me down. He has me working on a family law case, which I've never done before."

"Family law is rough," Will said, shuddering. "I'd rather stick with criminal."

Carson thought about how awful Jax's divorce case with Kristen had been for him. In fact, when she eventually opened her own practice, she was seriously considering focusing only on family law. Because, who else would fight for people like Jax in the courtroom?

"I actually have my first trial in two weeks," she informed him.

"Wow. Good luck."

"Thanks." She'd take all the luck she could get, though she was confident she was going to do well. Even her client, Jacob, was looking forward to the trial.

The song ended with a few plucks of a banjo, followed by a commotion on the stage in the far back. A live band had just finished setting up, and they began strumming guitars and pounding on a drum kit. Carson could feel the beat reverberate in her bones. More people congregated toward the middle of the saloon to dance.

"Please tell me they're going to line dance," Will prayed, eyeing the crowd excitedly.

"Would you expect anything less?" Carson asked, amused at Will's reaction to the saloon's atmosphere.

Sure enough, like a well-choreographed performance, men and women lined up and started to kick their boot-covered feet in rhythm, thumbs hooked in their belt loops and all. For a second, Carson thought Will was going to get up and join them.

"How's your boyfriend doing?" Will asked, tapping his finger to the beat of the music.

Choking on a sip of soda, the carbonation burning her nostrils, Carson coughed and cleared her throat, trying to regain control.

"Sorry, he's, uh, he's doing well. Just got a promotion at work," she finally shouted back, the live music banging around them. Perfect answer. Perfect recovery. She didn't have to confirm or deny if they were still dating, and she didn't have to fib. It was a win-win.

"What does he do?"

"He's a firefighter for the City of Prescott." Speaking of firefighters, there was a group of guys playing darts all wearing the Prescott's fire department emblem on the back of their shirts.

Will tapped a finger against his glass, pulling his attention away from the dancers to her. "So, he's buff," he joked.

She let out a laugh, and Will grinned, flashing his perfectly straight and very white teeth. But Carson's laughter stopped when she spotted someone walking through the front entrance. They locked eyes. The lights stopped flashing. The music died on the last note. Finally, it was quiet.

Jax looked at Will—who was still smiling at her—and back to Carson. His face wore shock, then a flash of anger, and finally disappointment. He pivoted and left.

Like a tidal wave, the next song blasted from the speakers, the lights continued to race across the room, and the conversations and dancing went on.

Carson tumbled off the stool, nearly knocking it over.

225

"Can you give me a minute? I'll be right back," she stammered, not bothering to wait for Will's response. Though she doubted he cared because he was still fixated on the line-dancers. She darted between the patrons and flew through the front doors.

Once outside, she spun, her eyes scanning every face, every person she could see. The dark of the night making it difficult. Finally, she spotted a familiar sweatshirt, familiar because she had worn it before, and took off running, grateful the sidewalks were clear of ice.

"Jax!"

When she was only a few feet from Jax, he turned around, causing her to almost smack into him.

"What?" he spat.

It was impossible to blame him for being upset. If she'd seen him laughing with another woman at a bar, she'd be too.

"It's not what it looks like, I swear," Carson wheezed, breathless. "He's another attorney who just moved here. He wanted to visit Prescott."

Ignoring Jax's glare, she studied his beautiful eyes, which were dark and sunken. Even his midnight hair seemed more unruly than she remembered it, wild as if he had just been in a haboob.

"How have you been?" she asked.

He let out a sigh. "I've been better."

"No thanks to me."

"I mean, you did break my heart," Jax teased, giving her a knowing smirk.

"I don't blame you if you hate me," Carson murmured, but glad that he could at least joke about their split.

Raking a hand through his hair, he then slid it down his face. "I could never hate you, Carson."

At the sound of her name on his lips, her heart faltered. She continued anyway, "Yes, but you have every right to hate me. There are not enough sorrys in the world to forgive what I did to you. Please know that I truly am sorry. At the very least understand that I had my reasons. I did it because I love you." Her tongue twisted and froze. Would he notice her use of present tense?

There was the tiniest glimmer in his eyes. He had noticed. Then he focused on the courthouse across the street. Christmas lights were still twinkling in the surrounding trees, like floating colorful lightning bugs. The city would soon be taking them down.

In her haste, Carson had forgotten to grab her jacket. The night air was freezing her skin, although the feeling was preferable to the stale smell of beer in the bar. Her fingers were going numb, so she shoved them in her jeans pocket and fidgeted with a piece of lint.

"Believe it or not, I do understand your reasons," Jax said. "That doesn't mean I agree with them. But I can understand why you ended us. I just hope that one day you'll realize how wrong you were."

Little did he know Carson was already processing her mistakes.

A car in the parking spot in front of them pulled out, and a new one took its place. A group of middle-aged women stepped out laughing and shouting at one another. Ridiculously large foam cowboy hats sat upon their heads. Carson hoped they weren't going into Mustang Saloon. She was in no mood to listen to woo girls.

"How's your family doing?" she asked, hoping to steal a few more minutes with Jax.

"Doing fine." He leaned against the two-hour parking sign they stood next to. "Except Beau."

"What happened to Beau?"

"I think he took our breakup harder than us. He really liked you."

A huge grin pulled her lips up, and she rolled her eyes. "Well, you tell your brother I really liked him, and tell your family I say hello."

"I will." Pushing off the metal pole, Jax straightened. "So, just another attorney, huh?" he ribbed, sounding like Raegan.

"I promise."

"Good," he said. "I was afraid I didn't make enough of an impression on you, if you could move on so quickly."

Cocking her head toward the bar, Carson said, "Yeah, well I better get back before he comes looking."

Jax nodded in understanding. "It was good seeing you."

"You too."

"Maybe we can catch up one day," he suggested.

"I'd like that," she said, hope filling her body. Maybe, just maybe, there could be another chance with Jax.

CHAPTER TWENTY-SEVEN

The anticipation was finally over.

Carson and her client, Jacob, sat in the courtroom as her opponent, Charles Patchett, rattled off his last questions to his client, currently on the stand.

"Now, Tiffany," Charles said, "the Petitioner, Jacob Phillips, alleges that your daughter has witnessed you and your boyfriend smoking marijuana on your couch. Do you own a couch?"

The witness leaned forward and spoke into the microphone, her voice sounding as if she gargled gravel before the trial. "No, I don't."

"Do you own a futon?"

"No."

"Loveseat? Sectional?"

"No and no."

"What about a chair, bench, ottoman, or anything that could possibly resemble a couch? Do you own anything like that?"

"No, I do not. I haven't been able to afford one yet."

"So, there is no way for your daughter to have witnessed you and your boyfriend smoking marijuana on the couch while in your custody?"

"No, sir."

"If there is no couch in your home, why do you think your daughter would tell her dad she saw this?"

"Objection, your honor," Carson interrupted before the witness could answer. "Calls for speculation."

"Sustained," Judge Halliday granted. "Next question, Counsel."

Charles peered down at his notes, scratched lazily onto a yellow legal notepad, then back up to the judge.

"No further questions, Your Honor," he said before turning to Carson and giving her a smug face. It was unprofessional and childish, but it didn't bother her because she had a wild card up her sleeve.

Judge Halliday took off her reading glasses and motioned to Carson. "Ms. West, your witness for redirect."

"Thank you, Judge." She grabbed the microphone and moved it closer to her, excited to finally present her biggest piece of evidence. "I only have one question for you, Ms. Phillips, and it should be an easy one. Does your boyfriend have a couch at his apartment?"

Tiffany's eyes grew big, darting between her attorney and Carson. From where she was sitting, Carson could see the gulp travel down Tiffany's thick throat.

It was satisfying seeing the witness squirm. Thanks to her dream about the couch, Carson had caught Tiffany. Their daughter had been restricted from going to the boyfriend's apartment.

"Please answer the question, Ms. Phillips," the judge ordered.

"Yes, he does." The confidence in Tiffany's voice was long gone.

"I have no other questions for the witness, Judge," Carson finished, throwing back the smug look to her competitor across the aisle. She was allowed to be childish sometimes too.

Wailing sirens sounded from outside the marble walls of the courthouse.

Everyone waited for them to grow quiet, but they continued, loud and close. Even Judge Halliday tilted her ear to the window behind her. Then she cleared her throat. "Let's focus back on this case. Counsel, your closing arguments."

Charles adjusted his wide tie, one probably bought by his wife. His closing argument was long and boring. Evidently, the judge was not entertained, as her focus was on the computer sitting on the bench. At least the muted sirens outside made for some sort of excitement.

Then it was Carson's turn. She always stood for her closing argument. Jacob tried to stand up too. Subtly, she motioned for him to stay where he was at.

"Judge, you heard the evidence today. I have nothing to add," she said. Garrett had taught her that closing arguments were for juries. He would say, "Presenting a closing argument to a judge is like explaining how a rocket works to a rocket scientist."

The hearing was adjourned, and Judge Halliday retired to her chambers.

"Do you think it went well?" Jacob whispered as Carson shoved the binder and file into her briefcase.

"I think it went as well as it could have," she said. "We'll have to wait for the judge's ruling now."

Internally, Carson believed it went very well. Especially for her first family law case. What she wanted to say was that the trial went almost perfectly in their favor. She couldn't wait to tell Garrett at the office. Junior partner seemed like it was getting closer and closer.

"Right." Her client stood, then jerked his chin toward the window where the sirens were still droning. "I wonder what happened."

"Probably a car accident," Carson guessed, slipping the briefcase strap on her shoulder.

A fresh blanket of snow greeted them outside. Large snowflakes floated from the gray sky like little feathers. The sirens were far away now, but a commotion was coming from the north. Horns blaring. Shouting. Glass breaking.

Carson quickly descended the courthouse steps, only slipping once in her heels and catching herself on the railing. Her client was following close behind. She saw the smoke before she saw the fire. Thick and gruesome it billowed from the atrium mall, The Village, across the street. The blazing flames licked at the windows. One, two, three fire trucks were there, lights spinning. Their hoses looked like snakes slithering all over the ground.

Police were holding the crowds back, attempting to secure the street. The shouts, the gushing of fire hoses, the roaring of the fire was chaotic and overwhelming. It was impossible to process what was happening before her.

Through a break in the mass of people, Carson caught a glimpse of one of the fire trucks: Engine 71. She recognized the huge, golden numbers, and worry began swirling within her.

"I've got to go," she shouted at Jacob before pushing her way toward the blockade. Her hands gripped the icy wood as she strained to see Jax. The heat from the blaze warmed her cold cheeks.

A familiar face appeared from around one of the trucks.

"Hunter!" Carson yelled, waving her hand. "Hunter!"

It took a moment for him to notice her, his eyes looking out over the crowd. Once he recognized who was calling out to him, he glanced at the burning building, then hustled over to the barricade. Sweat was trickling from his helmet and down his freckled face. She wondered if Raegan knew what was happening.

"How bad?" she asked.

"Bad," he said, his tone serious. Fun-loving Hunter was gone, replaced with on-duty Hunter. "We believe it was a gas leak."

Gasping, Carson thought about all of the people in the building, wondering if there were any casualties. She examined the flames that had completely taken over the roof. "Gas leak. Doesn't that mean there could be an explosion?"

When Hunter nodded, the flames reflected off his helmet's clear visor. "That's exactly why we're trying to keep the crowd back as far as possible. Which means you need to clear the area too."

"Wait, what about Jax? Is he here too?"

Hunter was looking up at the building. When he met her stare, he hesitated for a moment too long, causing her stomach to seize.

"What's wrong? Where's Jax?"

"The roof collapsed. Everyone got out, but—"

"He's still in there," Carson finished for him, feeling the blood drain from her face and fear encase her heart. Ducking under the barricade she stepped toward the building, wringing the strap of her briefcase between her hands.

"Carson." Hunter grabbed her shoulder and spun her around to face him. Then he gripped her other shoulder, determined to keep her put. The fire now heated her back. "The collapse just happened. He's only been in there for a couple of minutes. The team is ready to go back in. We're just waiting for the final command from the chief. Which should be any second now. They're going to find him, and he's going to be alright. We have to trust the process."

It seemed Hunter was saying the last part more to himself than to her.

Something caught his attention, and he peered over her head. "I need to go. They'll find him and get him." His voice didn't sound reassuring.

233

"Now get out of here. I need you safe."

He must have trusted that Carson would leave on her own, because he stepped past her and joined some of the crew huddled together, deep in discussion.

The inferno continued to snarl above her. Jax was just beyond those walls, stuck or worse. A tremor rolled through her body at the thought.

Taking a step forward toward the circle of fire personnel, Carson assumed they had the power to send in the rescue team for Jax. Straining to listen, she could only catch occasional words and phrases. It seemed the general consensus was to send rescuers in immediately. She breathed a sigh of relief.

A deafening eruption came from the adjoining building. Exploding glass showered the bystanders and first responders as shrieks and cries rang out. Terrified, Carson stood from her reactive crouch and shook pieces of glass from her hair, frantically focusing back on the rescue crew who were drawing further and further from the entrance, retreating to safety.

Was it too dangerous to go back in? Were they aborting the rescue?

Then Hunter began stomping toward the entrance. A couple of firefighters grabbed his shoulders, holding him back. He tried to shake them off until a burly man stepped in front of him. Carson recognized him as Bardot, the battalion chief she met at Station 71. His face was red, and he was shoving a massive finger into Hunter's chest, who was scowling and deflating by the second. She couldn't hear everything they were saying, but the chief was clearly ordering him to stand down.

It looked as though they weren't going back for Jax. That had to be why Hunter was fighting to disobey the orders.

Carson wasn't going to let that happen.

Eyeing the entrance, she saw that only a stream of white smoke was spiraling out. Maybe most of the fire was on the roof and the top floor. If she could sneak in and get a quick look around, she could come back and tell them it was safe. Maybe, with some luck, she could find Jax.

Before she could talk herself out of it, Carson crept backward and managed to scoot behind one of the engines, void of prying eyes. A compartment had been left open, displaying two spare turnout coats. Dropping her bag, she snatched a coat from its hook, surprised at how heavy it was, and folded it over her arm to make it less conspicuous. Then she opened and rummaged around a second compartment. Which was pointless because she had no idea what she was looking at, let alone how to use the equipment in front of her. The jacket would have to do.

Was she crazy? Yes. Brainless? Duh. But she was determined to do something. She couldn't let anything bad happen to Jax. When Luke and her child were killed, there was nothing Carson could have done. Now she had an opportunity to save a loved one. And she had to act fast.

Scurrying around the vehicles, she inched closer to the entrance of the mall. The beating in her chest was so hard, it was beginning to hurt. Even her nerves started to singe and fray, and a rock had invaded her stomach. Was she really about to do this?

You're running out of time. Jax is running out of time. Don't think, just do.

Sirens blared from additional emergency vehicles that were arriving, temporarily distracting the crew. This was her chance. Now or never.

With one last look at the courthouse and its beautiful stone architecture, Carson boldly entered the burning building.

CHAPTER TWENTY-EIGHT

The heat was unbearable.

Carson quickly slipped on the heavy coat and fumbled with the zipper. Though it kept the worst of the heat at bay, the intensity of the fire was unimaginably hot. Already she was missing the winter snow outside.

Carson's eyes stung from the fumes as she squinted around The Village's main foyer. Thankfully she was familiar with the layout of the small, four-story mall. Instead of a full floor on each story, the mall featured a deck-like landing that circled around the perimeter, where visitors could peer down to the ground floor. If she could reach the middle, Carson would have almost a three-sixty view of the entire building.

The Village's interior was surprisingly dark for a building on fire, as the smoke seemed to snuff out any usable light. And what was that roaring? It sounded just like a plane's engine. Carson crept forward, covering her mouth and nose with her sleeve. The air tasted thick and unbreathable from the smoke pluming above, its vapors finding every crevice to inhabit. Minutes. With this amount of smoke, Carson only had minutes to find Jax before her lungs would begin to suffocate and she would lose consciousness. She peeked down at her watch, one that Luke had bought her as a birthday gift, and noted the time.

When she reached the middle of the mall, Carson spun, analyzing the magnitude of the fire. It had fully engulfed the top floor, and tongues of flame teased the third to join the inferno. Red and white embers floated downward similar to the snow falling outside.

Toward the rear, Carson spotted the part of the building that had collapsed, settling on the second floor. Hadn't Hunter said the collapse was the reason Jax hadn't made it out? That was the first place she would look.

Once she found the stairs near the front, Carson sprinted up the steps to the second floor. The smoke became worse. Violently choking and gasping, she fell on her hands and knees, trying to get as low as possible, as she crawled toward the collapse. It seemed that her minutes would be shorter than she'd originally guessed. She needed to find Jax fast.

"Jax!" she called. Competing against the howling of the fire was useless.

Scuttling forward, she tried to avoid the glowing embers falling from above. The closer she got to the rubble, the stronger the heat became, like opening the oven door after preheating it to five thousand degrees. Like scurrying toward the sun. Sweat dripped into her eyes as she blinked away the stinging from the smoke.

The watch continued to tick. One minute gone.

"Jax!" she coughed out. "Jax!"

This was a dumb plan. Why did she think she could possibly find him in this catastrophe? Even if she did find him, what hope would she have of getting him out? The heat was nothing like she had ever experienced. There was no air quality because there was no air. There was no oxygen. It was smoke and only smoke.

Stupid. Stupid. Stupid. What the hell were you thinking?

A memory from Carson's childhood crept up into her mind. During a school fire drill a fire marshal taught them what to do in case of a fire. His first instruction was *not* to run back into a burning building, even to save someone. That piece of advice must have gone through one ear and out the other because Carson was doing the exact opposite.

As if the fire itself was trying to tell her how idiotic she was, one of the falling embers landed on the top of her hand, sizzling her flesh. "Ow!" she cried, hastening her pace. She needed to find Jax *now*.

Finally, when she reached the edge of the pile of collapsed building, she stood. "Jax!" she screeched, her voice hoarse. How much smoke had she already inhaled?

Then there was a beep, piercing and sharp. Not sure if her ears were playing tricks on her, she stopped moving. There it was again. It reminded her of the noise smoke detectors made.

She scuffled over a fallen metal beam, its surface scalding the palms of her hands. Even through the smoke, a tiny, muted red dot blinked at her. She lurched toward it, as the device continued to shriek, encouraging her forward. The red dot was attached to a . . . a person.

"Jax!"

He lay flat on his back, one of his arms stretched out above him as if reaching for her. A second metal beam was crushing his legs. His gloved fingers were limp.

Diving forward, Carson slid next to him. His helmet and face mask were on, and the glare from the fire made it difficult to see his features, but she knew it was Jax. He looked like he was sleeping, so peaceful amongst all the chaos.

Grabbing his arm, she squeezed his hand to her chest then pulled his sleeve down to expose the skin on his wrist. As she checked for a pulse her black fingers left marks on his clean skin. It was there, slow and steady, unlike her own erratic heartbeat.

Two minutes gone.

"Hey, wake up. We gotta get out of here," she croaked, shaking his shoulders. As soon as she disturbed his resting body, the shrieking from the device stopped. A TV show popped into her mind, *Chicago Fire*. In it, firefighters used gadgets that set off an ear-splitting alarm when still for too long. They were used as tracking devices.

Carson shook him again. Still, he didn't wake.

Okay, now what? Carson turned her attention back to the massive beam trapping his lower half. Were Jax's legs broken?

Her watch warned her that three minutes had passed. Time was running out.

Carson placed a hand on the side of Jax's mask. "I'm going to get you out of here. I promise."

Getting to her feet she used the sleeve of her coat like an oven mitt and grasped the metal. With all her strength, which wasn't much, she heaved. And yanked. And lifted. And pushed. It didn't budge. Kicking off her heels, she tried again. Nothing.

Four minutes.

Plan B, she thought, plopping back down and taking his hand.

Maybe she could make a mad dash back outside and tell the other firefighters she had found him. That may have been the easiest, most efficient thing to do. Then she remembered the battalion chief's angry command. A shudder ran down her spine, imagining them restraining her, like they did Hunter, once she was back outside, unable to go back in.

Back to Plan A then. It was up to Carson to get the beam off of him and drag him out.

Then there was a startling screech followed by a crackle coming from Jax's other shoulder. Was that a radio? Why hadn't she noticed it before?

The lack of oxygen was beginning to take its toll. Carson ripped it off his gear and pressed the communicator button, praying it would work.

"Hello?" Her voice was so hoarse! "I've found Jax. I'm inside the building." It took her a second to recall where she was. "I'm on the second floor on the back side."

The radio squawked at her when she released the button. Did that mean it wasn't working? She tried again. "We need help!" she screamed, her throat on fire. "There are two of us on the second floor on the north side, near the collapse."

No response. The radio gave a final chirp, then went completely silent. Worthless.

Five minutes.

A coughing fit climbed out of her lungs, practically choking her. Every time she tried to suck in a breath, she only made it worse. Her lungs were beginning to fight back, seeking the needed relief of oxygen. Remembering that some search-and-rescue squads carried spare masks for survivors, she turned back to Jax, hands fumbling around him. To her despair, she couldn't find one.

A cry escaped Carson's lips. The energy had finally drained from her body. There was nothing left inside of her. The place was spinning. In her vision Jax pulsed close to her, then far away, and her brain vibrated in her skull. By now, she didn't know if she could even make it back out. Would she even have the energy?

Running out of ideas, Carson laid herself next to Jax's still body, resting an arm over his chest. The air was a bit clearer so close to the ground. She followed the tempo of the rise and fall of his chest. Her lungs hurt with every breath, a scorched field inside her chest.

Eyeballing the swirls and bellows of the smoke and the dances and jerks of the flames above, Carson realized that she may have just sentenced herself to death. If not by suffocation, then by the fire itself. If the building collapsed, she would perish underneath its weight.

Time was up.

Closing her burning eyes, Carson considered the lectures she would receive if, by some miracle, they survived. From the fire department, Hunter, Jax, and Raegan. Raegan would be furious! Her friend would give her a good scolding. What would Dave think about her running into a burning building? He'd probably schedule even more sessions. And there went her dream of opening her own firm.

I guess I still have a lot to learn.

By now, it felt like Carson's body was floating. At any moment, the smoke or the fire would consume her whole. She was sorry she couldn't save Jax. That she hadn't been able to spend her last remaining weeks with him. She regretted wasting so much time unable to process the death of her family. Why had she waited so long to get help? If she could do it all over again, she would grieve their loss but cherish the time she did have with them. She'd use their love to build her life back up and be happy.

Shapes appeared above her. Luke and her son were there, ready to take her home. Then the smooth darkness swallowed Carson up.

Chapter Twenty-Nine

D éjà vu.

The quiet humming told Carson she had been there before. That, and the bed. After spending a copious amount of time in a hospital bed, she would never forget how it felt. Stiff, bumpy, and impossibly uncomfortable.

She peeled her eyes open, concerned at how irritated they felt. Everything looked fuzzy, but she was definitely in a hospital room. She recognized the spotted ceiling tiles and the plastic, buzzing light fixtures, the gray curtain drooping in the corner. The heart monitor next to her picked up its rhythm. The last time she'd woken up in a hospital, her family was dead.

Jax.

Various wires and tubes, including the oxygen hose on her face, tugged as Carson sat up, her head spinning. She was alone. No doctor. No nurse. No one was standing at the end of her bed, telling her that Jax didn't survive.

When she tried to call out to someone, she recoiled from the searing pain in her throat. She clutched her neck; it felt as though a hot branding iron covered in nails was being shoved down her throat. She was thirsty. Very thirsty. Was there any water? The bed tray next to her was empty.

Just then, a nurse pushed through the door. Apparently surprised to see her awake, he scurried over and began inspecting the machines, adjusting her oxygen hose.

"Ms. West? Do you know where you are?"

Carson opened her mouth to speak, then thought better of it and nodded.

"Do you know why you're here?"

Impatiently, she nodded again. Enough about her. What about Jax? Did he make it out alive? Did he die after she had lost consciousness? Was he home? In this hospital? In the morgue? Was he already buried? Did they even wait for her? What day was it? Question after question flitted through her mind like a mutoscope.

Luckily, the nurse was smart enough to understand her when Carson gestured with her hands for something to write on. Plucking a small notepad and pen from his scrubs, he handed them to her.

"Hmm. I don't have any patients with the name of Jax Miller," he said after reading her note.

She beckoned for the notepad again, writing down her next question.

"We have a phone you can use right here," he offered, pointing to a landline telephone on the counter to the left of her. "But I can page your friend. She's down in the cafeteria right now. I think her name is Raegan?"

Eagerly, Carson's head bobbed up and down before he had finished.

"Alright, give me a second," he said as he left.

Once again, Carson was alone. It was impossible to ignore her raw throat. Her mouth was still dry, like she'd licked a burnt log. The top of her hand pinched as she curled her legs underneath her. She looked down at the IV tube shoved under her skin. Then her eyes trailed up her arm and her heart stopped.

Her scars were out, saying hello to her and everyone. Her hospital gown couldn't hide them.

A smile teased Carson's lips. She had forgotten all about them. And at the moment, she didn't even care they were out on display. There were more important things to worry about—like the harsh reprimand she was about to receive.

Someone was running down the hall. Tap, tap, tap, tap, tap. Of course Raegan would be in high heels.

The door burst open, and Raegan stood frozen on the threshold, gaping at her in what appeared to be disbelief, as if she hadn't expected Carson to survive. Then tears sprung from her eyes, and she flung herself at Carson. Raegan's hug reminded Carson of the first time she'd hugged Shirley. Full of love.

Raegan drew away, her nose pink. "You are in *so* much trouble," she scolded. Carson's shoulders hunched.

"And Hunter is furious with you," Raegan added.

Carson slumped even more. *I know*, she mouthed.

"You're in luck, though. He's already forgiven you because you saved his best friend."

It took a second for the words to register. Saved his best friend . . . saved his best friend . . . *saved his best friend*. Like a crazed woman, Carson gripped Raegan's biceps, her fingers pressing deep into the muscle. The heart machine's beeping was starting to get annoying.

"Jax is *alive*," she rasped, fire ripping up her esophagus.

Raegan's brows fell over her eyes. "Yes. Didn't they tell you?"

Carson's head shook vigorously, as a lump painfully formed in her throat. Then her own tears of relief pooled in her eyes and started spilling over. Jax was alive. She had done it.

"Oh, honey." Raegan's tears started again, and she leaned forward to embrace Carson.

A torrent of emotions washed through Carson: relief, elation, and a bit of hysteria. This wasn't déjà vu at all. Not even close.

Releasing her friend, Carson mouthed a question. *Where is he?*

"He's upstairs in the TICU, the trauma intensive care unit," Raegan said, wiping the mascara that stained her cheeks with her fingers. "He's fine, though. His leg was crushed when the roof collapsed. He was in surgery all night, but they finished a couple of hours ago, and he's doing well."

The memory of the rubble on top of him, of not being strong enough to free him, flashed in Carson's mind. Again, more beeping. She glanced at the monitor until it quieted. Apparently, it only decided to beep when it detected her heart rate spiking.

How bad? she mouthed again.

"His femur was broken. They predict he fell unconscious from the pain."

Carson's mouth twitched with distress. *Can I go see him?*

Tucking one of her golden locks behind her ear, Raegan peeked at the open door, sniffing. "I don't know. None of us have been able to see him yet."

How long have I been here? Carson silently and carefully enunciated for her to understand.

"Both of you were brought in last night." Raegan's eyes darted to a clock on the wall. "It's about eight-thirty in the morning."

A knock interrupted their conversation. A woman with salt-and-pepper hair glided in, her white coat billowing behind her. Raegan got up to make room for the doctor.

"Good morning, Ms. West. I'm Doctor Hill," she said. "I heard the good news that you woke up." She took Carson's wrist and checked her pulse.

"Your throat may be very sore. That's to be expected from the amount of smoke you inhaled. Can you open for me?"

The doctor fished out a tiny flashlight, one that resembled a writing pen, and clicked it on. Her eyebrows furrowed when Carson obediently opened her mouth. "Definitely red and swollen." Clicking off the light, she placed it back in her breast pocket. "It's very important you understand that you were exposed to an extreme amount of smoke and the hazards that come with it. That means a liquid diet and no speaking. Let's do a forty-eight-hour observation and oxygen . . ."

Carson did her best to listen to the doctor and the hospital lingo spewing from her mouth. It wasn't easy, though. Her throat was in flames. No matter how many times she blinked, it still felt like sand was scratching her eyes. The machines hummed and buzzed annoyingly around her. Her backside was already hurting from sitting in the bed that might as well have been made out of wood. And she was anxious to see Jax.

After the doctor left, her nurse returned and gave her a small whiteboard and dry-erase pen before updating her chart. When he was gone, Raegan sat back on the edge of the bed. Her slow-growing belly protruded a bit more, making her look officially pregnant. It was a cute little bump. Carson wondered how big the baby was now.

"Man, you stink," Raegan said, wrinkling her nose.

Carson lifted her arm to sniff, but couldn't smell anything. Either the constant flow of fresh oxygen masked her odor, or her nose was so singed she'd lost the ability to smell. Her skin was still dirty, her fingers darkened from ash. Next to her IV there was a red spot where the ember had burned her hand. Lifting her shoulder once, she scooted back in her bed, the plastic mattress crinkling beneath her.

The door creaked open. Hunter pushed his way in and crumpled into the tiny recliner shoved in the corner of the room. His body seemed to melt as if his bones had turned to jelly. Smudges smeared his face, covering his freckles, and his red hair was wild and uncontrolled. He seemed to fight a losing battle with his eyelids as they drooped dangerously near closed.

"How are you feeling?" he managed to ask.

Using her new communication device, Carson scrawled her answer and faced the whiteboard toward him.

Great, but what happened? How did you find us?

"The radio," he said, puzzled by her question as if the answer was obvious. "You told us where to find you."

So, the radio had worked. Using her arm, Carson wiped the surface clean and wrote, *Start from the beginning.*

The fabric of the chair stretched when he leaned further back and put his hands behind his head. "I'm not joking when I say literally seconds after we got the command to go in, your voice comes through all of our radios." Then he laughed. "The looks on everyone's faces. It even took me a minute to recognize it was you on the other end. I had to piece together that you'd gone inside. The rescue team immediately went in and found you and Jax exactly where you said you were."

His arms dropped with a thud on the arm rests, his face now somber. "If they'd been even a minute later both of you would have been killed. As soon as they freed Jax, the whole area went up in flames. They barely made it out. If you hadn't told them directly where to go, they would have wasted valuable time searching. And you would both be dead."

Though the room was warm, goosebumps crept across Carson's skin. Only the humming of the oxygen device mounted to the wall disturbed the quiet. The three of them—Hunter, Raegan, and herself—let the reality of what had happened settle around them. Once again, death had tried to steal from them. Only this time, Carson had the chance to fight back, and miraculously, she'd won.

The black marker squeaked as she scribbled her next question. *Is the fire out now?*

Using his fingers, Hunter rubbed his tired eyes. "Barely. Two engines are still there. Raegan messaged that you'd woken up, so I came straight here."

A hundred more questions filled Carson's skull, too many to keep track of. A dull pain creeped from her neck to behind her eyes. There was so much to say, and ask, and do. But Carson knew exactly what she needed to do first.

Take me to Jax, she wrote.

Chapter Thirty

D^{*ing.*}

The elevator doors swooshed open, jostling Carson as her wheelchair maneuvered through the opening. The TICU seemed eerily quiet. Where were the nurses rushing back and forth? Where was the wheeling of carts and equipment? What about the codes being announced over the speakers? Wasn't this supposed to be a trauma floor?

She fished out the whiteboard wedged next to her thigh to write a question and held it up for her nurse.

"They purposefully keep it quiet so the patients can rest and recover," he said.

He pushed her down the dim hallway, passing room after room, patient after patient. It was almost creepy just how dead everything seemed. Almost like the building had been abandoned.

Thanks to the painkillers in her IV, the burning in Carson's throat had subsided to a warm ache. It took some silver-tongued, attorney-style persuasion to convince her doctor to not drug her into a zombie. She didn't want to relive her sluggish, drained hospital days pumped full of pharmaceuticals. She only wanted enough to keep the pain at bay. Enough to get her to Jax.

The nurse slowed as they approached the very last doorway at the end of the hall. Carson's leg began to bounce, and she let it. Nervously, she straightened the oxygen tube on her face, though it was already level, and smoothed her hand down her French braids.

While waiting for permission to visit Jax, Raegan had talked Carson into taking a shower. The clear water shooting out of the faucet had turned murky by the time it puddled at Carson's feet and slid down the drain. It hadn't been easy scrubbing off the soot with the tubes still hooked to her body. Thankfully, Raegan had been there to help wash her hair, hold the lines out of the way, hand her a towel, and braid her hair back. Raegan was going to be an amazing mother.

Jax's room was dark except for a glow emanating from behind his bed, much like the horizon just before the sun breached the sky. The amount of equipment stacked around him was intimidating and a bit nerve-racking. Wires, tubes, lines, and gadgets spilled out from under his gown as though the hospital was trying to transform him into a cyborg.

Under his blanket, a massive lump sat where his left leg should have been, making him look lopsided and deformed. Carson wondered what kind of break it was and how the surgery had gone. One of her clients from years ago had broken her femur once. She'd told Carson that by six months she was back to her normal activities, but even after two years she still didn't have full strength in that leg.

Even though his bed was adjusted to elevate his upper body, Jax was asleep, sporting his own oxygen cannula. But as Carson was wheeled right next to him, her muscles locked at how frighteningly unwell he looked. A thin sheen of sweat dewed on his face. His black mane stuck to his forehead, and a milky hue coated his skin. She reached out to touch his arm, half-expecting it to be cold and frozen, and she sighed in relief when it was warm.

Carson smiled gratefully at her nurse after he positioned her chair and locked the wheels. Once he left, she turned to inspect the machines, trying to interpret them. The buttons and numbers and symbols made her eyes cross, but no bells or alarms were sounding. She had to trust Jax was doing alright.

Seeing him alive was surreal. When the darkness had taken her, Carson had been convinced their bodies would be claimed by the fire.

This life was giving her yet another chance. How many times was she supposed to be dead? She should have died in that car accident. The pills and alcohol should have finished the job. Her body should have been smothered in flames. Three chances at life. It was finally time to start living.

Taking Jax's hand into hers, she lifted it to kiss the top, avoiding his IV. He didn't stir, and Carson had no idea how long it would be until he would wake. Using her arms as pillows, she leaned forward and rested on the side of his bed. Even though all she wanted to do was stare at his face forever, her eyelids began to droop. The exhaustion was strong, so she closed her eyes to rest.

The car was on fire. Everything was on fire. Carson was strapped to the front seat. It was so hot. Her esophagus burned. The flames danced closer and closer to her, so close that her skin was turning red.

Except the fire didn't scare her. Unbuckling the seatbelt, she lifted herself through the passenger door window. As she moved, the flames scurried out of her way, as if *she* was going to hurt them. Feet planted firmly on the road, Carson began walking away from the wreckage, leaving it all behind.

That was when a voice called her name. Looking around, all she could see was the blaze. Once again her name echoed around her—

Carson didn't know how long she had been asleep. Maybe an hour, maybe only minutes. She swallowed and cringed at the roaring pain. Why couldn't she dream about popsicles and ice cream? Her eyelids flitted as the hand she was holding squeezed.

"Carson."

Head popping up, she blinked away the irritation. After a couple of seconds, the blur before her sharpened into shapes. Jax was peering down at her, his beautiful blue eyes radiating. Eyebrows pinched in bewilderment, he looked at her, then at her hospital gown, then at her wheelchair.

"What are you doing here?" he croaked with labored breaths. The rise and fall of his chest was unnatural. He tried to shift in his bed, grimacing when the movement jarred his legs. A frown formed when he noticed the splint.

"Are you in pain?" Carson wheezed, ignoring the ache.

"A little," Jax said, clearing his throat. "What happened?"

Can't talk, she mouthed, pointing to her neck. Then she grabbed her marker and whiteboard, scribbled the most important facts she could think of, and handed it to him to read.

Fire downtown. You got trapped. Leg broken. You had surgery. Doctor says you're fine. Happened last night.

"I remember the fire. I remember them telling me about my leg and surgery," Jax said. "But that doesn't explain why *you're* here."

Grabbing the board out of his hands, Carson bit her lip. *I went into the building to find you. Smoke burned my lungs and throat. Not allowed to talk.*

As he read each word, Jax's sleepy eyes became more and more alert with

252

angst, triggering his heart machine to beep angrily.

"You *what?*" he hissed, then cringed at the pain that shot through him.

Frantically she waved her hands and shook her head, which made her a bit dizzy. Then she took his hand again and squeezed.

I'm fine, she mouthed, rubbing her hand down Jax's forearm and back up. The beeping quieted, but he continued to frown. Then he squeezed his eyes shut for a second before focusing back on her.

"Are you insane?" he asked.

Most definitely. Insane. Crazy. Stupid. All of it. She shrugged her shoulders.

Face softening, Jax relaxed his head into the pillow. "What am I supposed to do with you?"

A grin spread on her face, and she kissed his hand. A hushed voice floated through the hallway speakers behind her, something about a doctor needed at station six.

When the announcement was over, she stole back her whiteboard.

You look like shit.

After reading it, he let out a laugh, then sucked in a breath. "So do you," he said through the pain.

Wrinkling her nose at him she wrote, *HA HA*.

Footsteps sounded in the hall, and Carson's nerves shriveled. She wasn't ready to leave him. She still had so much to say. Who knew the next time she would see him again? Relief spread when the footsteps disappeared into the room adjacent to his.

No more precious seconds to waste.

I have something to tell you . . . The script looked like a toddler using a crayon for the first time because Carson's fingers were trembling so much. The board shook when she tried to hold it up, so she gently placed it on

Jax's stomach and controlled her tapping heel as it made the wheelchair creak. If she had still been hooked up to her heart monitor, it would have been dinging uncontrollably.

A single black eyebrow rose as Jax looked at the board, then her. "What?" His voice was deep and still, like the bottom of the sea.

Not bothering with the white board she took in a steady breath, even if the air scratched her blistered throat, and mouthed, *I love you*.

A groan rumbled out of his mouth. "I know that, Carson," he said, exasperated, causing her to draw her chin in. Weakly, his fingers reached for hers and interlaced with them. "I know you love me because when we first met, you were at your lowest, yet you still took a chance on me. You loved me enough to step away and let me decide for myself about having children of my own."

It must have taken all of his energy to talk, because he stopped to take in a few breaths. Carson was sure his doctor wouldn't approve of strenuous declarations of love until he was off bed rest.

"And it was your very stupid love that saved me," he finished.

Carson's gaze dropped to her feet, kept warm with a fuzzy pair of canary-yellow socks.

Unraveling their fingers, Jax used his knuckle to lift Carson's face. For the first time in a long time, he was smiling at her. Really smiling. Lines forming around his eyes and all. And it was clear to Carson that Jax had made his choice.

"Now, can you please let *me* love *you* this time?"

CHAPTER THIRTY-ONE

Eight months later . . .

Carson was baking in the hot sun. Her shoulders weren't used to the exposure, but the warm rays felt good on her skin. Thankfully, she had lathered herself with sunscreen before she and Jax left. It was freeing to relax and soak up Vitamin D in just shorts and a tank top, her riding gear slung over her dirt bike behind her. The breeze tickled her scars.

"Oh, I forgot to tell you. The leasing agent called this morning," Carson said, sitting on the edge of the rock and swinging her legs back and forth, toes barely skimming the surface of the Verde River.

"What did she say?" Jax asked, chucking a few pebbles into the bubbling current below.

"The office will be ready to move in by March. I should be up and running no later than April."

"Is that enough time to get a firm started?"

"It's more than enough time," she confirmed, wiping at a smudge of dust on her shorts. "Especially if I start building clientele now. Garrett has a law school buddy in East Houston who's going to start referring cases over to me. The only reason I'm allowing myself so much time is so we can get settled into our house before I really hit the ground running."

Garrett had had mixed emotions when Carson had turned in her resignation notice, but in the end, he was proud of her, and said if she ever was back in Arizona she had a job waiting for her. Dan, the third attorney, could have cared less. With a grunted good luck, he shook her hand and then scurried off to his office. Noah, on the other hand, was distraught, begging for her to reconsider and stay. Secretly, she thought it was because he'd never see Jax again.

A hawk screeched out in the distance. The deep valleys and cliffs before them stretched for miles and miles. She had spent many hours exploring them over her years living in Arizona. Now it was time to explore new lands, experience new adventures.

Leaning on her hands and letting her head fall back, Carson closed her eyes, the sun now kissing her cheeks. She was going to miss all of it. The sunsets that looked like they were painted by God. The spiny plants, beautiful and ominous. The chubby cheeks of Hunter's and Raegan's newborn baby. Her fingers were already twitching to pinch them again.

But Texas would bring opportunity. The opportunity to open her own law firm. To purchase a home nestled in the luscious trees. During the open house, Jax had to practically drag her inside to inspect the interior and not just the forest surrounding it. And Jax got to be closer to his family, his friends. With a referral from his battalion chief, he was able to submit for a transfer to a station only three miles from their new home.

Moving was bittersweet—ambivalent. Attraction and repulsion. But she was ready.

"It's going to be a busy few months for us," Jax commented, bringing her back to the desert, back to the Verde River.

"Yep." Carson popped the *p*.

"We definitely shouldn't add to it," he said.

"No, we probably shouldn't."

"So, you think throwing in a wedding would be too much?"

Carson's feet stopped kicking, and she looked over at him. The sun reflecting off his midnight hair made it appear almost blue. He was eyeing the tiny rocks still cupped in his hands.

"Wyatt and Emily's wedding isn't until the end of next year. I think we'll be fine," she said. Somehow, and she was still trying to understand why, his family didn't hate her after she'd broken up with Jax. Happily, Wyatt invited her to their Christmas wedding in Tennessee.

Fist clenching around the rocks, Jax peered out before him, toward the red cliffs of Sedona. "I'm not talking about their wedding."

Everything stilled. Her heart. Her lungs. The earth. Even the quail cooing in the bushes far to her left went silent. Carson wanted to see if the river continued to flow below her, but her eyes were stuck on Jax's face.

Exhaling, he tossed the stones into the river and turned to her, grabbing one of her hands. "I have so much to say," he started, his voice thick and melodic. "I just don't know how to say it all. But I want to love you for the rest of my life, Carson. I admire your strength and your growth. Because of you, I want to be a better person, not only for my family and for you, but for myself."

Pushing up off the ground, he pulled her up with him until they were standing, only wincing once when he put pressure on his left leg.

"What are you doing?" she whispered, her heart thrumming in her chest and her body tingling with electricity, threatening to puddle on the ground and slip into the turning waters of the river.

"What does it look like I'm doing, Mr. Hoover?" he teased.

"Are you—are you *proposing*?" she squeaked.

Bending until he was down on one knee, he looked up at her with his incredible blue eyes. "That's exactly what I'm doing."

Fishing around in his riding pants pocket, Jax pulled out a ring. Carson's loud gasp echoed through the canyon. It was the ring she had fawned over at the auction a year ago, the one with the inlay of raw turquoise squeezed between Apache tears. The copper glowed in the sunlight.

"But . . . ? How did you . . . ?" It was impossible to finish a question.

"I saw you bid on it at the auction," he said. "I figured it may come in handy one day. If not for you, then for another—"

Carson smacked his shoulder, which only caused an impish grin to spread across his face. "You had it this whole time?"

"Yes. Now would you stop asking questions so I can ask *my* question?"

Snapping her mouth shut, she nodded frantically.

"Carson, will you marr—"

"Yes!" she cried before Jax could finish. She didn't want to waste another second. Flinging her arms around his neck, Carson pressed her face to his and kissed him, breathing in his signature scent of dust.

The hawk squawked its congratulations. The sun blazed hotter. The breeze whipped and whirled around them. Somewhere a snake was rattling its cheers.

"Damn it, woman," he grumbled against her lips. "At least let me put the ring on before it goes flying in the river."

"Yes, yes. Of course." Carson pulled away, running a hand over her braids before offering her left hand to him. The jewelry slipped on with ease, hugging tight to her finger. The weight and feel of the band was familiar, like an old friend.

"Is it okay?" Jax asked, standing up.

Looking up at him, Carson smiled. "It's perfect."

ACKNOWLEDGMENTS

I want to thank my husband, Shaun. You've demonstrated that someone like me can be loved, and I will forever be grateful to you. Also, thank you for inspiring the whole kiss-down-by-the-river scene.

To my son, Johnny, thank you for telling me, "You're the best writer in the whole world." Because of your words, I believe in myself.

I need to thank my cousin, Heath (Hunter). If it weren't for you texting me every day for a month asking about my word count, I would have never completed this story.

A huge thank you to my best friend, Caleigh, for being my first responder insider. You helped make this story as realistic as possible.

Thank you to my beta readers who were kind enough not to say my manuscript was trash and instead pushed me to do better.

And finally, to my editors, thank you for answering my millions of questions. I have learned so much from you both and can't wait to implement this new knowledge into my future writing projects.

ABOUT THE AUTHOR

Maloree E Anderson is the last person you'd expect to write a romance novel. With her Wednesday Addams-like personality and one boyfriend that she married, her brain couldn't possibly draft up a HEA/HFN. To let you in on a little secret, she's a hopeless romantic and salivates at cheesy tropes.

If she's not writing or reading about love stories on the porch (with a Swig in hand) you can usually find her fishing or kayaking at the lake or off-roading somewhere in the desert. Maloree lives in Arizona with her husband, son, and three tortoises.

Attraction & Repulsion is her debut novel.

linktr.ee/maloree.e.anderson

Made in the USA
Middletown, DE
19 October 2025